Let Me Heal Your Heart

LILY FOSTER

This is a work of fiction. Names, characters, places and incidents are either the product of the author's imagination or used fictitiously. Any resemblance to actual persons, living or dead, events, or locales is entirely coincidental.

Let Me Heal Your Heart
Copyright © 2015 by Lily Foster

Cover by Cover Me Darling

First paperback edition January 2015

IBSN 9780990594161 (paperback)

* * *

Shorefront Books

Let Me Heal Your Heart

Chapter One

DECLAN

Silence.

Maybe the interminable stretches of silence are what finally did her in.

It's not that he doesn't speak to me at all, he does, but his overtures are weak, function-driven. *Did you eat? Do you have enough money? Do you need the car this weekend?*

Pulling up outside the dorm, he asked without looking my way, "Do you want me to help carry your things inside?"

Fuck no, my inner voice screamed. I wanted out of that car A-sap. Smiling to myself, I imagined him slowing down just enough for me to jump out of the still-moving vehicle with my stuff.

He surprised me when he made physical contact, putting his hand on my shoulder when he said, "Best years of your life. Study, but have your fun."

So it's all downhill after this? Always a ray of sunshine, aren't you, Dad?

It's not that I didn't appreciate the sentiment, I did, but talk about too little, way too late. Instead of telling him this, or telling him how much it hurt to even be around him because we no longer had any kind of a relationship, I managed a phony smile and said, "Thanks, Dad. I'll call you once I'm settled in."

I wouldn't call him.

He wouldn't be calling me either.

I made my way into Grafton Hall, my new home. I moved past kids flanked by a mother on one side, a father on the other, each one reluctant to let go of their baby. There were lots of hugs, moms speaking reminders about separating the darks from lights when doing laundry, dads handing over extra spending cash, and reminders from both to eat right.

I hung on their every word, envious.

My family, we used to be like that.

* * *

ANNA

"Did your father give you enough money, sweetheart?"

"I'm good, Aunt Margot. I have enough."

She tucked an envelope into my bag as we pulled up outside the dorm and grasped my wrist when I attempted to take it back out and return it to her. I was sure the envelope contained an ungodly sum.

"Don't you dare, Anna Banana. Trust me, you'll need some mad money for clothes, parties…Maybe some upperclassman will ask you to homecoming and you'll need a dress."

"You make this sound all very nineteen-sixties."

She gave my arm a playful smack. "Really? Try the eighties." She sighed and smiled. "I loved college. I want to go back."

"Be my roommate! You'll be heaps better than the potential serial killer I could be meeting in the next five minutes."

"I'm sure you're about to meet a best friend for life. I met Bunny my first day on campus."

"If my roommate's name is Bunny or Muffin I'm going to run out of that dorm screaming."

"Don't judge a book by its cover, Anna."

We each carried one of my two small bags. Most of my things were shipped here last week because that's how Margot Cole rolls.

My aunt practically scowled holding the door open for one parent wearing sensible walking sneakers and faded, high-waisted mom jeans, and then shook her head when the two of us were stuck in traffic behind the woman as she lugged several bags up the stairs at once like a pack mule. So much for judging book covers.

Margot Cole didn't lug. To my knowledge, Margot never physically exerted herself. No, she was the epitome of style and refinement. Today she was dressed college campus casual, and from her three-hundred-dollar driving moccasins to her five-hundred a month high-lights, she screamed money. All that aside, she was good to the core in my book.

Margot took me in at the end of my junior year of high school after my parents split up and were driving me to the brink of insanity. I was able to stay at the same high school, which made the idea of moving out a no-brainer, and I liked to think it served us both. After my cousin Dylan left for college, my aunt and uncle hated that empty nest feeling, and Margot got to dote on me like the daughter she never had. For me, having people in my life who accepted me as-is meant the world. Margot and Vince didn't bat an eyelash at my fashion choices, piercings or hair color du jour.

Loyola 231.

This would be my home for the next nine months. I was expecting a small room, but this was one-quarter the size of my bedroom at home and I was sharing this space with another human being. It was going to be tight, so I really hoped that I liked the person I was being stuffed in here with.

"Hmm, no roommate yet. Let's get you settled in."

We left the door open to catch the comings and goings in the hallway. Once every few minutes someone would glance in as they made their way to their own room, most with parents and siblings. I smiled and said hello to anyone who caught my eye. I hated being alone and wanted to make some friends here pronto.

I chose this school because of its academic reputation and architectural design program, but I struggled with the decision because my friends were all going to other schools, some of them going together in pairs. Only one other person from my high school was here, Vicki Knotts, and she was a prissy brat with a competitive streak. You know the type—the one who posts her kick-ass college board scores on social media? Suffice to say that Vicki and I would not be grabbing a latte together before class, like ever.

Being alone was my worst nightmare. Since Will died, I couldn't stand being alone in my empty house, or silence in general. The fear and loneliness were what drove me to leave home and go live with Margot and Vince.

I guess my parents had always been self-absorbed and distant, but their shortcomings became painfully obvious after Will's death. Dinner on the table? Showing up for parent-teacher conferences? Penciling in thirty seconds to ask how I was doing?

Wasn't happening.

Maybe I'm being unfair. After all, they say the death of a child is the most devastating event a person can endure. But in those dark weeks and months that followed Will's funeral, Mom still managed to get through spa days, shopping, and wine-soaked lunches with the ladies, while my father played golf like he was in training for a spot on the PGA tour, sipping whiskey and smoking cigars with his cronies at the club for hours afterwards.

My mother and father abandoned one another, and then they abandoned ship. It's not that their marriage was perfect before the accident, or that our home life was wonderful—it wasn't. But it was fine, it was normal. I had two parents, I had a stable home, and most importantly, I had Will.

Will's protective nature, his love and his humor made up for a lot of what my parents didn't contribute. Without him, our family was an already shaky house of cards bound to collapse.

And collapse it did.

* * *

DECLAN

My door was already open, so when I heard knocking, I turned my head, curious. I sent up a silent prayer that my roommate wasn't overly formal or weird in general. This guy looked ok, though, with his baseball cap on backwards, dressed like he'd just rolled out of bed.

"Declan Banks?"

"Yeah," I answered, sticking my hand out to shake his. I took in the guy's tight expression and wondered if I'd done something wrong. "What's up?"

"I'm Matt Parker, the resident assistant for Grafton. It's good to meet you," he said as he shook my hand. "Look, I got some sad news when I got here this morning. Your roommate's father had a heart attack a few days ago, a major one. He's probably not going to be moving in anytime soon. He lives fairly close by so he'll be commuting for a while."

"That's terrible. Is he coming by at all?"

"Don't think so. From what I gathered his father is still critical."

"Oh." I could think of nothing else to say.

"The bad news...I mean, I guess it's bad unless you like your own space, is that they won't assign you anyone else because his room and board is settled up and he may be back later on in the semester."

I looked over at the unmade bed on the opposite side of the room. The walls were painted an off-white color, but the surface underneath was cinderblock. The standard-issue desk and chair, the bare mattress and the cinderblock wall made that side of the room resemble a prison cell.

Hoped I hadn't just traded one jail for another.

* * *

ANNA

God bless Aunt Margot. Even though there was no Greek system here, she was hell-bent on making sure I had a sorority's worth of sisters before she left me today.

She bounced from room to room, popping in, introducing herself to other parents, making connections with them out of thin air. Once Margot asked where they were from, she could conjure up a link. "You're from Westport? We have a summer place next door to Carrie and Mark Spencer on the Vineyard, do you know them? Oh, you wouldn't be related to Ken Richter, would you? You are? He plays squash with my husband." And so it went. Margot had several new friends before she took off later that afternoon, and as a result, I'd befriended their offspring. She was a force of nature and I was grateful for her in ways that were too numerous to count.

My roommate materialized just as I was beginning to worry about the prospect of spending the night in my new room alone.

Fiona came off as shy and reserved when I introduced myself, and it was easy to see why. Her overbearing mother basically sucked the air from the room.

"Speak up, Fiona." Mrs. Fields butted in before her daughter had a nanosecond to answer my question. "Fiona," the domineering presence said as she rolled her eyes, "is from Ogunquit, Maine. You must come up in the summertime, Anna."

I felt pain on behalf of this girl. She looked as if she wanted to crawl underneath the flimsy twin bed frame and die on the spot.

I smiled right at Fiona and took her hand. "Only if you let me drag you to Connecticut first, Fiona."

The corners of her mouth turned up when she met my eyes. I think we both knew in that moment that we'd stumbled upon a friend.

Fiona's eyes were a rich, warm brown, and her dark brown hair hung in ringlets down her back. She had the kind of hair that other girls would kill for, while the owners of said hair generally lamented their plight, wishing they were born with stick-straight locks like every other girl in their grade.

She said, "So, um, I met Sarah, the resident assistant, and she said we had to be at the dorm meeting really soon, right?"

I checked my watch, noting that we had an hour, but then got her message loud and clear. "Oh my God, I lost track of time. Yeah, we have like five minutes. I'll come down to the car and we'll grab the rest of your things."

Mrs. Fields shot daggers at her husband. "Did you hear that, Max? Because you took so long getting here, now I can't even stay to help Fiona settle in."

He was meek in her presence, but I think Mr. Fields did his version of asserting himself when he said, "She's eighteen, dear. I think she can make her own bed."

She huffed, "Let's get the rest of your things and then I guess we'll just be on our way."

Mrs. Fields was hoping her daughter would ask her to stay longer, to need her in some way. From the look on her face, though, that would not be happening. Fiona looked as if she would buckle under one more minute of this woman's scrutiny.

The Fields' car finally pulled away from the curb. Taking in my gaping mouth and wide-eyes, she smiled and asked, "So, she's as bad as I've always thought?"

I put my hand on her shoulder and laughed. "I've never been so grateful for my distant, cold-hearted mother as I am right now. At least she doesn't bother with me."

"Ugh!" she cried out as she looked towards the sky. "All she does is bother me. It's like my grades are her grades, my friends dictate her social status, my place on the cheerleading squad is her achievement, not mine. Sorry," she laughed. "TMI for our first day?"

"No, feel free to vent."

"I feel bad sometimes because she left college during her sophomore year when she got pregnant with my brother. She wants to live vicariously through me and I feel pressure to let her do that." She shrugged and let out a deep breath. "And that's my life story. What's yours?"

"Parents divorced, self-absorbed and clueless when it comes to me. I actually live with my aunt and uncle now. I moved out when I was sixteen." In response to her shocked expression, I added, "See, thought you had me beat in the nightmare home-situation department, didn't you?"

By now we were back in our room, sitting across from one another on our twin beds. "I'm sorry."

"Don't be. My aunt and uncle are really good to me. You missed Aunt Margot, she left right before you got here. And my cousin Dylan is one of my best friends. My life is pretty great when I'm there."

"So you don't have any brothers or sisters?"

"I have a brother but he died three years ago."

She smacked her forehead. "I should just shut up with the twenty questions." Shaking her head, she added, "Ohmigod, I'm so sorry I brought it up."

I couldn't help but smile in response to her reaction. "It's ok. We might as well get all the awkward shit out of the way, right?"

She smiled back. "I just met you and I think you're pretty great, Anna."

"Right back atcha, Fiona."

Walking downstairs on our way to the dorm meeting, I felt an old memory rising to the surface, a memory that warmed me from the inside out whenever I let it in.

"Where in Maine did you say you were from?"

"Ogunquit. It's on the coast, York County."

"Maine," I said to no one in particular. "I've never been."

Chapter Two

DECLAN

After two weeks I was actually grateful for the few moments of solitude that my lack of a roommate provided. Just about every door on my floor was left open twenty-four-seven, and there was a constant flow of traffic between rooms. Calling them family may seem like a stretch, but after spending most of my waking moments either talking, drinking or laughing with these guys, it's how I felt in their presence.

Right across the hall I had Brandon Carter and Jimmy Walsh. Terrence Healy, Colin Watters and Frank Collagrazzo rounded out the pack I'd become closely associated with, while there were several other guys on the floor I could easily flop down next to at lunch, join in their pick-up basketball games, or fall into easy conversation with as we walked to class. I felt more at home in this new place than I did in the house where I'd spent the past eighteen years of my life.

All of them knew I was an only child, that I was from Maine, that I played hockey and that I lived with my father. They drew their own conclusions about my mother's whereabouts.

Only Brandon, my teammate and fellow finance major dared to ask, "So, did your mom die or just, like, leave?"

"She died."

That's about as detailed as I was willing to get on the subject.

"I'm really sorry. That sucks."

Right then and there I decided that Brandon was just about the most eloquent and articulate person I'd ever met. What happened that year did indeed suck. There was no other word in the English language that fit better.

Everyone had their shit, though, not just me. My phantom roommate, I heard through my RA, was basically assuming the head of the household role in his family and would not be returning to school. Brandon had an older sister, who at age twenty already had a three-year-old child, and Terrence hinted more than once or twice at his mother's alcohol problem. I was more at ease knowing I wasn't the only one who came from a screwed-up background, but I still couldn't help but feel that every one of these guys had it better than me.

I doubt that any of them went home to a house that was devoid of life in any form. My house was clean, there was food in the fridge, there were basic amenities and some luxuries, but there was no life. There was no music playing, and if I played mine without headphones, I'd typically get a soft rap on the door indicating that I needed to cease and desist. There were no parties, no visitors. I avoided the place unless a shower, meal, or place to crash compelled me to walk through the front door.

I became a competitive hockey player thanks, in part, to my father's shitty parenting skills. In an effort to avoid him, I'd play pick-up games for hours after school no matter the age or skill level of my opponents. Because I hung around the rink so late, this often meant that at fourteen I was playing against sixteen and seventeen-year-olds. Rough around the edges, these kids didn't come from families where mom called you home for dinnertime, and walking in the door late at night with the faint odor of weed on your clothes was no biggie where they came from.

They were stronger and tougher than I was at the time, and seemed to believe that how hard you checked someone into the plexiglass was as important as the number of goals scored. Playing with them made me skilled at evading checks, but as a result of the many I'd failed to duck from quickly enough, I became bloodthirsty to inflict at least some measure of pain on others as payback.

After they left to smoke and to flirt with the girls who wasted their time at the rink, I would stay. I'd take the cones the figure skating coach stashed underneath the bleachers and line them up, making a narrow path leading to the net. With less than an inch of space left to clear the puck on either side, I'd take slap shots from every angle. Line up the cones, shoot, repeat. For hours I did this, making me just about the most accurate wing in my town, able to shoot both left and right-handed.

In Maine, much like in every other bitterly cold, godforsaken part of the world, hockey was a religion. My skill on the ice became well known as I grew and packed on more muscle. The starting spot on my high school team as a sophomore was a nod of recognition.

Aside from the rink, my only other haven was Tess. When my mother died, I pretty much tuned out of the high school social scene. I used to be like everyone else. I used to be happy, oblivious, hanging out after school, hitting the beach all summer, always up for a good time. But after my mother's death, I lived and breathed loss. It changed me.

At the beginning of junior year, Tess moved to my town and we gravitated towards one another, kind of like two lost souls. Her father lost his big job in Boston, so the family had to come live in a house inherited by Tess's mother. They had to downsize in a major way, and Tess had a hard time adjusting to the smaller house, small-town high school, and the quiet off-season life of a coastal town. I grew up here and have to admit, it's an acquired taste.

Tess and I became a full-on couple by Christmas. We were pretty much inseparable, holding onto one another the way drowning people grasp onto driftwood. We spent that winter at the rink. Tess would sit in the bleachers on the far side away from those other girls, waiting patiently for me to finish. We would do homework holed up in her room, or watch movies in my den huddled underneath the blankets, beginning to explore one another's bodies. That next summer was spent at the beach, at my pool, and playing tennis at the courts down the street from my house—feeble attempts to teach a very uncoordinated girl to swim and to play sports that required eye-hand coordination. Watching her splash around awkwardly or swing the racquet and miss time after time, I thought she was freaking adorable. For a long time, nearly an entire year, I had no need or desire to be with anyone else.

Maybe it was time, maybe it was Tess, but by senior year my outlook improved and I was happier. I felt a gradual pull towards my old life again, a desire to belong. I let friends who I'd all but cut out of my life back in, and I started to say yes more often when I was invited to parties.

Tess wasn't from here so I couldn't really blame her for being reluctant. Small town girls could be really nice or really bitchy, and Tess never seemed to have much luck fitting in with the crowd. She preferred the nights when it was just us, no one else, and she dug her heels in when I tried to draw her out. She would give in occasionally, but when she did agree to go out, it wasn't with any enthusiasm. Tess was glued to my side at the bonfires or the house parties our classmates threw on cold winter nights. Did I feel like she was holding me back? A little, I guess, but there was a part of me that felt as if I owed her. Tess was my first, and when you're seventeen and in love that is a powerful bond.

There was another girl, but God, that was a lifetime ago. If you asked me at the time, I'd have told you that I loved her. We were young, though, and what we had was short-lived, so referring to it as love seems kind of ridiculous and stupid. But even now, years later, sometimes I find myself thinking back to that summer.

I still think about her.

ANNA

"Hello...I'm waiting!"

"Easy, bitch!"

Fiona had clearly morphed into a new, free-spirited girl now that she was out from underneath her mama's watchful eyes. The girl cussed more than I did, and that was saying something.

"Fiona, you take so long to get ready. C'mon, Danielle and Lauren have been waiting on us. I don't even know where this party is, so we need to go with them."

"All right, I'm ready," she said as she made a pouty face in the mirror, checking out her make-up.

"You're beautiful, let's go!"

"Hey, usually I'm the one waiting on you as you insert your... Let's see, *five* earrings," Fiona said as she trailed her finger up my right earlobe. "Cut me some slack."

Fiona and I had become overnight best friends—like soul sister, attached at the hip kind of friends. We had several other great girls on our floor, and I found myself loving being a part of this makeshift family we'd formed in our dorm.

All in all, college was a good fit for me. I was a student who never really struggled to make good grades, so that wasn't what I'd feared. I was basically leery of moving again, of leaving what was familiar. Specifically, of leaving the emotionally safe, accepting cocoon that was my Aunt Margot's home. For as composed as I seemed to my friends now, I bore the battle scars of a damaged kid whose emotions could shift directions as quickly as the wind.

The rash, impulsive decisions I'd made in those instances had resulted in no less than six changes in hair color and the multiple piercings I now sported. I was a chameleon. It could be black hair, biker-bitch clothes and every hole on my ear lobe filled with tiny, tarnished silver hoops, or I could go back to blonde—my natural color—swept over the empty pierced holes, pearl choker at my neck, Burberry ensemble head-to-toe. The auburn hair, dark brown with hombre-tinged ends, or the rare but occasional streak of crayon-colored hues were my in-betweens.

After the accident, it was done in an effort to shock them—a blatant rebellion aimed at my suck-ass parents. But now it was no more than a hobby, something I did occasionally when I felt the urge to shake things up.

Tonight I was somewhere in between. My hair was currently my natural honey-colored blond. Piercings were in but my outfit didn't scream, "Back off or I'll kill you." I was wearing battered boyfriend jeans, a snug long-sleeved black t-shirt and some worn Vans. In other words, I blended in just fine.

Another thing I loved about Fiona was that she treated me the same, regardless of what cover my book was sporting that week. I couldn't wait to drag her home with me on holidays, suspecting that Margot, Dylan and Fiona were like-minded, kindred spirits.

We were giggling as we made our way through the woods, tripping over stray branches and teasing one another about the probability of a Freddy Krueger-type jumping out and slashing us all to pieces.

Thank goodness we had Danielle leading the way. She'd been hooking up with some guy Frank since the first week of school and he was running this shindig tonight.

Since we were underage, parties were relegated to a far-off clearing in the woods behind where the freshman dorms were located. It had probably taken these guys the better part of the day to coordinate this, rolling kegs the quarter mile or so from the nearest road.

After walking for over ten minutes, I was relieved when I saw a faint light in the distance and could finally pick up on the sounds of people laughing and music. I'm sure the school knew what went on back here every weekend but chose to turn a blind eye. It was fairly unrealistic to think that a bunch of college freshman, many of whom had been drinking since age sixteen, would be content to talk and dance at the non-alcoholic campus "mixers" that were university sanctioned.

Frank lived in Grafton, which was the dorm where most of the freshman male athletes were housed. As a result, this party seemed especially rowdy, even at this hour. The shots were more readily available, there were some drunken wrestling matches in progress, and the girls who were intent on snagging themselves a division-one basketball, football or hockey player were in nauseating abundance.

Being from Maine, Fiona had been around hockey players her entire life, and her brother was currently a star senior defenseman at Northeastern. The puck-fucks, as she'd so kindly dubbed them, were the girls who seemed to cling onto the hockey players, happy to wash their sweaty gear after practice or bandage their boo-boos, all in the hopes of bedding them.

"Be nice, Fiona."

"I am being nice, it's just that they're borderline ridiculous," she said as her lips curled into an unpleasant snarl. "Just look at them.

They have to be fairly intelligent to be at this school, but they act like mindless, vapid females around those guys. From the looks of them, you'd think they couldn't do basic algebra or comprehend a fifth grade-level book. Are they afraid the boys won't be into them if they show their true colors and demonstrate intelligence?"

Lauren chimed in, "Most of those guys, sadly, aren't interested in what's in your head, only what's in your pants."

Danielle's back was up. "So not true! I dated a football player in high school. He was great, a total gentleman. And Frank isn't a douchebag either."

"My brother is a good person," Fiona said. "But I've seen the girls at his games and he's no saint. I'm pretty sure he's partaken in some of that."

"Wouldn't know and don't ever care to know," I said. "Jocks, in general, are not my thing."

"Since when?"

"I shouldn't say I've ruled them out entirely, but I do seem to gravitate towards the non-violent, brainy types."

"What's Jonathan like?"

"He's...good."

Lauren coughed, covering her hand with her mouth to murmur, "Sounds hot."

She got a hip check from me for that one, nearly knocking the red cup out of her hands. "He *is* hot. Good, though, is the best word to describe him. He's always been really good to me."

She teased, "So when are we going to meet Mr. Jonathan Good?"

"Jonathan Wallace, you wise ass. He's at Marquette. I don't even know if I'll see him before Thanksgiving."

"I don't know why you girls didn't come to college free and easy like I did," Colleen, another girl from our hall, added.

"You're easy all right," Fiona teased.

As Colleen dipped a finger into her beer and then flicked it at Fiona, she said, "I mean it. I was in *love* in high school. We went to prom, had our last summer together and all, but Jason and I were realistic. He's at Penn, I'm here. I knew I'd be tempted and so would he. I have no regrets about breaking up with him."

"How did he take it?"

"His status was single last week and he's now *in a relationship*," she said, smiling. "So I'm gathering he's ok."

Breaking up with Jonathan had crossed my mind. Not just before leaving for school this year, but once earlier this summer, once last fall, and—if I'm being completely honest—about one month into the start of our relationship.

Jonathan was like a comfy, well-worn sweater: familiar and warm. He was smart, supportive, honest, kind, didn't care if my hair was neon green or if I put a barbell through my septum. I hadn't, by the way.

I knew Jonathan before the accident, and after it happened, he seemed to be the only one who knew what to do. While everyone else said, "Sorry about Will," as they grimaced uncomfortably, dying to get that over with and then get away from me, Jonathan said nothing. He hugged me tight at the funeral, not letting go for a solid minute. Then he moved my hair aside and kissed my cheek. It wasn't hot or romantic in any way. No, Jonathan's gestures were intended to make me feel cared for and accepted, and they did. That crushing hug and that kiss sustained me.

I wasn't deemed fit to go back to school on the Thursday or Friday following the funeral, so I spent the time locked away in my room. It's not like the locked door was necessary, as neither parent was seeking me out. They'd each decamped to their own corners of our cavernous house and were busy drinking themselves into a stupor. I stayed in bed staring at the ceiling, so devastated and lifeless that I couldn't even muster the energy required to cry.

Saturday morning Jonathan called and asked if I wanted to go to the movies with him. I did. He took me to see some mindless comedy, took me out to lunch and then bought me ice cream. The next day I hung out at his house, his mother making us lunch and making small talk. He met me at my locker that Monday morning, sensing that being back at school would be difficult for me. He practically shadowed me that first week, making jokes, talking about everyday nonsense, and making certain that I didn't fall down the rabbit hole.

As a result, my life returned to normal—at least it looked that way from the outside. I returned to cheerleading at my teammates' insistence and went out for tennis later in the spring. I attended parties, and even though I tended to cut out early, I maintained my place in the social strata of high school. That was all thanks to Jonathan.

Jonathan was incredibly patient with me and he was accepting to a fault. After what I pulled at the end of that summer, everyone else basically dropped me. The fact that he remained friends with me said a lot about his character.

I basically went off the rails.

Following a month of hanging out with my girlfriends, spending days at Jonathan's house lounging by his pool, and taking long meditative runs—all in an attempt to get my head back on straight—my parents sat me down and announced that I would be attending a two-week summer grief camp in the Berkshires. I sat there dumbfounded, staring down at the brochure on the dining room table.

Heart Songs?

Could they come up with a stupider name? What does that even mean?

I looked back up to my parents, wanting to revolt but totally speechless. I noticed that for once they were side by side, a united front.

"Why?" was all I managed to say.

"Anna, we know this has been so difficult for you," my mother crooned. The slow speech and saccharine-sweet demeanor were a dead giveaway she'd been popping Xannies. Same shit, different day. And how would she know it had been difficult? I'd hardly seen the woman since the night Will's head was blown off.

Dear old Dad chimed in, "We think you need counseling. This place is highly regarded. It's very upscale so you won't be forced to mingle with any, you know—"

"Common folk?" I'd intended for it to sound sarcastic.

My father was a pretentious prick, which is fairly common among those who do nothing to earn their money. He seemed relieved, though, to think that for once we were on the same page. "Yes, exactly. It's just for two weeks, Anna. Beautiful grounds, lots of different activities…It will be good for you."

"What if I don't want to go?"

He looked to my mother, lips in a tight line, and then looked back to me. "We think it's best. You're going."

If they tried to pull that shit now—well, let's just say they wouldn't dare. Back then I was a fifteen year-old honor student and all around do-gooder. I'd just lost the one and only person in this world who mattered to me. I simply did not have the strength or desire to fight with them. Back then, disobedience was a foreign concept.

I held the tears back until I closed my bedroom door and flopped onto my bed. Even at that age I knew in my heart that I'd been coping pretty fucking well, and it was my mother and father who were in dire need of mental health services.

After letting myself wallow in it for an hour or so, I got up, packed my largest duffle, turned off my lights and went to bed.

A car was waiting to take me away at nine the next morning. I wasn't foolish enough to expect that either one of my parents would drive me to camp. I was actually shocked that my mother was even home to see me off. She flitted about, which was her time-honored strategy of avoiding conversation or meaningful connection of any kind. *At least she isn't high*, I thought to myself as I sat on the couch waiting for my ride.

When the horn sounded, she met me at the door and held me in a stiff hug. "I love you, Anna. Be good, ok?"

I nodded and smiled at her before turning to leave. My mother didn't walk me out. Says a lot, I guess. She was about to let her teenage daughter get into a car with some guy, a complete stranger, but didn't even feel the need to venture into the driveway to introduce herself or check him out.

It's not like there was some lightbulb moment, a sudden realization that my relationship with my parents had withered to nothing. No, it was a gradual process. I do remember family vacations when I was younger, holidays, birthday parties—the trappings of family life. I do not remember, however, feeling a sense of warmth radiating from my mother or my father. I don't remember being hugged frequently by anyone other than Will, and he was the one I instinctively went to for comfort when I was upset.

I didn't notice how odd this was until I got a little older. I saw how the other mothers doted on their daughters, stroking their hair or hugging them when they picked them up after school. I saw my friends' parents cheering on the sidelines at our field hockey games. My parents, meanwhile, probably couldn't even tell you what sports I played. And no, I don't ever recall opening my lunchbox to reveal a napkin with a heart-encased note like my classmates did.

That day I returned from camp, my relationship with them changed irrevocably. I no longer felt young, I no longer felt innocent, and I no longer felt capable of tolerating their bullshit attempts at parenting me.

DECLAN

"Hi."

"Hi yourself. What are you doing up so late?"

"I can't sleep. My roommate is annoying. She's sleeping now with her earbuds in, like I can't still hear her music playing. *And* she snores. I should have insisted on a single."

"I'm betting the singles are a lot more money, though, right Tess?"

Her laugh had a hard edge. "Yes, and extra money is something I definitely do not have. Thanks for the reminder."

"When I sign my NHL contract you'll have a big house with as many rooms as you like."

"Right...You'll probably drop me for some bimbo groupie." She paused. "You won't do that, will you, Declan?"

I hated when Tess talked like that. Always with the subtle accusations, always looking for me to reassure her, to pledge my love. I started to think I should hold back on making those pie-in-the-sky statements. I only did it to lighten the mood, to make her happy. And I figured most girls would take it that way, laughing it off as good intentions and nothing more. Not Tess, though. No, she took them as blood-sworn promises.

Two minutes into this conversation and I was already pinching the bridge of my nose. "Never," I practically chirped. "I hate bimbos and groupies."

"Speaking of, am I going to meet all of your friends this weekend?"

"Yeah, but don't call anyone besides Brandon a bimbo, ok?"

"Right, like you haven't met any cute girls at school yet. I'm sure they're following you around just like they were in high school."

Why couldn't Tess have more confidence? She was beautiful and had a big heart. She had no reason to feel inadequate compared to the other girls. Sometimes her insecurities felt like a weight bearing down on me, and her constant need for reassurance pissed me off.

"Did I even notice them, Tess?"

"How would I know? For all I know you were thinking about one of them while you were with me."

"Cut that shit out."

Once my tone changed and she knew she'd gone too far, she'd backpeddle. More upbeat, she said, "I'm just joking. I can't wait to meet your friends. I'm betting your campus life is better than the nonexistent social scene here."

"You're at Southern Maine, not some community college out in the boonies. There have to be some cool people and some things to do around there."

"Not really. I feel like I'm in the middle of North Dakota. I wish we could have gone away to school together."

It went unsaid, but she had neither the grades nor the money to attend this university. Not that I'm a genius, but I never struggled academically. I also had the added bonus of being a sought-after hockey recruit. It didn't matter if my college board scores were just a little bit lower than what was typical for this school.

"So I'll meet you at the bus on Saturday?"

"Three more days, Declan. I cannot wait to see you."

"Love you, Tess."

"Love you too."

I laid back and stared at the ceiling, trying to fight off this growing sense of unease. I was looking forward to seeing her. Missed the person I'd spent every last waking moment with over the past two years. Missed her in my bed too, if truth be told. Four weeks had passed since we said goodbye, and I'd replayed that last night together out in my pool house over and over to sustain me. But I was wary of mixing my two worlds. I'd made a nice little life for myself here. I had friends—mostly guys but some girls. They were only acquaintances, but if Tess knew girls were sitting with me at lunch or popping by my room to swap class notes, it would *not* go over well. I could picture it now: Tess cold and resentful, me groveling and pledging my love until she let up.

Good times.

My best strategy would be to avoid the parties on Saturday night. I'd take Tess out for a nice romantic dinner in town instead. Sunday morning I'd tour her around campus and then see her off before my two o'clock practice.

Wasn't a good sign that I was planning Tess's departure before she even arrived.

* * *

ANNA

"Danielle, are you ok?"

Last night we were at another party in the woods, and Danielle's boy Frank proved that yes indeed, he did fall into the douchebag-jock category.

She'd just given it up to him the weekend before, right after he drunkenly proclaimed his love for her. Love my ass. Love must not be a word he reserves for the special women in his life. Maybe Frank also bestows the term on things like cheese fries and Xbox, because loving Danielle did not prevent him from making out with some other girl right in front of her face just one week later.

After witnessing that train wreck, we all decided to get wasted in an effort to show solidarity with Danielle. Now, the next morning, we were all paying the price.

"I'm going to be sick," Danielle whispered before bolting out of bed and running for the bathroom.

Just the thought of her barfing made my stomach churn. Never, I thought to myself, will I drink like that again.

I wasn't a big drinker, smoker or anything else. My high school, located in one of the more affluent enclaves of New England, had its share of privileged kids with unlimited disposable income. Drugs and hard liquor were readily available at anyone's home any day of the week and at every party. I wasn't a total abstainer, but more kids did partake heavily than those who didn't. Jonathan was no saint, but he was never out of control and that was fine by me.

When Danielle crawled back into bed, Lauren asked, "Are you going to confront him?"

"Not my style," she replied, still only capable of whispering.

"I'd march right up to that asshole in the cafeteria and dump a plate of scrambled eggs right onto his head," Colleen said as she filed her nails. She was the only one of us who gave the impression of being pain-free.

I knew it was a long shot but I had to ask, "Are you sure it was him, Danielle? It's always so dark out there in the woods and there were like a hundred people. Could you have mistaken him for someone else?"

She shook her head like she was moving in slow motion. "I walked right up to him, Anna. I tapped his shoulder, looked right into his eyes."

"And he didn't say *anything*?" Fiona asked.

"He smiled at me...Like a lazy, friendly fucking smile. He was obviously drunk, but that's no excuse. It's also pretty obvious that he isn't into me."

"Who was the girl?"

"I didn't catch her name," she said as she broke off crying. "I'm never doing that again. I'm never giving up the goods unless I know for certain that it's for real."

Colleen reached over and took her hand. "Don't beat yourself up. He's the jerk here. You did nothing wrong except trust a dumb-ass jock."

Fiona said, "Well, I can say for certain the guy isn't dumb. He's in my bio class and he's a science whiz." She looked to Danielle. "A science whiz but an absolute dickwad."

"Come on," I said. "I have to put some food in this belly. I'm dying right now."

Fiona and I went back to our room to change, and then we all made our way to the cafeteria looking rough: unshowered, hair up, dressed in sweats and t-shirts. Danielle stopped in her tracks when she spotted Frank. Lauren whispered in her ear and nudged her reassuringly when she stood in place staring at him.

I didn't even know Frank, but now I thoroughly disliked him. Since we were a month into school already and he'd hooked up with Danielle repeatedly, you would think he'd be well acquainted with all of her friends. But this wasn't the case because Danielle was someone Frank seemed to sneak off with at the end of the night, not someone he spent time with during the daylight hours. She fell for his bullshit and he used her. I'd witnessed those one-sided relationships too many times to count in high school. Maybe I was smart, or maybe I was just shrewd and jaded from the environment I grew up in, but I knew that if a boy didn't want anyone to know about me or didn't want to hang out with me unless he was buzzing, then it was bad news. I felt sorry for Danielle but wanted to shake her at the same time.

We filled our trays with greasy breakfast food and sat down, taking our places around Danielle, trying to create some kind of barrier between her and everyone else. She put on a brave face. Lauren and Colleen were making jokes, making her smile whenever they noticed Frank or one his friends looking over in our direction. I sat with my back to the group of boys seated three tables over, not trusting myself to play nice. I did turn once, but only saw Frank looking our way for a split second before one of his asshat friends said something that made him and all of the other guys at the table erupt in laughter. He clearly wasn't broken up over what he did last night.

* * *

DECLAN

Tess groaned as she pulled the comforter over her head in an attempt to block out the noise coming from the hallway. "Is it like this every single weekend?"

"Pretty much."

It was *loud*. Guys and girls were carrying on, obviously drunk, laughing—the sounds of Saturday night on a college campus. Every so often someone would bang on my door. "Banks, where the fuck are you?" Or even better, "Oh, his girlfriend is here?" I heard Jimmy and Terrence then, doing their version of a chick's voice. "Oh, Declan...Do me, Declan!"

Tess was on the verge of an aneurysm by two-thirty. "Seriously? Are you in this kind of shape every weekend, too? Falling down wasted?"

"No!"

I *was* drinking more since starting college, but I didn't go as hard as most of my friends did. I took my training seriously, and although I could still perform after a night out, I wouldn't run the risk of showing up to practice dragging.

I turned on some music in an attempt to drown out the noise coming from the hallway, but it was useless. I was just praying that none of my friends who happened to be female decided to pop over tonight and say hello in a drunken state. I'd been one hundred percent faithful but I was still nervous. Friends who possessed boobs and a vagina? That would not have been cool with Tess.

I rolled over onto Tess, caging her in between my arms in an effort to distract her, to make her happy again. "Come on, baby, it's got to be like this in your dorm too, right?"

"I guess. I just hate that you're here and I'm so far away. Sometimes..." She started to cry. "I just don't think I can take it."

"No, don't say that."

Anything along the lines of being unable to cope scared me. I couldn't bear to hear it, so I distracted her with sex, showering her with kisses and telling her how special she was to me the entire time. I was trying to get back to that place where it was just us and she was all I needed.

After, as I lie with Tess sleeping in my arms, I told myself I was happy. It used to be this good feeling that overwhelmed me every time I was with her, but now it was something I repeated like a mantra. *I love Tess. Tess makes me happy.* I was trying to make myself believe it.

Tess and I were up earlier than everyone else on campus the next morning. No one was in the cafeteria except for the few odd stragglers who were actually pumped to get their day started early on a Sunday. After we ate, Tess and I walked all over. I showed her where my classes were, where she'd be coming to see my hockey games, and other places, like the bookstore and library.

"You're a great tour guide, Declan. What other fun things do you have planned for us?" Her tone was playful and she pinched my ass when she asked, "Will I get to watch you type a paper next, maybe watch you clip your fingernails?"

I backed her up against a wall and pressed into her. "Fine. Next time you're here we're hitting parties all weekend long. You asked for it."

"Why didn't you take me last night?"

"I don't know. You were never into that kind of thing at home, so I figured it would be torture for you. Especially here...You know absolutely no one."

She shrugged. "So next time you come up to see me."

"We talked about this. I can't leave with practices and training. I'm on scholarship. They practically own me."

Here we go, I thought. Now her arms were crossed and the petulant pout was firmly in place. "So I'm going to have to come *here* all the time?"

"Only when you can, Tess. I know you're busy too. We're in college now…It's a little different."

"Maybe I can't do different. Maybe I need you more than you need me." She looked so goddamn sad. "I think you really like it here."

"I do, but I love you, Tess, and I need you."

She nodded her head, accepting my words. Thankfully she wasn't up for a fight.

I was in a deep funk after she left. Felt so damn guilty. The real reason I didn't take her to the party last night was because I was different here. I was closer to my old carefree, happy self. Day by day I was shedding that brooding, needy side of myself, the one that clung to his sadness like a lifeline.

Tess didn't know the "me" that existed before my mother's suicide. And I couldn't shake the feeling that she wouldn't really know what to make of that person.

Chapter Four

ANNA

Another small gripe about college was the need to do one's own laundry. At home, my clothes magically made their way from the ball on the floor where I'd left them, back to my closet, perfectly clean and pressed again. Didn't know exactly when or how it happened, it just did. But here my clothes accumulated on the floor until I picked them up, and my clothes got clean only after I hauled them to the laundry myself.

We all did our laundry in the basement of Fisk Hall. There were probably fifty washers there, as four dorms used this same facility.

I hated doing wash for several reasons. First and foremost? Clueless boys. I'd never operated a machine prior to coming here either, but you didn't see me sidling up to people acting all pathetic and begging for help. For crying out loud, they had stick figure drawings showing you how to turn the thing on. Do you *really* need to have some babe show you how to press the start button? Or show you how to measure out a capful of detergent? Seriously, would these boys dump an entire bottle in if not *closely* supervised, or would they dump the detergent on top of the machine *after* closing the lid, rather than in with the clothes? It was nauseating.

For the guys, the laundry room was a major hook-up spot. Some of the heaviest flirting on campus happened there. I wasn't having it. I mean, I resented having to do my own wash; I certainly wasn't taking on yours too. I also didn't like that I had to stay there and watch my stuff. There were some truly obnoxious people who couldn't wait five damn seconds. They sat like vultures, ready to dump the contents of your washer or dryer into a bin the second it stopped. I certainly didn't want some guy touching my undies, so I typically sat there with a book. And that—you guessed it—would leave me open to multiple overtures from clueless boys looking for either a hook-up or a wash maid. Ugh!

An hour and twenty-seven minutes later—but who's counting? —I finally finished up and was lugging an overloaded basket of my clean, folded clothes back across the lawn towards my place. It was a beautiful day and people were hanging out outside, reading and playing ball. I was calling out to a girl I knew when a Frisbee practically decapitated me. Stunned, I dropped my laundry, spilling the contents of the basket out onto the grass. *Where's the asshole*, I thought as I looked around to see who had the bad aim. I saw some guy trotting towards me, cocky smirk on his face, and then another, who practically stiff-armed the first guy and said something that made him stop in his tracks. As he got closer, I noticed his build. He was tall and muscular. And his face? Well, let's just say that his face, body, smile—he was hot. As he came into better focus, he also struck me as familiar.

Holy crap.

It can't be.

* * *

DECLAN

It was a relief to get back to my routine after Tess left. Trying to shield her from what she might not like about my life here, and trying to keep her happy and reassured in general was an effort.

I like it here, I thought to myself one morning as I was getting dressed for class. I liked my routine, loved the camaraderie of my teammates and friends, and I liked the social life. The simple things, like talking with people before class and eating lunch and dinner with my group of guys and girls, made me feel like I belonged here. I even enjoyed study groups, as they were usually fifty percent study, fifty percent just hanging out. And despite what I'd told Tess, I loved the weekends. I loved the parties, and loved lazing around on Sunday mornings talking about all the crazy shit that happened the night before.

When we spoke on the phone, I only relayed stuff about classes and what went on between me and the guys on my team and in my dorm. Like I said, I'd been faithful, but there were girls who expressed a not so subtle interest in me.

Melissa was a friend of Brandon's from home and lived one dorm over. Melissa and her roommate, Paige, typically sat with us at lunch and we'd often hang out with their crew of friends on the weekends. On two separate occasions, Paige had all but mauled me after consuming a few too many drinks, to the point where I had to peel her off of me. Their other friend, Charlotte, was more subtle about it but I noticed the lingering looks and the frequent attempts to get my attention.

I wasn't blind and wasn't completely unaffected. Those girls were beautiful, and they were also carefree and fun to be around. But whenever my thoughts veered in that direction, I'd stop myself. It felt wrong to compare those other girls to Tess. It made me feel like a cheat. I wasn't doing anything wrong, but in my heart I knew that having even a passing desire for someone else was cheating in its own way.

Making my way back from class later that day, I took in my surroundings. This campus was just how you'd expect a top, old-school New England university to look: expanses of green lawn where preppy coeds sat cross-legged, talking and laughing with one another or reading underneath the branches of an ancient sycamore.

No doubt about it, these kids of all shapes, sizes, races and backgrounds were a cut above—the best of what America's high schools had to offer. I laughed, realizing that I sounded like a bit of a douche to my own ears, but whatever, these were my people now and I liked it here.

I ran into Terrence, Jimmy, Colin and Brandon outside of our dorm. They were playing Frisbee, but now the four of them were standing side by side, all staring off in the same direction.

"See anything you like?" I broke in.

Terrence kept his eyes fixed straight ahead. "Yes, me sees something me likes a lot."

Brandon chimed in, "Terrence has been talking up this girl from his advanced calculus class since the first day of school."

"Yeah," Colin added. "She's been the inspiration for his nightly jerk-off sessions. Do you know what it's like rooming with this guy? He's a fucking pig."

Terrence served Colin with a low roundhouse kick, taking his legs out from under him and landing him on his ass. "Do *not* talk about my girl like that."

"Your girl," Brandon mocked. "You haven't even spoken to her."

"No, but I have admired her every day from afar. Damn, she is *hot*. She comes to class wearing prim little hipster-girl clothes one day, then rocker chick outfits other days, and she has these piercings snaking up her earlobe. Makes me think she's a saucy little minx in the sack."

We all laughed at that one.

"What's her name?" I asked.

"Prof doesn't take attendance so I don't know."

"Holy crap!" Jimmy was doubled over. "You don't even know her name?"

"Nope. I just know she's beautiful. And I consider myself a math whiz but she blows me out of the water. Last week we got back a test that was just...brutal. I leaned over and snuck a peek at her grade. She got an A. To me that makes her even hotter."

Colin laughed. "That's 'cause you're practical, Terrence. You're hoping she can fuck you *and* tutor you."

"Enough of this bullshit." Brandon snatched the Frisbee from Terrence's hand. "Incoming!" he shouted as he whipped it right at the girl.

Terrence looked to Brandon. "I'm gonna kill you."

"Oh shit," we said collectively as the Frisbee whizzed by full speed, missing the girl's face by no more than a few centimeters. Startled, she dropped a giant basket of laundry all over the grass.

"You're such a dick," Terrence muttered as he started off towards her.

She glared in our general direction, searching for the guilty party. *No way.*

Before I knew it I was breaking into a jog, and when I caught up with Terrence my left arm instinctively went out and knocked him back, stopping him mid-stride.

"What the fuck, Declan?"

I vaguely remember offering up some explanation. *I know her.* Maybe I absently threw out something like that. Terrence didn't matter. In that moment, nothing and no one else mattered but Anna.

"I'm sorry about that."

My heart was beating out of my chest. Her mouth fell open, no words, no sound.

"Declan?" she finally whispered.

"Anna, I can't believe it's you," I said as I picked her up off the ground and hugged her close to me. I didn't even think about it before I grabbed her. The level of emotion running through me at that moment overwhelmed any sense of rational thought I might have had. Seemed to be the same for Anna, as she clung to me for a long moment before I felt her body shake with...sobs?

I put her down and studied her face, my hands resting on her shoulders. She wiped at a stray tear and then laughed. "Sorry 'bout that. I guess I wasn't prepared for the shock."

I noticed then that Terrence, Brandon, Jimmy and Colin were standing around, looking back and forth between the two of us curiously. Jimmy broke in, "Introduce us to your friend, Banks."

I cleared my throat, annoyed they were interrupting my moment with her. "Uh, Anna, these are my friends." Making next to no effort, I gestured to each and muttered, "Brandon, Colin, Jimmy...And I think you know Terrence from calculus."

They all exchanged hellos and then Jimmy added, "I think our boy Terrence here wants to take you out in exchange for some tutoring sessions, Anna."

Anna's eyes went wide for a second and then she laughed. "Does that actually work for you guys? Do girls give up hours of their time to tutor you in exchange for the *honor* of snagging a date with you?"

Terrence pushed Jimmy square in the chest. "Yeah, shut up, Jimmy. When I ask Anna out, I'll be doing it solely for the pleasure of her company."

Anna smiled at him, letting him down easy when she said, "I have a boyfriend, Terrence, but if you're having a hard time with calculus, I'll help you."

Terrence looked visibly disappointed while I could have ground my teeth down to dust. Standing by as my friends openly flirted with Anna? Fighting to keep a relaxed smile on my face as she casually dropped that nugget about having a boyfriend? What the fuck?

I still felt territorial over her, and that was crazy. I knew that.

Anna and I spent two weeks together that summer and one very special night. More than three years had passed since the last time I saw her, but crazy or not, it still felt like I was connected to her, bound to her in every way that was important.

I stood there staring at her as the other guys bent down, falling all over themselves to pick up the laundry that had spilled out of her basket.

"You boys better not say anything if you see me wearing clothes with grass stains this week. I'm *not* rewashing any of it."

Colin said, "Brandon's the one who aimed for you. He should have to rewash them."

She looked at him, eyes wide. "You did that on purpose?"

He just shrugged and laughed. "Terrence has been drooling over you for weeks. Just wanted to help him out."

Terrence's cheeks were flaming red. "Fuck, Brandon, are you trying to kill me?"

When I noticed Jimmy trying to sneak a pair of her panties into his back pocket, I kicked him. He shoved them back into the basket but his grunt got Anna's attention. Guess she saw what had happened because her expression changed and she seemed uncomfortable when she said, "I've gotta go. It was nice meeting you guys." Then she looked to me. "Declan? I guess I'll see you around?"

I cleared my throat but didn't say anything, just nodded. I watched her walk towards her dorm, making a mental note that she lived right next to me in Loyola Hall. This entire time she'd been living in the dorm next to mine?

Brandon was eyeing me. "What the hell was that, Banks?"

I ignored him. "Seriously, Jimmy, you were stealing her underwear?"

He shrugged. "I was trying to snag a souvenir for Terrence."

Brandon shoved Jimmy from behind. "That's the kind of souvenir you deserve after bagging a girl, not after knocking her laundry all over the ground. Anna probably thinks you're a freak with a weird fetish."

Colin said, "You're right, Terrence, there's something about her. She's gorgeous."

"I know," he said, sounding far off and sad. "I sit there in class and watch her every day. She has a sick body, I love the way her hair smells, and she just seems nice, you know?"

"And she has a boyfriend," I said in an end-of-story kind of way.

Brandon kept at it. "Fess up, Declan. Why did you two look like sappy, star-crossed lovers when you first saw each other?"

"Did you get with her?" Terrence asked.

I wasn't telling them shit. I couldn't even process the fact that she was here yet, that she still existed, that she was real.

"Declan?" Colin prodded.

"I haven't seen her in years."

I turned and left them standing there. When I got back to my room, I closed the door behind me and locked it. I needed to be alone.

Anna Clarke was here, at my school, sleeping in a bed not more than fifty yards away from mine.

Holy.

Shit.

Chapter Five

THREE YEARS AGO...

ANNA

The humongous black SUV made its way down a winding, tree-lined path that seemed to stretch on forever after we passed the sign that signaled our arrival at Camp Heart Songs.

I focused on the words and the font they used, certain that it was all wrong. I was always tuned into design, how certain shapes and patterns evoked feelings, and I thought the sweeping script used on the sign just screamed funeral home. And that awful name. Why not call it New Beginnings? No, that sounded like a drug rehab place. What about Camp Hope? Nah, that sounded hopeless. Whatever—Camp Heart Songs, Camp Heart Strings, Camp Heart Break—it was all the same.

I stayed in the car when we pulled up to the entrance, taking it all in from behind the tinted windows. It *was* posh, I conceded. So my father was right, there would be no impoverished grieving children at a place like this.

The central house was impressive, like a grand Adirondack-style estate. I noticed the other cars parked out front were all of the Benz, BMW and Land Rover variety. A few kids who looked to be around my age were walking about, smiling and talking. All of them were decked out in the same style clothes the kids in my neighborhood wore. I giggled, thinking of a new slogan this place could print on their marketing materials: *Camp Heart Songs, when you're looking to grieve in style.*

How was I going to survive this? I didn't want to talk about it. What was there to say? It was awful, fucking awful. There was no making this better, no bringing Will or Drew back, no undoing of that night. My life sucked and that was that.

I wasn't sure how I did manage to get through my days, but I did. My grades had dropped considerably, but given the fact that I rarely slept through the night and was basically incapable of sustained mental effort, I thought my B-minus average was pretty fucking great.

I'm sure I was scowling as I got out of the car, my thoughts focused on my mother and father. The nerve, the absolute galling nerve of them. I needed help? *I needed help?* They were unbelievable. Un-fucking believable.

"You must be Anna."

Startled, I looked up to see a middle-aged man with a kind face standing in front of me. When he moved in to shake my hand, I flinched like a freak.

"Sorry, Anna." He stepped back. "I'm Doctor Benjamin Roth, but everyone here calls me Doctor Ben. You've been assigned to my group."

My mind was too busy racing to come up with a response. No *Nice to meet you* or even a simple *Hello*. Nope, I had nothing. Way to make a stellar first impression.

"I'll let Cheryl show you to your room, and then I'll see you at one o'clock group after lunch, ok? It's your first day here so feel free to just hang back and listen. Typically campers arrive on Saturday and have an individual session first, but since you were enrolled last minute, your schedule is a little mixed up. You and I will be meeting later on this afternoon for an individual, all right?"

This time I did manage to nod, even though my thoughts were now spinning. I was last minute? What did that mean? My parents had probably paid double just to get rid of me, to shove me off on someone else. And, oh crap, did I have to really sit through a group therapy session? I was envisioning lots of emo-type adolescents pouring their hearts out.

The driver followed me to my room and placed my bag onto my bed. I realized that, one, I had not spoken a word to the guy yet, and two, he'd just heard that awkward exchange between me and Dr. Ben.

I turned to him and tried my best to smile, reaching into my bag for my wallet. "Thank you. Did my parents arrange for your gratuity?"

I don't even know why I bothered to ask. My parents were thoughtless and they were cheap. Don't get me wrong, they dropped obscene amounts of money on themselves—my parents were all about making an impression—but on the hired help? Please, if they could get away with an indentured serfdom arrangement in this day and age, they would.

"That's unnecessary, Miss Clarke." Ugh, his expression was sympathetic, pitying. "Do you need anything else?"

"No, thank you," I said as I met his eyes and placed a fifty in his hand. "I appreciate it."

He nodded, his smile warm, and squeezed my hand for a beat before extricating his hand with the bill. "I'll be going then. Take care of yourself, Miss Clarke."

Flopping down onto the bed, I thought about how sad and odd it all was. The driver offered me more comfort in that one short exchange than my own parents had in the weeks and months since my brother had died.

My room was small but well appointed. It wasn't the Four Seasons, but it was not your standard camp bunk quarters either. I had my own room, a queen-sized bed made up with quality linens, and a bookshelf filled with an array of upbeat, motivational titles—Sylvia Plath need not apply. Didn't matter, I packed my own books and magazines. At fifteen, I preferred Architectural Digest over Teen Vogue. That's not to say I was completely disinterested in fashion or pop culture, but I did feel somewhat different from my friends in that respect. I loved math, I loved drawing detailed sketches of structures, and I loved designing rooms in my mind. Layouts, window placement, lighting, patterns, fabrics, art—you name it. While other girls were on social media twenty- four-seven, I was on homebuilding sites where you could create mock plans, or on interior decorating blogs soaking it all in.

Already unpacked, I was flipping through a magazine when someone knocked on my door.

"Anna?" the girl asked.

"Yes," I answered, my tone guarded but managing a smile.

"I'm Beth. Dr. Ben asked me to come for you. We'll grab lunch and then I'll take you to group after."

"Great," I answered, trying to muster up some enthusiasm. "Thanks, Beth." I took a quick look in the mirror to make sure I didn't look like a total basket case, then grabbed my key and followed after her.

"You just got here today, Anna?"

"Yeah, what about you?"

"Oh, I'm here for the entire month," Beth said, rolling her eyes.

"I'm here for two weeks, or slightly less, I guess. I think I'm a day late."

"Yes, you missed orientation yesterday." She paused for a moment. "I was just about to make some lame, snarky comment, but as much as I hate to admit it, being here has helped me."

"Oh, nice," I said, while simultaneously praying she wouldn't elaborate. I didn't want to know. Didn't want to know why it helped, how it helped, or what circumstances had landed her here in the first place.

We walked into a dining hall where I estimated there were no more than seventy-five other people eating lunch. Some kids sat alone at the long communal tables, some in groups of two, and some in larger groups of five or six. It was just like high school: the loners, the people with one close friend and the social butterflies.

In fifth grade I learned that a group of butterflies is called a kaleidoscope. They're also called a swarm, but kaleidoscope is a way cooler word. I used to be one of them, but I hadn't felt colorful or peppy or excited about anything in months. It's like the oranges, yellows and bright blues were nothing but water-based paint on my wings, and after it rained so hard for so long, I was left with nothing. I barely had enough energy to flap those drab brown wings. I would still hang out, show up for the parties, and I'd laugh even though I generally didn't catch on to what was so damn funny. So I guess I still looked like a butterfly on the outside, but I sure as hell didn't feel like one.

Beth led me through the line and we took our trays to a table where two other girls were sitting. She introduced me, and I murmured my hellos without taking note of their names. They were all going into senior year of high school, I learned. All of them were in Dr. Ben's group.

"It's your first day? We'll go easy on you," the redhead said with a warm smile.

"Dr. Ben told me I could sit back and just listen today."

Short girl with the freckles said, "Today you can get away with that, but tomorrow? He's subtle, he doesn't push, but there's something about him that—"

"Makes you want to spill," Beth interjected. "It's an experience, Anna, you'll see."

And that first group session *was* an experience. I didn't make one peep, and noticed that the only two boys in the group kept quiet too. Dr. Ben gently prodded the one who looked to be about my age to join in at one point, but he just shook his head and kept his eyes fixed on the floor. When he moved on to the older boy, he just smiled and said, "Maybe next time, Dr. Ben."

Paulina, a slim, pretty girl, was the focus of most of the session. She went into detail about her mother's death. She described how the house smelled when she walked in, a mixture of what she would later learn to be gunfire and blood. She described what it felt like to pick her mother's head up off the floor and rest it in her lap. How limp and still her mother's body was, and the way her mother's blood soaked through her own clothes. A long time passed, she thought, as she just sat there doing nothing. The police finally arrived, and she was surprised to find out later on that her screams had alerted the neighbors. She didn't recalled making a sound.

I sat there utterly rapt, unable to take my eyes off her as she told her own personal horror story. But at one point I felt eyes on me, and looked over to see that boy staring. His eyes shot right back to the floor.

I don't remember exactly what Dr. Ben said to Paulina, but I recalled thinking that I liked him. I was no longer petrified by the thought of sitting down for a one-on-one.

I left with the same girls after group and went to the pool with them before my session with Dr. Ben.

"Is everyone that open?" I asked as we lounged on floats side by side.

"No," Beth said. "In fact, those were the first words I've heard Paulina speak since she's been here...Almost two weeks. It seemed like she needed that, right?"

"Yeah," Jane the redhead answered. "Seemed very cathartic for her."

"That was intense," I said.

Maggie, formerly known as short girl, said to no one in particular, "Heart Songs is nothing if not intense."

"So how was group, Anna? I hope that wasn't too much, too soon."

"Um, it was a lot to take in, but interesting I guess. It's hard to wrap my head around the idea that everyone here had something so shitty, uh, I mean terrible happen to them."

Dr. Ben nodded. "Yes, everyone has some heavy stuff to deal with." He gestured to himself. "Yours truly included."

We sat in silence for a moment before I asked, "So now, is this when I'm supposed to tell you my life story, why I'm here and everything?"

"I know why your parents sent you. It's all in your file." He kept his kind gaze on me. "I know about your Will."

The way he said *your* Will made my heart ache. That's who he was, *my* Will. My brother, my protector, my best friend.

"Is this going to help me?" I whispered.

"Time helps. Time does help. And talking helps for me, sharing things about the person I loved with others. I don't ever want to forget, even though thinking about that person and remembering can be painful. But that's just how it is, Anna. It's hard."

"It is hard," I repeated quietly, using both hands to wipe my wet cheeks.

I did cry in the days following his death—cried silently, screamed into my pillow, broken things in my own controlled, quiet way. Now, though, I was sobbing. I was six tissues in before he said, "Tell me about him."

The full ninety minutes passed in a rambling monologue. I barely stopped to take a breath. I told him all about Will, about my parents, about the circumstances surrounding Will's death and the fallout from it. It was as if the dam had been breached, and I couldn't stop the flood of my thoughts, my words or my tears.

I walked out of his office feeling as if a giant weight had been lifted, but I was flat-out exhausted. It was nearly dinnertime when we finished, but I planned on just getting a cold drink from the cafeteria and then crashing in my bedroom. I couldn't be a butterfly tonight.

I was the first one there. I grabbed a flavored water drink and was about to leave when fatigue took over. The cafeteria had the air conditioning cranking and it felt so good. I plopped down at a table and closed my eyes as I gulped the cold drink.

"You look like you've been through hell."

My eyes popped open to see that boy from group sitting across from me, smiling down at his tray.

When I recovered from my surprise a moment later, I asked, "You got enough food there?"

He shrugged, never taking his eyes off his plate. "I'm a growing boy."

"You can't put away that much food."

"No?" He smiled when he finally lifted his head to look at me. "Why do you think I'm here so early? I'll be back here for round two before they close the kitchen later on."

He was cute. No, he was beautiful when he smiled. He had a dimple on his left cheek and his blue eyes twinkled. Back in group I really didn't get the chance to see his face. As he stared holes into the floor, all I could see was a mess of dark brown hair that was nearly black, stiff shoulders and hands clenched into fists. He looked like a storm cloud then, but he looked nothing like that now.

"What are you, in training for the Olympic sumo wrestling team or something?"

"Hockey, but I don't know about the Olympics or anything. So far, just Cape Elizabeth High School."

"Where's Cape Elizabeth?"

"Maine."

He didn't ask me where I was from, and I sat there feeling disappointed for a second, thinking he wasn't interested. Then the smell of his food grabbed my attention. I barely took a nibble from that sandwich at lunch and had no appetite whatsoever this morning. I was suddenly starving.

"Whatever that is, it smells delicious."

"Kale, orzo and lamb chops."

"I'll be right back."

I grabbed the same for myself and was ridiculously happy to see he was still sitting at the table. I was afraid he'd scarf his food down and then bolt.

We ate in silence for a few minutes before he asked my name.

"Anna," I answered.

"It's weird, right, how they don't introduce you to the group? *It's up to you to share*, Dr. Ben says. I've only been here two days, but it's weird that no one knows my name."

"All right, I'll bite. What's your name?"

He smiled at me again, and I do believe my heart actually fluttered. "My name is Declan Banks, I'm from Maine, I just turned fifteen yesterday, and I'm a Leo."

He was funny. "Wow, a guy who knows his Zodiac sign? I'm beyond impressed."

"My mother used to read our horoscopes every morning."

"Don't you want to know my sign, baby?"

"No, let me guess." He pretended to study me, cocking his head to one side. "You're a Virgo, right?"

I tossed a dinner roll at his head. "Is that your lame way of asking if I'm a virgin, you creep?"

He raised his hands in surrender. "No, just a lame attempt at humor. I'm sorry. So what *is* your sign, Miss Anna..."

"Clarke, Anna Clarke. I'm fifteen as well, I'm an Aries, I'm from Connecticut, and...I can't believe you got sent here on your birthday, Declan."

He laughed. "I like you, Anna." He looked at his plate again before he said, "I don't think my father remembered it was my birthday. He's kind of, uh, been in a fog."

"I'm guessing it was your mother who died?"

"Yep." He pouted and played air violin when he asked, "And what brings you to Camp Heart Songs?"

"I guess that name induces nausea in everyone, not just me?"

He laughed. "It's terrible."

He didn't press me to answer, but for some reason I wanted him to know. "I'm here because of my brother, Will."

"Oh." He nodded and left it at that.

We sat in comfortable silence as more people filed into the cafeteria. Maggie and Beth waved to me but took a different table.

I was glad.

I wanted Declan all to myself.

* * *

DECLAN

I've been through worse. That's the pep talk I gave myself as we pulled up outside of camp whatever the fuck. I was essentially sentenced to two weeks here, so best to just suck it up and get on with it.

It says a lot about how I'd been acting, not to mention the downside of living in such a small town, that my high school guidance counselor confronted my father in the middle of the summer to impart her two cents.

I knew Mrs. Sullivan was concerned about me and she meant well, but I didn't like being her pet project. And since my mother offed herself over Christmas break last winter—December twenty-second to be exact—that's what I'd become. Mrs. Sullivan regularly stopped me in the hallway to check in, to remind me for the umpteenth time that her "door is always open" and she was "ready when you are." She was a nice woman and all, but I didn't want to talk. I just didn't want...anything.

One day she cornered me on my way to class, late, as had become my habit. I was generally moving in slow motion.

"Please let me help you, sweetheart," she said, her expression truly pained. "Your grades are falling, Declan. And it's more than that...I know you're hurting."

"I'm ok," I said, shaking my head as I pleaded with her silently to just stop talking. Her concern and her tender care were about to break me. I was right there on the edge. If Mrs. Sullivan had reached out and put her hand on my shoulder at that very moment, I just might have collapsed against her in tears.

"Ok." She retreated, clearly disappointed. "Don't take this the wrong way, Declan, but you need a shower."

That comment, believe it or not, made me chuckle. I detoured to the bathroom, and when I took in my greasy hair and the clothes that had seen better days, I had to concede the point to Mrs. Sullivan. I hadn't bothered to take a shower since leaving the rink the night before, and I always smelled pretty rank after sweating in my hockey gear.

The security guard looked up from his newspaper when I passed but said nothing. I made my way across the track and hopped the fence, walking a mile or so across the fields before cutting through my neighbor's backyard. I stood outside our house, the biggest one on the bluff overlooking the beach. The bright pink tulips my mother planted a few years ago were in full bloom, and the sign that read: *Welcome to Our Home* was still hanging next to the front door. I stopped for a moment and took it all in before fishing the spare key from under the mat. Such a nice house, so perfect looking from the outside.

As I turned the doorknob, I prayed that my father hadn't decided to play hooky. I was in no mood to see him.

Since my mother's death, Dad had morphed into a zombie. He

worked, came home, ordered food for us that just sat on the counter, locked himself in his study to work some more—so he said—and then drank until he passed out. Every. Single. Night.

It's not like he was ever in the running for Dad of the Year. Not even close. When I was a kid he was often gone, always away on business trips. When he was home I guess he made an effort, went through the motions, but he was distant.

I always wondered how they'd gotten together in the first place, my parents. My mother was sweet and bubbly, attentive and loving, while my father was cold. I always felt slighted on my mother's behalf when he ignored her. She'd say something funny but he wouldn't laugh. She'd ask what he wanted for dinner and he'd just shrug and say he didn't care. She'd dress up and style her hair when he came back from those business trips, but he wouldn't even spare her a second glance, let alone compliment her. I wanted to throat punch that motherfucker so many times.

He never raised his voice, he wasn't a mean drunk or physically abusive. I'd hear them argue occasionally but they never really fought. At the time I didn't have much to compare their marriage to other than the fake shit you see on television. So I just assumed they were like a lot of other real-life married couples. They coexisted.

Standing under the stream of the shower, I wondered how I'd gone from a kid who liked his hair cut every three weeks, to one who didn't care enough to even comb the sweaty, greasy strands that now hung in his eyes. I raked my hands back and forth over my scalp, sudsing up twice, then let the near scalding water wash over me. It felt good.

As I toweled off, I made an executive decision to put forth an effort in at least one area of my life. Offending my classmates with noxious bodily odors just wasn't fair.

I put on deodorant and dressed in one of the neat collared shirts from my former life. I tried to put on some chinos but they were now floods. Come to think of it, so were the jeans I'd been sporting for the past four months. Must have had another growth spurt since Christmas. I settled on a t-shirt and sweatpants for my outing.

First stop, the barber. Benny seemed overjoyed when he caught sight of me walking through the door. "Well it sure took you long enough, but I'm glad to see you, son."

"Hey, Benny. Give me my regular, ok?"

"I'm not gonna ask you why you ain't in school, 'cause I don't much care. Just glad you're not turning into one of those punk kids with the long hair."

As Benny buzzed and clipped, we bullshitted about town news, which in this town meant hockey and little else.

"That fellow that runs the Zamboni down at the rink told me he never saw no one that shoots like you, kid."

"C'mon, that old dude is half blind, Benny."

"Don't you be modest. You scored a whole mess of goals this season. I was there. Every game. After what happened to you, boy, that's a miracle in its own right." He cleared his throat and said, "Sorry about that, kid. Just meant to say you're tough, you got the true grit you'll need to make it in that sport."

"Thanks."

"What do you think?" he asked as he handed me the mirror so that I could inspect his work from every angle.

"It's good, Benny. Makes me feel better."

"Always," he said as he slapped me on the back. "A man always needs to look his best. Now I better see you again in the next four weeks, or else I'm gonna come down to that ice rink myself with the buzzer. Got that?"

"Yep." I smiled as I stood up, took off the apron and dusted the stray hairs off my shirt. "Thanks, Benny."

Benny reached over then, and instead of his usual handshake and clap on the shoulder combo, he hugged me, brief and tight. "Take care of yourself."

Benny had been cutting my hair since I was a toddler. We weren't super close or anything, but over the years I'd shared more of my personal thoughts and news with him than I had with my own father. How sad was that?

Next stop was going to be for some clothes, but without venturing to Portland my choices were limited. I decided to go home and ring up some purchases on the credit card my father kept in his study. I—or should I say Dad—even bucked up for one-day shipping. Pants, shirts, shorts and a few sweatshirts. I'd even been walking around in sneakers that no longer fit, so I ordered some new ones, some deck shoes and some flip flops—all one size bigger than what I currently owned. Then I ordered new skates, new hockey pants and gloves. I didn't go crazy. Spent a little over eighteen hundred in total. Dad wouldn't even notice.

I decided to take Friday off and return to school on Monday a new man. I'd finish out the remaining two months of school, if not acting normal, at least dressing the part.

I thought making those changes would get Mrs. Sullivan off my back, but apparently I was wrong. So when Heart Songs was forced on me against my will, I was more than a little resentful. Hockey camp was the only type of camp my father should be bucking up for. I didn't express that to him, though. That would require actually speaking to one another.

I reasoned that if I said anything or asked a question, then I might not be able to stop. There was so much I wanted to know. *Was it an accidental overdose? Is there such a thing in a case like hers?* I mean, you either take one pill as prescribed, or you swallow a handful of them with vodka like she did. I don't see how that could be construed as an accident. He held the answers, he knew why. I didn't particularly think my mother was happy or fulfilled, but I didn't think she was depressed either. Was she? Had she been suffering? Was I too wrapped up in my own life to notice? I could go crazy some nights, my mind racing with questions as I rummaged through her things looking for clues.

Other kids were arriving, duffel bags slung over their shoulders like me. They walked away from whoever sat in those cars, the family members who still remained. I had a sudden urge to cry, but thankfully kept myself in check.

A woman approached with a clipboard, smiling as if she was never so happy to see someone in her life. It didn't succeed in making me feel special. "Hi, I'm Cheryl. What's your name?"

"Um, Declan Banks."

"Ok Declan, I can see that your dad is, uh, gone now." I turned to see my father's car speeding away in the opposite direction. *Nice going, asshole.* No need to check in with me, to make sure I was ok, to make sure this place checked out and wasn't really some cult run by a nutcase. The lady leading my very own welcome committee was extra chipper when she said, "Let's get you settled."

The first day was interesting. I had a one-on-one counseling session with a psychiatrist, Dr. Ben. The fact that I was seeing a psychiatrist made me a little uneasy at first, but the guy turned out to be pretty easy going and non-threatening. I didn't say much. Although he was probably trained to wait his patients' prolonged silences out, I was a master at enduring them from living with my dad.

Dr. Ben caved first. "Tell me about playing hockey, Declan. Is it an escape for you?"

He was good, I'll give him that. In that roundabout way he got me to share what playing hockey did for me, how it made me feel. How I'd rather be at the rink than at home any day of the week, and how skating and shooting pucks for hours on end helped me to forget.

The group session was weird. It was five girls, another guy named Trent, and then me. Trent introduced himself without being prompted, then told us he was about to leave for college somewhere down south. He added his hope that this experience would help him to "get a handle" on the anxiety he'd been experiencing since his twin brother died last year of leukemia. When Dr. Ben asked him to share about his brother, he declined, which seemed odd after just spilling that much personal info without so much as being asked. But hey, who was I to judge?

We spent that next hour listening to a girl named Maggie talk about her mother, who died after a six year-long battle with cancer. Everyone else in the group said something, whether it be a word of acknowledgement, some words of comfort directed at Maggie, or to share what they had in common with her. I said nothing. I barely even looked at anyone. Everyone else in the group was a few years older and didn't seem to have much interest in meeting me. I left group without anyone even knowing my name. You would think the anonymity would have been a relief, but it wasn't. I felt incredibly lonely sitting there among them and then again staring at my ceiling later on that night.

I took a long run that next morning, then showered and made my way to breakfast. I sat down next to two boys who weren't in my group. I wasn't usually so forward but something about yesterday had me rattled. I really didn't want to be alone.

"Mind if I sit here?"

"No, go ahead. I'm Kevin. You got here yesterday too, right?"

"Yeah, yesterday. I'm Declan."

"I'm Shane," the other one offered. "You play hockey?" he asked, gesturing to my shirt.

"Yeah, do you?"

"All-state last year."

"Wow. Where do you play?"

"Jersey, you?"

"Cape Elizabeth in Maine."

"Damn, if you're even halfway decent then you're better than most of the guys I play with. I went to camp last summer in Bangor. Tough, nasty motherfuckers," he said with an admiring laugh. "You know they called me Southern Boy? Like I was from Alabama or something. Can you believe that shit?"

"Yeah, people from New England, the Dakotas, Minnesota…We take our hockey hard-core."

"I should be at hockey camp right now instead of here," he said, shaking his head.

"I hear you." Looking over to Kevin, I asked, "Where are you from?"

"Hingham, Mass. And no, I don't play hockey. As you can see, I still have my original grill," he said, flashing his teeth.

"I do too!" Shane and I said that at the same time, and the three of us laughed.

"I'm built more for basketball," he said, rising from his seat. "I'm going in for a refill. Be right back."

He wasn't joking. Kevin looked to be about six-five. "How old is he?" I asked Shane.

"Fifteen. He said his dad is six-eight."

"Wow. How old are you?"

"Seventeen. This is my big year, as far as college recruiting goes. What about you?"

"Fifteen. I'm going into sophomore year."

"A baby," he said, smiling. "How's your team looking?"

"Good. We don't have JV, but I got some playing time last season on varsity."

"As a freshman?" When I nodded, he said, "You *must* be good."

"I'm all right."

"Maybe we'll cross paths in college one day, Declan."

I shook my head. "My grades were horrible this year. My hockey coach basically told me he'll bench me if I don't get my shit together. I think he's bluffing but I've got to do better."

"As long as I pass, and I mean with a D, I'm golden."

"Really?"

Shane nodded. "I'm my high school's great white hope for the state championship again. My teachers let me slide even when I don't deserve it."

"Not the case for me. They know I can be an A student so they don't cut me much slack. I pulled C's across the board last semester."

"Hard time concentrating?"

"Yeah."

He looked away. "Yeah."

We broke after breakfast, making plans to play some basketball after our morning group activities. I was happy to have found some friends here because eating alone really sucked. And Heart Songs was a cell phone-free environment—couldn't even pretend to be occupied staring at my screen like I did every day in my high school cafeteria.

I shuffled in and took my seat, planning for a second day of hanging back and just listening, when I saw her walk in behind the others. A new girl. She was smiling, as if one of them had just said something amusing, but she looked uneasy. After staring at her for way too long like a dork, I made myself turn away.

She was sun-kissed. Blond hair and tanned skin that made the whites of her teeth and her blue eyes pop. She caught me looking and smiled in a friendly way before I shot my gaze back to the ground. *You ass*, I said to myself, *that was smooth*. I couldn't help sneaking looks, though. She was, by far, prettier than any girl I went to school with. Prettier than any girl I'd ever seen in person.

She didn't say a word, just sat listening as some girl told us about finding her mother after she'd committed suicide. It didn't resonate with me as you might expect. All that blood and gore made our experiences vastly different.

When I found my mother, I thought she was asleep. She was neat. The vodka had been put away and the pill bottle was back on its shelf in the medicine cabinet. She was sitting up in her bed, eyes closed, peaceful. She looked as if she'd just nodded off. I actually left the room and went downstairs to play video games for two hours before checking on her again. I only went back upstairs when I noticed that, one, I was hungry, two, no one else seemed concerned that dinner wasn't being prepared, and three, that the sun had set. The fact that she'd been up there for two hours—that she might have been alive when I first came and knocked on her door—turned her death into something I would always feel guilty about.

I caught that girl looking my way later on when I walked past the pool on my way to the gym. Was this what chemistry felt like? I didn't even know her name, but just the sight of her had my stomach flipping and had me feeling warm and buzzed all over.

When I saw her sitting in the cafeteria later on that day, I immediately wanted to put my arm around her, to comfort her. She looked tired, overheated and emotionally drained. She sat with her eyes closed, head turned towards the ceiling, the cold drink bottle pressed against her neck. I grabbed a tray full of food and then decided to take a chance and sit down across from her. I was risking being shut down, but something in the way she looked at me earlier had me thinking she was kind.

Anna, it turned out, was not just kind, she was sweet. And she was even more beautiful up close, when her smiles and laughter were directed at me. I liked her sense of humor. She was a bit of a wise ass, like me. And I liked that when I got up to leave after dinner, she looked disappointed.

"I guess I'll see you at group tomorrow?" she asked.

"Yeah." I stood there thinking. "What are you doing later on?"

"I don't know. What do you wild kids do at Heart Songs?"

"Well, they had a movie last night." I broke out my serious face when I added, "Nothing with death, drug addiction, gratuitous violence or sadness of any kind, of course."

"Of course."

"And there's a game room."

"What kind of games?"

"Ping pong, pool, board games...It's crazy in that game room."

"Are you going there?"

"If you want to go, I will."

She looked relieved. "I'll go. And don't worry, I'll take it easy on you in ping pong."

I couldn't help but laugh. "*You'll* go easy on *me*? No, no, no little girl, it's *me* who's going to have to go easy on *you*."

"Little girl, my ass. You're going down, Banks."

I walked her back to her room after barely hanging on that night, winning three out of five games against her.

"You're like one of those lethal little North Korean table tennis players, you know that, Anna?"

She hip checked me. "You're pretty good yourself. I demand a rematch tomorrow night."

I checked her back, liking the contact way too much. "No way. I'm not playing you in ping pong again. I'm going out on top. Tomorrow we'll move onto pool."

"No fair, I don't know how to play."

"I'll teach you. I have a feeling you'll be a shark within thirty minutes."

The thought of showing her how to shoot, standing close by as she aimed for the ball, made me think of kissing her. God, I wanted to kiss her.

"I'll see you tomorrow?" she asked.

"Anna, you're stuck with me for the next two weeks."

She smiled that sweet smile again. "We don't have group until after lunch, right?"

"Yeah, individuals all morning."

"Lordy, I don't know if I have it in me again."

"Yeah, those can be pretty brutal." I put my hand on her shoulder to reassure her, and I wanted to make her feel better, I did, but I also really wanted to touch her. "See you tomorrow," I said before turning and walking away.

I drifted off into a peaceful, deep sleep that night, dreaming of Anna Clarke.

* * *

ANNA

I was sitting on the bench outside of Dr. Ben's office when Declan walked out of his session. Just the sight of him made me straighten up and smile, but his pained expression and red-rimmed eyes took the wind right out of my sails.

I didn't know him well enough to do it, but in that moment I wanted to take his hands in mine and give them a reassuring squeeze. I wanted to hug him, wrap him up in my arms. I wanted to kiss him, to help him forget. He looked at me and forced a lopsided smile before walking away.

Dr. Ben came out to greet me. "Hello, Anna. How was your first day?"

"Good. Everyone here is really nice. I'm friends with Declan."

"Oh."

I'd never been in therapy before, but I watched enough television to know the basics. Neutral tone, no leading questions, no helpful opinions. And I knew about confidentiality before Dr. Ben gave me the introductory speech yesterday. So fishing for intel on Declan wasn't going to get me anywhere.

We spent the session talking mostly about my relationship with Will and about Drew also. Drew was a complicated topic.

Everyone wants to help after a tragedy. *I'm here to listen. Do you need anything? Tell me what I can do.* But the truth is that no one wants to listen. Despair, grief, depression—it makes most people really uncomfortable. I'd been keeping everything bottled up inside for the past few months, so an hour one-on-one with Dr. Ben on a daily basis was cathartic, like Jane said, but it was draining. I practically staggered out of my session an hour later.

I gravitated towards the pool, lured by the sounds of the waterfall and a few kids playing volleyball. A dive into that cool oasis, yeah, that was just what the doctor ordered. I didn't even take a chair or grab a towel. I just kicked off my sneakers and stripped out of my shorts and tank as I walked towards the pool, dropping garments as I went. I dove right in, grateful for the silence and the cool water on my skin as I swam underwater. When I came up on the opposite side of the pool for a breath, Declan was crouched down on the deck waiting for me.

"*You* are a slob."

"Huh?"

"You must have a cleaning lady at home, Clarke. You just took your clothes off and discarded them over a half-mile radius."

I was trying to think of a snarky comeback, but I had nothing. So when he reached his fingers into the water to splash me, I grabbed his wrist and pulled him in.

"Jesus," he sputtered as he came up for air. "You're dangerous."

"You called me a slob, you deserved that."

"I don't even have a suit on."

"Lesson learned. Next time you'll think twice about insulting me when you're poolside."

"Fair enough."

He was less than a foot away from me. When he reached his hand out to tuck my hair behind my ear, I must have looked foolish, closing my eyes in anticipation. I thought he was about to kiss me, which was ridiculous being that it was the middle of the day, he hardly knew me, and there were at least six other kids in the pool with us.

"Hey," he said softly. "I'm sorry about before."

"Are you apologizing because you were upset after your session?"

When he didn't say anything, I flicked a little water his way. "We *are* at a grief camp, Declan. Crying is not only expected, it's mandatory."

His lopsided smile made me feel accomplished, as if making Declan happy was an achievement on par with curing cancer.

"How was your morning?"

"You saw me on my way into the pool, didn't you?"

"It is rough, but there's something about it...I like it even though it makes me feel like I've been hit by an eighteen wheeler."

I nodded. "Yeah, no one talks to me at home. It makes this really hard because I'm not used to it, but at the same time it's such a relief to talk."

He nodded his head in agreement and then said, "So you saw the schedule for later, right? They've messed with my plans to teach you nine-ball."

"The schedule?"

"Get with the program, Clarke. You get a schedule under your door every morning, which dictates your life. Tonight we're separating into groups, girls and boys."

I tried not to sound too disappointed but I'm sure it showed on my face. "Oh."

"You want to meet up after? We'd have to sneak out after they do bed checks, so if you don't want to I understand."

Sounding more than a little too eager, I didn't even think it through before I said, "No, I'll meet you."

"It's probably for the best anyway. I didn't want to beat you in two sports, one night after the other. I mean, damaging your self-esteem while at grief camp could affect your long term mental health."

With that, he ducked underwater and swam away from me. Little did he know, the pool was the one place I could almost certainly kick his ass.

Just as he was getting to the other side of the pool, I caught up and snagged the hem of his shorts, giving them a yank before I pulled ahead and surfaced.

"Hey, that wasn't fair." He was out of breath and splashed me in the face for good measure.

"So now we're even. You're better at ping pong and I'm a far superior swimmer."

He didn't say anything, just kept treading water and looking at me. I wanted to know what he was thinking but couldn't read his expression. He ducked under for a few beats, and when he came up he'd snapped out of whatever that was.

"Tennis or basketball next. You pick."

That was a no-brainer. He was nearly a foot taller than me, and while I wasn't good enough for a singles spot on my high school team, I was decent. "Tennis it is."

"You're not some junior national champ or something, are you?"

"You'll just have to wait and see, now won't you?"

"Ugh."

He put his palms on the deck and lifted his body out of the pool in one swift motion.

"You look older than fifteen," I said, looking up at him.

"You think? Is it the beard or the massive muscles?"

When he grasped my hand and pulled me out as if I weighed no more than a wisp of air, I'll admit I was a little swoony over the muscles.

"Well," I said, as I touched his cheek, "since you don't have so much as a whisker, I'll have to say it's the muscles."

He was surprised by the compliment, and as soon as the words left my mouth I felt exposed and more than a little uncomfortable. I could feel my cheeks turning red and I suddenly wanted to cover up my body, on full display except for the string bikini I was wearing.

Struggling as I looked around the deck, I asked no one in particular, "Where are my clothes?"

"Maybe the cleaning lady came by after all," he joked. But when I didn't laugh, his smile dropped. "Wait here, I'll run and get you a towel."

He jogged over to the other side of the pool and grabbed a towel from the shed. He tossed it to me and said, "I think I see your stuff on a lounger. I'll check."

The pool was like the kind you'd see at an upscale resort, with a waterfall feature, a hot tub in a nook off to the side, and teak loungers with plush cushions situated all around the large deck.

"I was joking before but I think one of the attendants did fold your stuff for you, you brat." He handed me the pile of clothes. "Are you still up for meeting tonight?" I nodded, shaking off my discomfort because I *really* liked him. "Ok, if you walk out the back door of your building and then keep going straight, you'll hit the lake. It's less than a quarter mile. Take a flashlight with you, but don't turn it on until you're at least fifty yards away."

"I don't have a flashlight, Ranger Rick. You actually *packed* a flashlight?"

"There's one in your nightstand drawer, wiseass. I'll be on the dock waiting for you, ok?"

"Ok."

I didn't trust myself to say anything else. I felt awkward, nervous and excited. *Tonight could be the night.* I was hoping for my first real kiss.

* * *

DECLAN

Group was uneventful, or maybe I just thought it was because I was hardly paying attention. I was fidgety and restless, using every ounce of willpower I possessed to keep my eyes off the girl sitting right across from me.

I'd never fallen for a girl. It was an unfamiliar feeling, one that was wild and potent and exciting. Anna was pretty, and I'll admit, seeing her at the pool considerably upped my already high opinion of her looks, but it wasn't just that. I hung on her every word and studied every change in her expression. Her smile and her laugh made me feel like *I* could laugh again. Like I could finally breathe again.

I ate about half of my regular king-size portion at dinner. It was still enough to nourish a normal kid, but the butterflies in my stomach were really messing with my appetite.

It took Shane tapping a fork on my plate to snap me out of my daze. "Hello there, Declan. I see *someone* has caught your attention."

"Huh?"

He laughed. "Over there," he said as he just barely nodded his head in the direction of Anna's table. "And she keeps sneaking looks over at you." I shrugged, brushing him off. "She's cute, Declan."

"I guess."

"You guess, my ass. Seeing you two young lovebirds makes me miss my girl. Jess acted like I was going away for six months when I left on Saturday."

"What's she like?" Kevin asked.

I was glad he asked because I wanted to know, too. Shane was like this worldly, fascinating guy. The two years he had on us made him seem more knowledgeable about everything in life.

"Jessica? She's beautiful, inside and out. After what happened, she was the only one who helped me keep it together. Without her, the drinking and the drugs would have gotten a whole lot worse." He looked to me when he added, "I would have been kissing school, hockey and everything else goodbye."

I nodded, thinking to myself that I wanted a girl like that. Someone beautiful inside and out, someone like Anna.

"Do you think you two will go to the same college together?"

He smiled at me and shook his head, as if that sort of question could only come from someone with a naïve and sunny outlook. "Jess can go anywhere. She's seriously the smartest person I've ever known. She wants to be a biomedical engineer, whatever that is," he joked, obviously proud of her. "But I'm a different story. I go wherever hockey can open a door for me. She's been tutoring me for the college entrance exams, but I think she's wasting her time."

"What about your friends? Do they play hockey? Anyone with prospects like you?"

He stood and picked up his tray. "Besides Jess, I don't have any friends."

Kevin filled me in after he left. Shane was here because five of his friends were killed in a drunk driving accident last winter. He was supposed to be with them, would have been the sixth kid crammed into the SUV, but his coach kept him late for practice.

It hit me again just how odd this place was. At first glance we seemed like your average everyday teenagers, but we were *not* normal. Every single person here was a shell of their former self.

We were all damaged goods.

I was sitting on the dock waiting, palms sweating, when I heard the crunch of pine needles getting closer. I hopped back up and walked the length of the short pier and called out to her. She emerged from the trees, shining the flashlight right into my eyes.

"Turn that thing off, Anna. You're blinding me."

"Sorry," she said, laughing as she shut it off. It was pretty dark out there, but the moon cast a glow off the water, enough so that I could see clearly. "I was petrified walking here! A quarter of a mile is a long way in the pitch black. I almost turned around I was so scared."

"Thank God you didn't. I would have been sitting here all night like an ass."

"We have a lake near my house," she said, looking around. I noticed she was twisting her fingers together. She was nervous.

I took one of her hands in mine and led her out to the dock. "C'mon, we can put our feet in. The water's warm."

She sat with one leg tucked underneath her, the other leg dangling over the side of the dock. She swung that one leg back and forth, back and forth, back and forth. I was staring down at her toes as they made soft ripples along the surface of the water with each pass.

"So, Declan..." She smiled when she angled her body towards me.

"So, Anna..."

My breath was caught in my chest and my heart was hammering like I'd been out on the ice for three periods straight without a break. I wanted to kiss her lips so badly I thought I could taste that plump sweetness already.

"Let's play twenty questions."

That broke me out of my trance. "Huh?"

"You know, we ask each other questions to get to know one another better." I knew what the game was, just didn't know if I was up for it. "I'll go first. Declan Banks, what is your favorite color?"

She was telling me not to worry, that she'd keep it light, and that put me at ease.

"Blue."

She reached down into the lake and flicked a few drops of water my way. "Predictable."

"What?" I asked, pretending to be insulted. "The best things in life are blue...Blue sky, blue ocean, my hockey team's jerseys are blue."

"Ok, ok, Declan. I just broke the rules, anyway. You aren't allowed to critique someone's answers."

"Yeah, that was bullshit," I teased. "Ok Anna Clarke, tell me *your* favorite color. Wait, forget it, I know it's pink."

"I'll admit it, I'm a girl and I like pink, but my favorite color is green."

"Why green?"

She rolled her eyes. "The best things in life are green...Green grass, green olives, green money, and...What's that next big town over from Cape Elizabeth?"

"Portland?" I asked, confused.

"Yeah, Portland High School's hockey jerseys are green."

I grabbed both of her wrists and gently wrestled her back to the dock. She was laughing so hard, like I was tickling her. "That was mean. I can't have that vision in my head, of you wearing my biggest rival's jersey." As I let her back up, I said, "I'm going to have to send you one of my jerseys now and make you snap a picture of yourself in it."

"I'll have to think about it. I'm very loyal to Portland." When I made a move to grab her again, she held both hands up, laughing, requesting a truce. "Okay, you ask the question now."

"All right, the pressure's on." After a moment, I said, "Favorite food. I'm keeping things safe."

"Up until the day I met you, I would have said falafel, but now I'm thinking lamb chops."

"Falafel?"

"Yeah, middle eastern, fried chickpeas in a pita with that yummy yogurt sauce."

"You're very sophisticated, Miss Clarke."

"You've obviously never had one, Declan. When they're good, they're really messy. You wind up with half of it on your face."

I was thinking about how much I liked her, how much fun I was having just sitting there talking to her. I hadn't had fun in over six months. I was lost in that thought when I felt her nudge me. "Favorite food, space cadet?"

I recovered quickly. "That's not an easy question. I'm thinking."

"I think you like all foods, *so much*, that you can't narrow it down."

"Maybe. But if I was stranded for a weekend, say, and knew I could only have one meal over and over for two days, I'd go with spaghetti and meatballs."

"Solid choice."

"Your turn." I was having more fun with this than you could

imagine.

"Ok Mr. Banks, who was your first kiss? I'm *not* keeping things safe."

"Ugh."

"What? Was it bad or something?"

"No, it was just...nothing." I shrugged, trying to shake off the memory of that weird night. "Some girl from school named Melody, last summer one night on the beach."

She was looking down into the water, watching her foot move back and forth when she said, "Sounds romantic."

"Not. There were three boys and three girls. We just paired off, no big deal. Then she started showing up at the ice rink. It was annoying."

"So you've had your first kiss *and* your first stalker. That's hot."

"There's something the matter with you," I teased. "Ok, even though I don't really want to know, who got your first kiss?"

"If you *really* don't want to know, you can ask me a different question."

I thought on that for a moment. "No, now I'm curious. Tell me."

She hesitated before she said, "Never been kissed."

"Are you for real?"

"Yes, I'm for real." Before she turned away I caught the hurt look on her face. "Don't make me feel like a freak."

I shook my head and reached for her hand. "I didn't mean it that way. It's just that you're so pretty...I figured you'd have all the boys chasing after you."

I'm sure I was a deep shade of red at that moment, but I didn't care because she was smiling again. I could feel it even though I was looking away, looking out over the lake.

She gave my hand a gentle tug. "Thanks."

"For what?"

"For telling me I'm pretty."

I looked back at her. "You're more than pretty, Anna."

Now she was embarrassed, looking down into her lap. "I have an idea," she said softly. "Why don't you be my first? That way it will always be a good memory for me."

She didn't have to ask me twice. We were sitting side by side on the dock, feet in the water. I scooted over a few inches so that our legs were touching. It wasn't the most comfortable position I guess, with our lower bodies facing one way and our faces turned towards each other, but I only remember how good that kiss felt. We didn't break apart for a full five minutes.

When we did finally come up for air, Anna looked blissed-out and dreamy when she said, "You see? I will happily remember that kiss for the rest of my life."

"How about this one, think you'll remember it?" I asked as I went back in for more.

She had one hand resting on my cheek, while the other was laced with one of mine and resting in our laps. Her touch felt so good, so gentle. I knew for sure that I'd remember because that kiss was the start of the best few days of my life.

* * *

ANNA

I was floating on air by the time we made it back to my cabin.

With each and every one of my senses in overdrive, the crickets peep-peepy chirps sounded like some mad chorus, the stars were neon-bright against the sky, and the heady pine-laced air made me feel goofy in the best possible way. And his hand, each finger laced and interlocked with mine. I pictured an atom splitting right at that spot where our hands were clasped together, an explosion of color and electricity invading my veins, zipping up my arm and spreading throughout my entire being.

He whispered, "Goodnight, Anna," before bending down to kiss me again.

In bed that night I relived his goodnight kiss over and over again. I pictured his face and touched my fingers to my lips, trying my best to recreate the sensation of his lips on mine. After months of insomnia, I fell into a deep and peaceful sleep.

And after that night, we were pretty much inseparable. I mean, we weren't attached at the hip completely. Sometimes I ate with Maggie, Jane and Beth, and sometimes I sat with Declan, Kevin and Shane, but I wanted to be with him, just him, every second of every day.

Unless I was sitting across from Dr. Ben, I was either with Declan or thinking about him. But this *was* grief camp, so there were many hours of therapy to contend with. So I was either riding a euphoric high or delving into the lowest of the low points of my life. Dr. Ben made it bearable. He was patient, understanding and *so* different from my parents.

I told him that people don't change during one of our sessions, and that I hated my parents and knew my relationship with them would never be a good one. I was bracing myself for some generic *Oh honey, you don't mean that* crap, so I was surprised and relieved when he told me that I might be right. He cautioned me to always leave the door open, but that it was true, you can't change people. Some people, he stated simply, are blessed with wonderful parents, others are not. He told me the way to make it right was to be a good parent to my own child if I decided to be a mother myself one day.

Talking to someone who didn't bullshit me, or try to sugar coat the clusterfuck that was my life, was a comfort and a relief.

Being in group with Declan wasn't awkward either. We both started to pipe up here and there. One day at the beginning of the second week, Declan went ahead and shared the story of his mother's suicide with the group. He often looked to me, almost as if he was speaking to me alone and no one else was in the room. Later that night when we were down by the lake, he told me that having me there gave him the strength to keep talking. I kissed him with everything I had that night, wanting to comfort him, love him, and make my way into his heart.

Our time was running out. Maybe it was because he made me brave, or maybe it was because I wanted him to know everything about me, but I decided to share my story. Only four months had passed since that awful night, so I wasn't very smooth. I had to stop a few times. Declan was sitting on one side of me and Beth was on the other. When I looked down at one point, I noticed that she had one of my hands and he had the other. I hadn't felt cared for or protected like that since Will had died.

When I went to sneak out of my cabin that night, I saw Declan waiting next to a tree just a few yards from my door.

"I thought you'd be down there already."

"Yeah, I was thinking I'd walk with you tonight."

I knew he was there waiting because he was concerned about me. To be honest, I was so tired from the session that I almost fell asleep before it was time to meet up with Declan. But I wouldn't have missed this. It was our last night together. Right after breakfast tomorrow we had individual sessions scheduled. Family sessions were to follow with departure immediately after. It went unsaid, but we both knew we might not see each other again after breakfast.

We were quiet as we made our way to the dock. You could only hear pine needles and leaves crunching underfoot, the occasional call of an owl, and crickets calling out to one another.

We were holding hands, lying on our backs and staring up at the stars. Declan took my hand and raised it to his mouth to kiss it. He rested my hand against his heart then and said, "I'm going to miss you, Anna. I wish you lived in Cape Elizabeth."

"Me too. I'd hang around the ice rink after school just to annoy you."

"That would *never* annoy me."

I was twirling my hair, lost in thought. "It would be nice, though, wouldn't it? I have a lot of friends, but they don't know me like you do. I guess everyone feels misunderstood, but what happened to me..." I raised myself up on my elbow to look at him. "I mean, what's happened to people like *us*, it sets us apart from everyone else. Only one of my friends even mentions my brother's name around me. The others get really uncomfortable if I bring him up."

"How do you think it is for me? You think any of my hockey buddies are there to listen? I got a few grunts of condolence at the funeral but that was it. I didn't get much more than that from my father, come to think of it."

"Dr. Ben told me I'll be a better parent to my children because of how sucky my parents are. Do you believe that?"

"You? Definitely. You'll be a great mother someday."

His words made me blush. I shook my head. "It's stupid to even think of something like that now, but...I do hope that he's right. I hope I don't morph into some cold bitch."

"You won't," he said as he moved my hair behind my ear and then leaned up to kiss me. When he lowered me down onto him so that our upper bodies were pressed together, I wondered if he could feel my racing heart. He pulled back slowly, looked at me and said, "I don't think I've ever seen anyone as beautiful as you are, Anna. You know that?"

"That's good," I whispered. "I want to be the most beautiful girl you'll *ever* see. Please don't forget me, ok?"

"I won't."

I laid back on the dock again, holding his hand, lost in good thoughts. I must have drifted off for a while. When I woke, Declan was up on his elbow looking down at me, gently running his fingers through my hair.

"Do you want to go back up to the cabin? You fell asleep on me."

"No," I said, yawning. "I can sleep tomorrow. I want to stay here with you tonight. Is that ok?"

"It's more than ok," he said as he leaned down to kiss my forehead.

The idea hit me suddenly. "Let's go swimming."

"Yeah?"

"Why not? The lake's warm. You're here to protect me from any creepy lake things."

"We don't have suits."

"Swim in your undies. That's basically the same as a suit."

"Ok, crazy Anna. I'm game if you are."

I poked him in the ribs. "You first."

"Fine with me."

Declan took center stage on the small dock, then pretended to do a strip tease, complete with dancing and humming a burlesque tune. He flexed his muscles like a brute after the shirt came off.

"How can you even get through doorways with that big head of yours? I've never seen a boy who loves himself more than you do, Declan Banks."

"Puh-lease, you're loving the show." He slid off his gym shorts and did a cannonball into the lake wearing only his boxers.

I pretended to yawn then, stretching my arms above my head. "On second thought, I think I will hit the hay." I got up and walked a few paces down the pier, back towards the cabin.

"You wouldn't dare."

I turned to him and smiled. "Well, I'm *not* doing a striptease, if that's what you're waiting for."

"No need for that, just get in here."

"Aren't you going to turn around so I can get undressed?"

"What happened to," he switched to a god-awful imitation of a girl's voice, "undies, same as a bathing suit." He splashed water my way. "What happened to that, Anna? And I don't recall you looking away when I got undressed. Noooo, you made me feel like a piece of meat the way your eyes never left me."

"My eyes never left you? You practically begged me to watch!"

I was laughing, but inside I was a messed up tangle of nerves. No boy had ever seen me before. And it's not that I hated my body or felt ashamed of it or anything, but I did wish that my damn boobs would grow already. I had something there, but I was a late bloomer compared to everyone else I knew. I was the last of my friends to get my period, and a few of them already looked like grown women compared to me. So standing there on that dock, I felt exposed and shy and scared.

I gave myself a quick pep talk and decided to just get it over with. I shimmied out of my shorts and lifted the tank over my head.

My plan was to get a running start and jump in quick, but just as I was about to take off Declan whispered, "Stop. Just stay there a minute." So I did what he said and didn't so much as breathe. He looked at me with wonder in his eyes. "I want to remember what you look like." His voice broke a little when he said, "I'm afraid I might not ever see you again."

I sat down on the edge of the dock and slowly lowered myself into the water. I was no more than a foot away then, treading water like him. "No, don't say that. I know that I *will* see you again someday."

Declan moved closer and kissed me, turning me so that my back rested against the ladder and he was able to use it as leverage to hold us up. His kisses were gentle and he left just the slightest distance between our bodies. He reached up between us and waited for me to nod before sliding the strap of my bra off my shoulder. He ran his fingers back and forth over my shoulder and then traced the skin over my collarbone. It felt like every one of my nerve endings was wired. Declan continued kissing me, his hand slow and tentative as he skimmed my breasts. He moved in to close the distance between us, and my breath hitched when I felt his body press against mine. I'd never felt a boy before, and Declan's lower body couldn't hide his want. He backed away, embarrassed for a moment, but came closer again when I leaned back in to kiss him. We stayed like that, kissing, our bodies slick and just barely touching, for what must have been close to an hour. We got out only when Declan caught sight of my pruned fingers.

We didn't speak as we got back into our clothes, but he took my hand once I was ready and led me back down the pier towards the shore. We walked in silence until we got to my cabin door. By then it was just beginning to get light. He looked tired and sad. I'm sure I did too.

"Get me a pen and paper, ok?"

I grabbed my sketchbook and a charcoal from the desk. I tried to make a joke even though I wasn't feeling the least bit cheerful. "Do you want my autograph, Declan?"

He rolled his eyes. "I want your phone number." He looked unsure when he asked, "Can I call you?"

"You'd better," I said as I wrote it down. The tears I'd been holding back started to come then. It was partly fatigue but mostly it was the sure knowledge that my time with Declan had come to an end. I knew that his face, his words, and the feelings I had when I was with him would all blur and fade into a distant memory, just like Will and Drew were fading away. I choked out the words as I handed him the folded paper, "I don't want to leave you."

He tilted my chin up. "I know. It's crazy, isn't it? I feel like my heart's breaking." His eyes were wet with unshed tears, and everything, everything in this life suddenly seemed so un-fucking-fair.

Declan kissed me again, deep kisses that stung my lips and took the hurt away at the same time. In that dizzy haze, I imagined that I was warm maple syrup or melted chocolate, that I had the power to melt right into him, to seep past his skin right into his veins. I wanted to stay with him. I didn't want to go back to being alone.

When Declan broke the kiss, he rested his lips against my forehead and whispered, "My Anna," before he turned and walked away.

Chapter Six

ANNA

The basket hit the floor with a thud right before I collapsed onto my bed. My pulse was racing and my heart was hammering in my chest.

I'd just seen a ghost.

Declan Banks.

Three years since we left camp. Three years since he kissed me goodbye as the sun rose. Stretched out on my bed that morning, I decided that I was in love with him. That I loved him and that one day I'd marry him. I smiled at the thought, smiled at the naïve, fifteen-year-old girl I used to be.

My mind replayed those two weeks, replayed as many of the conversations, the kisses and the feather-light touches that I could remember.

I missed dinner and was surprised when I checked my phone to see that it was nine-fifty. I had this ritual of taking a short run every night at ten. It was my time to meditate, to get a handle on any problems or stress, and it was my time to reconnect with Will.

At the risk of sounding unbalanced, I had conversations with

Will during my nightly runs. I would tell him about my day, ask what he thought about this or that, or I'd just tell him how much I loved and missed him.

I was walking out the back door of Loyola, making my way towards the road when I heard him call out to me from a ground-floor window, "Anna?" He hopped out through the open window, and as he got closer I could see that he was shaking his head. "I see this girl running every night at the same time, and I always worry about her. I always think to myself that she shouldn't be running alone at this hour. It's been you every night, hasn't it?"

"I can take care of myself, Banks. I've been doing these nightly runs for years."

"Why? I mean, why so late?"

"When it's dark or when it's late, that's when my mind stops spinning, or slows down enough for me to think." I spoke before he could weigh in on that weird admission. "I couldn't believe it when I saw you today. I still can't believe it."

He nodded, his hands shoved deep into his pockets. "I had to lock myself away in my room for a few hours just to wrap my head around it."

"Yeah, I just emerged from my trance a few minutes ago."

"Hey, let me get my sneakers on. I'll run with you."

"No, I'll be fine." I took a few steps back. "Maybe we can meet for lunch one day?"

He looked disappointed for a moment before he recovered. "Yeah, I'd like that."

I ran. I ran so fast and so hard that night. Usually this was a jog, nothing crazy. I wasn't in training for anything. Tonight, though, I wanted to run, to scream, to cry—to push myself until I couldn't breathe anymore.

Why was seeing him again so hard?

An hour later I was back. When I came to a stop behind my dorm, I just about collapsed into myself, resting my elbows on my knees. I stayed like that for a few minutes until my breathing evened out. I made my way to the second floor, grabbed my shower basket and then proceeded to stand underneath a stream of steaming hot water for a full half-hour.

"What happened to you?" Fiona asked when I came into our room and flopped onto my bed.

"Just tired."

"Are you sure? You look, I don't know, devastated or something."

"I saw someone today that I haven't seen in years."

"Boy or a girl?"

"A boy."

She rubbed her palms together. "Ok, this is getting interesting."

"It's nothing, Fiona, really."

"C'mon, you're killing me. Gimme the dish, spill it."

I rolled over onto my side to face her. "A boy I met three years ago. It just brought up a lot of feelings. I met him right after Will died."

"Oh, Anna, I'm sorry."

"No really, it's ok. Seeing him just threw me for a loop." I pulled at my blankets, snuggling them right up under my chin. "You mind if I just crash? I feel like I can barely keep my eyes open."

"Go ahead," she said as she gathered her books and grabbed a pen. "I'll go to the lounge. Get a good night's sleep. You'll feel better in the morning."

I cried myself to sleep that night. Not really sure why. Maybe it was the pain of reliving those good memories with Declan, knowing they were just memories and nothing more. Maybe it was being thrown back to that time again, the pain of losing Will so fresh. Or maybe it was the heavy sadness of that awful homecoming. I didn't have Will, I didn't have Declan, and I no longer had a home.

What a shitty year that had been.

* * *

DECLAN

My Econ professor was probably saying something interesting and important, but I wasn't paying attention.

"Who's Anna?" There was a sharp edge to Charlotte's voice. "I thought your girlfriend's name was Tess?"

"Huh?"

Charlotte nodded towards my notebook, and when I looked down I was surprised to see that I'd been writing her name over and over again. I shut the notebook and closed my eyes.

Shit. Why did it hurt so bad? Anna backing away from me last night, acting as if being within ten feet of me was unbearable. The look on her face damn near killed me. It felt as bad as it did three years ago, when my texts went unanswered and my calls repeatedly went to voicemail with no response. I couldn't wrap my head around it then, just as I couldn't accept it now.

My desk was by the window. Nearly every night I would notice that girl stretching and then taking off for a run at exactly ten o'clock. It annoyed me to no end because I couldn't completely relax, didn't feel as if I could leave my spot at my desk until I'd see her amble back up the hill, safe and sound, usually half an hour later. Last night, when I saw it was Anna and she practically fell backwards trying to get away from me, I sat there staring out the window after she left. Thirty minutes stretched to forty, then forty-five, then fifty minutes. Didn't she know she was putting herself in danger? When my phone screen read eleven, I laced up my sneakers. I was sliding the window open, about to hop out, when I saw her bent over and pulling for breath. A moment later she was walking in the back entrance of her dorm, out of sight.

Charlotte was nudging me playfully after class as we walked towards the cafeteria. She kept asking if I was excited about my first game, which was coming up that weekend. She was pouring the flirt on heavy and it was irritating.

"Everyone says you'll get playing time."

"Unless my coach says it then it really doesn't matter, right?"

She linked her pinky finger with mine and batted her eyes when she said, "Well, I'll be there hollering your name if that'll help."

I freed my finger from her grip and used that hand to hitch my backpack up onto my opposite shoulder. I didn't want to be rude, but damn. "I don't think that's how the coach sets the roster, but whatever, knock yourself out."

I paused when we got to the table. When Charlotte sat next to Paige and then looked to the empty seat on the other side of her, I didn't acknowledge the invitation. I took a seat at the opposite end.

"What's up, boys?"

"Big weekend, right?" Brandon asked.

"I know, I'm pumped."

"Is Tess coming in?"

"No, she'll be here next weekend for the game against BU."

Terrence slapped my back. "Ok, so since the mouse is away, the cat can play. We're thinking a big bash in the woods."

"Which is different from every other weekend, how?" I asked.

Frank popped a fry in his mouth. "Every other weekend has been pretty damn good, no?"

"This will be different," Terrence said. "This will be the first of many victory parties."

Brandon was frowning down at his plate. "I wonder how it's going to feel winning now, when my ass has splinters in it."

"I know, right? To go from playing nearly every single minute to just watching. It's going to be weird," I said.

He let out a tired breath. "It's going to suck."

"We just have to wait our turn, Brandon."

"Easy for you to say. Coach gets a hard on just watching you during drills."

"I'll be riding the bench just like you."

Frank grimaced. "Shit. Disgruntled female, twelve o'clock."

I looked up to see some girl eyeballing Frank, and she was clearly upset. I recalled seeing her leave his room in full Walk of Shame-mode on at least two of the past few Sunday mornings.

"Who is she?"

Charlotte looked to me smiling. "One of Frank's booty call girls."

He smirked and then Paige said, "She looks crushed."

Charlotte flipped her hair to the side and said, "That's what you get for being a slut."

The entire table turned to her, surprised by the mean-spirited comment.

"That's fucked up," Colin said.

Brandon tossed a fry at her. "And could you have screamed that any louder?"

"Yeah," Frank added weakly, "Danielle's all right."

Charlotte shrugged, making a half-assed attempt to defend herself. "It's just that some girls are like cling-ons when it comes to you athletes."

"Yeah," Paige agreed. "They don't even know you and just come on to you at parties. It's sickening."

Colin rolled his eyes and I shared his opinion. Didn't Paige and Charlotte realize they'd just given a very accurate description of themselves? They were clueless.

I checked my phone at nine, nine-twenty, nine-thirty, nine-forty-five, and then I just sat there staring out the window.

I didn't have some premeditated plan, but I was still wearing my sneakers even though I'd been back in my room for over two hours. When I saw her making her way towards the road, I hopped out the window and jogged in her direction.

"Let me guess, you just happened to get the urge for a run, right?"

"Yep. And the urge just happened to hit at exactly ten o'clock. Go figure."

"I guess it's a free country. I can't stop you."

"I figured I might as well get some exercise instead of staring out the window for the next hour. Last night you were late, you know."

"Late?" she asked, stretching her quads.

"You usually run for exactly thirty minutes, but last night you were gone for an hour. I was just about to get a search party going when you came back."

"You've kept watch for me?"

"I told you I saw you before last night, just didn't know it was you. It actually pissed me off that I couldn't relax until I saw that girl get back home each night."

She smiled at me and held my gaze for a moment. "Sorry I worried you last night."

"You should be."

We jogged together in near silence that first night. When we got back, we sat on the grass stretching for a few minutes, talking about mundane crap—what's your major and all that. The next night I ran with Anna again. I was outside waiting again at ten o'clock the night after that.

Talk slowly drifted from polite conversation to the kind of familiar talk you can only have with people who know you well.

Anna told me she moved out of her house and was living with relatives now. She smiled and reassured me when I asked if she was all right, but I knew the look, the battle scars. She asked about my father, and I told her what little there was to relay on that subject. She squeezed my hand and smiled up at me when I told her about my first day here, about my dad dropping me off at college without even cutting the engine.

When we got back Thursday night, Anna said, "Ok stalker, just so you know, I take weekends off. I'm not running again until Monday night."

"What are you doing this weekend?"

"I'm not sure yet."

I thought about telling her that my first hockey game was on Saturday, but figured that might sound a little bit desperate. I wanted to keep things casual, right? "My roommates are throwing the party in the woods this Saturday." *Please, please come*, I silently begged.

"Maybe I'll see you there," she said as she stood up to leave. "Goodnight, Declan."

"Sleep tight, Anna."

My phone was ringing when I walked back into my room. "Hello."

"Where have you been? I've been trying to get you for an hour."

"I was out running. Is everything all right?"

Tess let out a tired breath. "I'm fine."

"So what's going on? Did you change your mind and decide to come down this weekend?" I felt a flash of guilt thinking that I really didn't want her to.

"I have commitments too. I can't just drop everything for you all the time."

I shot back, "Didn't ask you to, Tess."

She broke the silence a moment later when she said, "I'm sorry. It's just...When I call you and I can't get you, my mind starts racing with these thoughts." I stayed quiet. "I hate being apart. I hate that other girls are getting to see you and talk to you every day. You're going to move on."

"Stop it," I pleaded, tired of this conversation that we seemed to be having over and over and over again.

"I won't be able to take it, Declan. I have no one without you."

I felt like I was being strangled. "You're not losing me, ok?" Anxious to change the subject, I asked, "What are you up to this weekend? And Tess, I'm happy you've got things going on there. I don't want you to feel like everything's about me, ok?"

"I know." She yawned, so I looked to the clock to see that it was already past eleven. I was hardly listening to Tess, more focused on the fact that I'd be getting less than my minimum requirement of eight hours sleep before tomorrow's morning skate. "It's nothing really, just homecoming weekend. A bunch of people from my dorm plan on tailgating before the game and then there's a few parties that night."

"That sounds like fun." I heard homecoming, people and parties, so I figured that was a safe response.

"Yeah, I guess. What are your plans after the game?"

"I can't think beyond the game. I probably won't get any ice time but I'm nervous anyway."

"I'll be thinking of you."

"Love you, Tess."

"Love you too."

* * *

ANNA

"I wonder what we're going to do in January. I mean, it's going to be too cold to be partying in the woods when it's ten below," Fiona said.

"It's freaking frigid today and it's only mid-October."

"Danielle isn't coming tonight. She said Frank and his boys are running the party."

Frank and Declan must be buddies then. Interesting.

"I don't blame her. I wouldn't want that thrown in my face."

Lauren, Colleen and Danielle walked in, taking the empty spaces on our beds with us. Fiona asked Danielle, "What are you going to do about tonight?"

"If you're not going then I can bail. I'll stay back with you," I offered.

"Thanks, Anna, but just because I'm home licking my wounds doesn't mean you have to miss out."

87

Colleen wrapped her arm around Danielle's shoulder. "Don't let what that bitch said bother you, ok?"

"What happened?" Fiona asked.

Colleen rolled her eyes. "Frank and his goons sat down two tables away from us at lunch yesterday. One of the head cheerleader wannabes who follows that crew around like a puppy begging for scraps said something stupid."

"She called me a slut," Danielle whispered.

"She was talking about you? Are you sure?" I asked.

"Seemed that way," she said.

Colleen nodded in agreement. "I was going to yell something over there but Danielle begged me not to. I personally hate that girl, Charlotte. She thinks she's the shit."

"I seriously would have *killed* you, Colleen. Promise me you won't say *anything* tonight, all right? To her *or* to Frank."

"I won't, even though calling another girl a slut is borderline criminal." She put her hand up in a pledge. "I'll keep my trap shut, swear to God."

Looking to cheer my friend up, I changed the subject. "Who's up for going to the hockey game? It's at six, the first game of the season. My cousin Dylan bought me a bunch of tickets and I don't want to waste them."

The only reason I was even entertaining the idea was because I was suddenly a little preoccupied with all things Declan Banks. He never mentioned hockey during our runs, but maybe he did play on the team. I was curious.

"Are they the kind of seats Dylan splurged on for football?" When I nodded, Fiona said, "They're probably center ice, right behind the glass. I'm in."

Looking at a picture on my desk of me with Dylan and Kasia, Lauren said, "That girl is *so* lucky. Could you even imagine having a guy like this for your boyfriend? He's gorgeous."

"That reminds me. Check these out," I said as I dragged a large box out from underneath my bed. "Kasia sent me a care package."

Inside were some of her Sweet Betty Threads winter pieces. A cute black dress, two funky-patterned shirts, and a fitted pencil skirt with an applique overlay.

"I love her designs," Lauren said as she ran her hand over the skirt, probably cooking up plans to hijack my stuff. "It's like retro, hipster, nerdy but funky."

"When her store finally opens we'll have to make a pilgrimage to Brooklyn."

"I'm out on hockey tonight but definitely in on that plan," Lauren said.

"Danielle, come with us. Watching those guys check each other into the boards will take your mind off your troubles. Hockey is a total rush," Fiona said as she tickled Danielle's feet.

"All right, I'm coming," she said, tucking her feet back in underneath her butt. She didn't exactly sound pumped, but getting her to leave the dorm was a start.

"Who are you going to root for when we play Northeastern, Fiona?" Colleen asked.

Fiona was a die-hard hockey fan. "Northeastern, duh. I'd never root against my brother."

"Well, tonight you can cheer for the home team." I dug the tickets out of my drawer. "They're playing Michigan."

Fiona took the tickets from me and smiled when she saw where they were. "Tell Dylan I love him, ok?"

"Will do."

"That's bold. It's not Saint Patrick's Day, you know," Fiona said, taking in my outfit.

"What? You don't like the shirt?" I asked, looking down at the fitted, kelly green knit top I was wearing.

"I like it. I mean, the shirt makes your boobs look big. It's just a different look for you...Plain long-sleeve top, jeans, tennies. You usually look like you just walked out of In Style. Your outfit is, dare I say, ordinary," Fiona teased.

"My boobs look big?" I asked, checking myself out in the mirror. Thankfully, they had grown some. I was not exactly busting out of my B-cups, but I was perfectly adequate—not too small, and not too big to make running uncomfortable.

"Yes, you're *huge*," my very well-endowed friend teased. Looking down at her shirt, she said, "At least one of us is wearing school colors...Rah, rah, rah."

When Fiona, Colleen, Danielle and I took our seats in the arena, I was surprised to see it so packed. Nearly every seat was taken. And most people were not only wearing school colors, they were waving flags or crazy giant foam fingers. Some rabid fans down in our section even had their faces painted maroon and white.

The crowd went bananas when the team came out and did a skate around the rink. I saw number twelve's jersey with the name Banks on the back, and I was done for. My heart fluttered, my breath hitched, you name it. He was beautiful, gliding effortlessly across the ice, tall and strong.

"That's the freshman my brother said to watch out for. Banks, some kid from Maine. My brother played against him in high school. Said he's so good it's unlikely he'll finish college. He'll go pro early."

"They do that?"

"Yeah." She looked at me like I was a total dumb ass. "It's just like the NBA or the NFL. More and more of them are being drafted right out of high school. I'm not sure if my brother is even at that level, but my parents were adamant about him getting his degree."

My eyes were on no one but Declan for the duration of the game, even though he spent most of it on the bench. But with six minutes remaining in the third period, score tied, Declan was put in.

"Oh, yeah," Fiona said, nodding her head. "Frosh must have the goods if he's getting in."

I'd never watched a hockey game before, but it wasn't that hard to follow. Fiona said he was a right wing, or maybe she said winger—whatever. He was aggressive, and he seemed like he was better than most at getting out of the way of the hits those brutes were landing on one another. The one time he did get checked, I clutched my chest because it seemed barbaric. Fiona looked over at me and laughed. "This is hockey babe, not golf."

With one minute left on the clock, Declan's teammate broke away and took a shot that deflected off the goalie's skate. As Declan swooped in, Fiona rose to her feet and screamed, "Shoots, and he scores!" Everyone around us jumped up, and then we were all screaming our heads off. It felt like the arena was literally shaking. I'll admit, the game as a whole was exciting, but seeing Declan score was mind-blowing and... pretty freaking hot.

After getting mobbed by his teammates, Declan skated backwards, getting ready to play out the last thirty seconds of the game. Once he was back in position, he looked directly up at me, gave me a head nod, tugged at his own shirt and then shook his head in disapproval. Yep, he remembered the joke.

"What the hell was that?" Colleen asked, looking directly at me. "Do you know him?"

All three of them were now staring at me. "It was a long time ago."

Colleen waggled her eyebrows. "I'd say that boy is into you."

"He's friends with Frank," Danielle added despondently.

They managed to hold Michigan off and took the win. The other guys, probably because Declan was only a freshman, raised him up on their shoulders and skated him around the ice. The entire arena was going wild cheering for him.

As we made our way back, Fiona drew me a few steps behind the others. "The other day when you came in and said you'd just—"

"Yeah, it was him. We met a few years ago at a grief camp." In response to her raised eyebrows, I said, "Yes, *grief* camp. Anyway, we became friends and then we lost touch. I was just shocked to see him again, that's all."

"What was with that thing he did? Does he like you in tight green shirts that show off your boobies?"

"My *boobies*? No, you freak. I don't know what that was. And I had no boobies to speak of back then anyway."

I didn't want to share that memory with Fiona or anyone else. Anything that Declan and I had told one another, shared, or did back then was off limits, private...sacred to me.

Now Fiona was excited. "So, we're totally going to the party. Banks is going to be the man of honor tonight."

"Um, no," I said quietly, gesturing towards Danielle. "I'm hanging back with her. I can't explain it, Fiona, but I don't want to go."

She was quiet for a minute before she said, "Ok. I don't get it but I'm sure you have your reasons." She saluted me then and said, "I will gather a full report and give you all the drunken details tomorrow."

This was one of the many reasons I loved Fiona. No annoying, pushy nonsense. She wouldn't try to convince me to go just because it served her, because she needed a wing-man or wing-woman—whatever. She just was good, through and through.

DECLAN

I spotted her midway through the second period. My mind was completely focused on the game, believe me, but when Coach called me up, I admit that I wanted to show off for her.

That green shirt? She was still a wiseass. But more importantly, I thought, it was her way of telling me: *I remember*. God, I remembered everything about her—everything she'd said to me, every look, how her skin felt and how her mouth tasted.

I pushed thoughts of Tess out of my head as me and the rest of the freshman players made our way to the party in the woods after we'd celebrated for a couple of hours with our team. I needed to see her.

There was a bigger crowd than normal out in the woods tonight, and when me, Brandon and the other guys showed up, the place erupted. It was a rush. I drank a beer with my buddies, smiling and giving a "thanks" to everyone who slapped my back and congratulated me. Scoring my first college goal was a big deal. I was walking on air.

I looked around every few minutes, scanning the large crowd for her. I figured she was here somewhere, but I also knew Anna, and I was pretty certain she wouldn't come to me when I was surrounded. I told the boys I was going to take a leak then made my way around the perimeter of the party. If she was here, I couldn't find her. Twenty minutes later I gave up and went back to my friends. Charlotte and Paige practically tackled me when they grabbed me around the neck for a hug simultaneously.

"You were beyond amazing," Charlotte gushed.

"And you skate lightning fast," Paige added as she rubbed her hand along my forearm.

Brandon and Melissa were standing behind them, Melissa pretending to gag while Brandon simulated a blow job. I was trying my best not to laugh because I didn't want to hurt the girls' feelings, but their praise was a little over the top and a lot nauseating.

"I cannot believe Tess wasn't here to see your first goal. I feel so bad for her," Paige said looking up at me.

That was so not sincere. Paige was aiming to highlight the fact that Tess was not here, but *she* was, ready and willing. Her comment did remind me to check my phone, though. I had my head so wrapped up in seeing Anna that I'd probably missed the twenty calls Tess had made to check in after the game. I had a pit in my stomach knowing I'd have hell to pay.

No missed calls. That was beyond odd. I excused myself and moved off to a more secluded, quiet spot.

"Hello!" a giggling, tipsy Tess answered.

"You sound like you're having a good night."

"I am!"

There were voices in the background, guys and girls. I was happy, relieved she was having fun, when I heard a male voice say, "Hurry the fuck up, Tess!"

"Who the hell is that?"

"Just...no one, a guy from my dorm. Ohmigod, I almost totally forgot! How was the game? Did you win?"

I heard her slam her door shut. Probably to drown out that dickhead's voice.

"Yeah, Tess, we won."

"That's great, baby!"

"I scored."

I felt aggravated all of a sudden. Not because of that guy's voice, although that did piss me off. No, it confused me. I would tear any guy to shreds who touched Tess. She was mine, right? But then again, I'd been dreaming about kissing and touching a girl who was not Tess every single night this week. What really annoyed me, though, was that Tess was always making me feel bad for enjoying myself, guilty for having fun without her. Now here *she* was having fun and I was happy for her. Why couldn't she let me have that too?

"Did you say you scored? Declan, that's amazing!"

Now I could hear multiple people banging on her door, yelling for her. "Tess, go. It sounds like I'm interrupting a good night. I'll talk to you tomorrow."

"Ok, g'night."

That was quick.

I proceeded to drink my fill that night, never stopping my scan of the crowd for her. She didn't come. I woke up the next morning with a raging headache and Paige sprawled across my phantom room-mate's bed.

Great.

I tossed a rolled-up sock her way and called out, "Hello, sunshine," in an attempt to wake her. My memory was foggy, but I remember Paige situating herself right behind me as I opened my door last night and then making a drunken attempt to kiss me—again. I ignored her and went right to sleep fully clothed, but woke up when she crawled into bed with me practically naked. I rolled over so that she was deposited directly onto the floor, landing with a thump. Guess that's when she moved over to the spare bed.

I liked Paige as a person, especially when she was sober, but she was getting to be a pain in my ass. "Paige, get up."

"Declan?" She looked around, acting all innocent and confused. "How did I? Did we?"

How did she get in here? Was she joking? I felt like telling her she was here because she tried to sexually assault me last night, making it two times this month.

"Nothing happened. You slept there, I slept here," I said, gesturing between the twin beds. "You can't come here late-night again, Paige. I have a girlfriend."

That did it. She was sufficiently embarrassed and seriously pissed. "Don't worry, I won't be," she snapped as she put her jeans and sweater back on. "Later, Declan."

A minute later Brandon walked in, wrapped in a towel after his shower. "Did you hook up with Paige?"

"No! She landed herself in here and tried to maul me. I passed out when she refused to leave."

"She is *fine*, Declan. Not too many guys would pass when she's offering it up on a platter."

"Not interested. How was your night?"

"I actually met a very cute girl and had an excellent make-out session. Her name's Victoria."

"Nice."

He smiled. "Yeah, she is nice. She runs track."

"You'll have to point her out to me."

"Will do, will do. I am so fucking glad we have a day off from practice, aren't you?"

"Yeah, I'm beat. I can't drink like that again after a game. I feel totally dehydrated right now."

"Breakfast in ten minutes?"

"I'll be out of the shower in five."

I spent most of Sunday lounging around, trying to read but unable to study due to my lingering hang-over. Drinking just wasn't worth it. I laid my Econ notes on my chest and closed my eyes.

I went to my favorite visual, the one of Anna standing on the dock, shy and innocent. Anna carefully lowering herself into the water. Anna's face an inch from mine, our breathing audible as I traced two fingers over her shoulders and then down, exploring places on her that I'd never ventured to with any girl before. Everything new and beautiful.

I wondered what would happen if Anna and I were on that dock again now. I pictured us lying on our backs looking up at the night sky, but older like we were now. Holding hands and talking, I imagined it would feel just as good as it did back then. And if we took another night swim, how would she look now? My body had changed in three years and so had hers. I wanted to see, wanted to be granted access again.

I was burning with the need to kiss her, but more than that, I wanted to go back to that feeling. I wanted it to be me and Anna against the world again, just the two of us, connected in the best possible way.

Chapter Seven

ANNA

Declan had another home game coming up, but I gave my tickets to Fiona and Colleen.

I saw Declan every night this past week at ten o'clock sharp, for the nightly run that had gone from being mine to ours. The conversations flowed more easily with each passing day, and I no longer felt anxious when I saw him hop out of that ground floor window. No, now I happily anticipated it.

We still kept to safe topics for the most part, but he might throw a zinger at me occasionally or I might lob one at him. Thursday night he started the jog off by saying, "So, you said you had a boyfriend. Why don't you tell me about him and then I'll tell you about my girlfriend?"

"What is this? You want to play *I'll show you mine if you show me yours* like we did in the lake three years ago?"

"Don't you even *try* to tarnish the memory of that night, Clarke. I still consider that one of the best nights of my life."

I smiled when he said that, the kind of smile that comes from feeling warm all over. But those good vibes didn't last long. "Who says I want to know about your girlfriend?"

He shrugged. "I want to know about your boyfriend."

"Why?"

"I don't know. I guess a part of me always felt like you were—" He stopped mid-sentence, shrugged again and shook his head. "You don't have to tell me if you don't want to."

After we jogged in silence for a minute, I rattled off some basic, boring stats. "His name is Jonathan. He's at Marquette. He's a freshman, recruited for tennis." When he didn't comment or offer anything up in return, I started to ramble. "I guess we didn't officially start dating until junior year, but we've been friends since ninth grade. We became close friends after Will died. He was one of the few people who treated me like I was normal. He made sure everyone kept me in the loop at school…Made sure I didn't fall into some self-imposed exile. And I did try to crawl under a rock, believe me. Sophomore year, even when I went off the deep end, he stood by me. He's always been really patient and understanding."

Our run had morphed into a very slow jog. Declan might be a well-conditioned athlete, but I couldn't keep a fast pace and simultaneously recite that soliloquy.

Declan looked straight ahead, and his tone was just slightly clipped when he said, "He sounds great."

"Your turn…You show me yours."

I was trying to act like this was no biggie, when in reality I was fighting the urge to scream *lalalalala* and cover my ears like a pissed-off nine-year-old.

I would rather have had my fingernails forcibly removed than listen to Declan talk about his girlfriend. And I knew exactly why he was doing this. I knew she was visiting this weekend. I'd already gotten the breaking news alert, and kind of wanted to punch Declan for thinking he needed to brace me for it or something.

"Wait. What did you mean when you said you went off the deep end sophomore year?"

Even though it was one of my least favorite topics, I was happy to keep talking if it meant that I didn't have to hear about Tammy or Bess or whatever the hell her name was.

So I put my hand on his shoulder, because if I was going to launch into that story, I was going to need to walk. "Do you know why my parents really sent me to Heart Songs?" I couldn't help but roll my eyes as I said that fruity name and he laughed. "First of all, they never showed up for the family counseling session on the last day. It was so fucking embarrassing, but Dr. Ben tried to make me feel like it was no big deal. When I got home, though, they were both sitting on the couch waiting for me. A united front of stupidity. Not two minutes after I walked in, they announced they were getting a divorce and selling our house. Just like that. No welcome home, no easing into it. Then they start with the living arrangements while my head is like, spinning. Oh yeah, the *great* visitation schedule they've already drawn up with the attorneys, all the *fantastic* vacations I'll be taking. Both of them grinning like idiots, trying to pass a giant pile of shit off as caviar.

"Four months. Sixteen *weeks* after I had to watch my brother's body being lowered into the ground, Declan. And it's not like I really cared whether or not they were together. I didn't care if they loved one another anymore, it wasn't that. It was the abandonment, that feeling of having the rug pulled right out from underneath you. I didn't just *feel* alone...I really and truly was."

I looked down then and noticed that Declan had taken my hand at some point. He had his fingers interlaced with mine and it felt really nice.

"So I turned around and walked out of the house. I left without a key, without my phone, without any money. They didn't find me for a week."

"Holy shit. Where did you go?"

"I just ran towards the woods behind my house and then started taking trails, staying off the main road. Later that night I was probably five miles from my house. My feet hurt and I was hungry, but there was no way I was heading home. A guy I vaguely knew, a friend of Will's, happened to drive by and pick me up." When Declan squeezed my hand, I reassured him. "Jeremy's a good guy, totally honorable. He played football with Will in high school and he'd been at our house a few times. I remember my mother making a snide comment about him once. Jeremy wasn't like the other boys I went to school with. His family wasn't wealthy. His father lives on some rich guy's grounds doing the maintenance work. Anyway, that night when I told Jeremy that I couldn't go home, he understood." I laughed when I said, "He told me my parents were assholes. I guess my parents had made it clear that they didn't approve of their son associating with *his* kind. My parents could be like that." I looked up at Declan, nodding and smiling. "They're assholes."

"He just let you stay with him? You were fifteen and he was..."

"Eighteen. Yeah. His father lived in a carriage house on the grounds and Jeremy had his own separate tiny quarters on the other side of it. All we did was hang out, talk and listen to music. He let me try some of his premium cannabis after I begged, and—best memory ever—he helped me dye my hair black."

"I don't think I'm liking Jeremy."

"No, he's a good person. He had a girlfriend. She was there the entire time and slept over too. There was nothing...My virtue was safe, Declan. It's like Jeremy gave me a vacation from my parents and a makeover."

"The hair?"

"Jeremy dyed my hair, Vanessa did the piercings." I lifted my hair to show him my ear. "I also had a lip and an eyebrow piercing when I came home, but I eventually got rid of them and let the holes close. I'm not that much of a badass."

"How did you wind up back home?'

"The cops got a tip, came and searched Jeremy's place, and alas, I was rescued. That's how the story first went. I raised hell and insisted that I ran away, so Jeremy wasn't charged. My parents freaked, of course. Not because they were frantic with concern, but because I'd disgraced them socially." I couldn't help but laugh, recalling their reaction. "They were so embarrassed! Word had gotten around that I'd shacked up with a bad boy from the wrong side of the tracks. And to make things worse, I refused to change my hair color and I started dressing in black, head to toe. I went back to school that September looking like Marilyn Manson's demon bride, whereas I'd once been Sandra Dee."

"How *was* that?"

I smirked. "You mean, how did it feel to hear *everyone*, even people I'd known since first grade, whispering behind my back that I'd been fucking some eighteen-year-old loser who worked as an electrician's assistant?" I looked up at him, eyes as dead as I'd felt back then. "I didn't even care."

His thumb was rubbing along the back of my hand. I felt like I was right back in Dr. Ben's group, with Declan holding my hand as I told everyone about Will. It made me feel safe. "I still feel like spilling if you think you can take it."

"I've got all night, Anna."

We walked, probably for a total of an hour. I told him all about Jonathan. That despite my best efforts to push everyone out of my life, Jonathan didn't let me. And since he was the school's golden boy, people followed his lead. If he was nice to me, they were. If he had his arm around me—black hair and piercings or not—then I was golden too.

"Sounds like he loves you a lot."

"He's loyal and he's a really good person."

We were back behind my dorm. "Are you all right, Anna?"

I nodded and smiled. "It feels good to talk to you like this again."

"It feels good for me too."

As I went to open the door, I turned back to him. "Did you ever try to call me?"

"What do you mean?"

"Three years ago. Did you ever try to get in touch with me?"

"You don't know?"

I shook my head. "My parents wouldn't give my phone back after that week on the run. They were holding it ransom until I stopped acting crazy. Which meant until I lost the black hair, the plethora of earrings, and the slutty clothes." I added air quotes for the last two words. "They gave in eventually, but I was given a new phone with a new number. They're so clueless they thought a new number would prevent me from having any further contact with the oh so very wicked Jeremy." He was looking up at the sky. I couldn't tell if he was angry, sad or just lost in his own thoughts. "Did you?" I asked again, hoping the question didn't sound like the wishful plea that it was.

He looked back to me, forcing a weak smile. "I did."

* * *

DECLAN

Tess was on my bed flipping through the Freshman Directory, a book with every incoming freshman's picture, hometown, favorite quote and major. Terrence, Frank and Jimmy had rated nearly every female in my copy with the rankings: *hell yes, if drunk,* or *fuck no.*

"Your friends are entertaining," Tess dripped sarcastically as she studied the pages.

"I'm glad you at least have the sense to know I didn't write that crap."

She looked up but didn't return my smile before focusing her attention back on the book.

I heard giggling outside my door followed by knocking. It was Melissa and Charlotte, all smiles, rolling out the veritable welcome wagon. "Hi, Tess!" they said, ignoring me as they walked right past me into the room.

"Hello?" Tess said, unable to hide her uneasiness.

"I'm Melissa and this is Charlotte."

"Hi!" chirped Charlotte.

Melissa said, "We figured you could hang with us when the boys leave, and we'll go to the game together later on."

It was a good idea and I trusted Melissa. "Up to you, Tess, but I do have to be there two hours before the game."

I could tell she'd rather eat glass, but she forced a smile and said, "That sounds great."

Melissa smiled at Tess while Charlotte looked her over from head to toe. As they turned to leave, Melissa said, "Come over when Declan leaves, ok? Next door, Bryant Hall, room 312. We'll see you later."

When I closed the door behind them, Tess flopped back onto the bed. "Looks like I have a new set of friends. Ugh."

I laid on top of her, caging her in. "You'll like Melissa. She's genuinely nice. She's a good friend of Brandon's from home."

"You don't have to tell me that I won't like the other one. I already know that."

"You're perceptive."

"Perceptive enough to know she'd like to keep your bed warm?"

I laughed. "You think?"

"Yes. She screams skank, Declan. Stay away from her."

"Done," I said as I pinned her arms above her head and kissed her.

I left for the arena with Brandon an hour later, Tess reassured while I was uneasy. I loved her, I did. And when it was just us two alone, we were good—better than good. It's when we were outside of that bubble that things got complicated. And truth be told, I was coming to realize that I wanted out of the bubble.

I didn't like the idea of Tess spending time with Charlotte and

Paige. I was so concerned about it that I went out of my way and asked Melissa to please stick to Tess like glue. I knew she'd do that for me, but I still wasn't one hundred percent focused on the game so it's a good thing I spent most of it on the bench. I kept looking up into the stands to where the girls were, and I was also looking to the VIP seats where Anna was sitting the week before. No sign of her, which eased my mind some. I didn't want to run into Anna tonight, didn't want her to see Tess's hand in mine.

I knew I'd been treading into dangerous territory these past couple of weeks, but I couldn't stop. Nothing could have kept from jumping out my back window at exactly ten o'clock every Monday through Thursday night. The force that drew me to Anna was more powerful than a nor'easter undertow.

The other night when Anna asked if I'd tried to call her way back when? I was so frustrated and angry that I wanted to hit something, but wanted to cry tears of relief at the same time. I needed to ask her again. I needed to be sure. She never knew? She never heard the voice-mails? Never read the texts?

Back then it hurt like hell. I felt stupid and foolish, caring so much when her silence made it clear she felt nothing for me in return.

Maybe I'd gotten it all wrong.

Tess was waiting with Melissa and Victoria when we came out of the locker room. Brandon, boy, he had it bad. I liked that Brandon didn't hide how he felt about this girl, Victoria. He grabbed her hand and kissed it when he saw her, sighing dramatically. "I promised you a goal and I didn't deliver. I am so sorry, milady."

"You looked good in your uniform, if that's any consolation. Anyway," she whispered in his ear something that sounded like, "that's not the only way you can score."

Brandon burst out laughing and then grabbed her tight, spinning her around. Melissa raised her eyebrows looking at me and Tess, but I just smiled. I liked how the two of them made each other laugh.

We split our night between an off-campus party thrown by a few of our sophomore teammates, and the weekly gathering in the woods. It was colder now but not unbearable. Tess acted as if the night wasn't entirely painful. She didn't let go of my hand once, but she was friendly whenever someone came over to talk to me and seemed relaxed when they introduced themselves to her.

I saw Anna's roommate and a few of her friends at one point, but no Anna. Fiona and I had become friendly over the past few weeks. She was funny, and the girl could talk hockey with more sense than most of the guys on my team. When I saw her making her way over towards us, my palms started to sweat. Nothing had happened, I hadn't been unfaithful or anything, but still, I was praying Fiona wouldn't bring Anna's name up. Running buddies, friends, the fact that we were linked by our weird, sad past—the mention of Anna in any context would leave me with a lot of 'splaining to do.

"What's up, Declan?"

"Hey, Fiona." I gestured between them. "This is Tess. Tess, Fiona."

They exchanged hellos, and then Fiona started in on how I was "going down" next week against her brother. I felt Tess's hand relax in mine as Fiona made an effort to include her in the conversation, explaining how her brother played for one of our biggest rivals and how Fiona's entire family was coming next week to "witness the bloodbath." The only reference to Anna was when Fiona said, "I have to see if I can con Anna out of those center-ice seats again next week. Maybe I'll play the pity card and say my father's eyesight is going and he needs to be up close."

"What does everyone think about you rooting against the home team?" Tess asked.

She shrugged her shoulders and smiled. "Blood is thicker than water, right?" With that, she turned her empty cup over and said, "Duty calls." Before Fiona turned to go for a refill she said, "It was nice to meet you."

"Now *she's* nice," Tess commented.

"Very," I agreed. "Sometimes I think she knows more about hockey than I do."

"Does she have a boyfriend?"

"I don't know."

"On second thought, stay away from her."

"So maybe I should just avoid any and all persons with boobs."

"That works for me," Tess said as she pinched my side, hard.

Walking back later on that night, I was so relieved. Maybe Anna was there, looking on from the edge of the crowd, but I didn't think so. I was taller than most, so I'm pretty sure I would have caught sight of her. I don't know what I would have done.

My feet were so firmly planted in this world. Boston, my team, my friends, my classes, the runs that I looked forward to every freaking day...and Anna. My life here was so different from my life at home. Having Tess here was like trying to jam the wrong missing piece into a puzzle that was otherwise perfect.

Tess turned me down, telling me she was tired when I made a half-hearted move for her in bed. I was only going through the motions anyway. I didn't want to be with her in that way.

I was awake long after Tess's breathing became deeper and more regular. No surprise, I was staring at the ceiling thinking about Anna. Thinking back to that day right before we left camp, when she told everyone in group what happened to her brother. I remember how her hands shook as she recounted each detail—so badly I felt the need to grab her hand to steady her, while the girl on the other side of her must have felt that same impulse.

With her voice cracking, Anna spoke about the last time she saw him alive. They were sitting on his bed and he was reassuring her about some long forgotten pre-teen drama. She rattled off fragments of memories: his startled reaction to a text, pushing his arms through the sleeves of his jean jacket, kissing her head before he rushed out. Anna shuddered as she recounted walking downstairs the next morning, listening in as the police officers spoke to her parents in hushed tones. She choked out a laugh when she recalled her confusion at the sight of her father's arms wrapped reassuringly around her mother, knowing then and there that something was most definitely *very* wrong. She bit her lip open then, just slightly, and there was a faint trace of blood on her lip as she angrily recounted how everyone in the room was ignoring her. Her tears fell unchecked when she relayed the officers' theory, developed from the physical evidence and from the recovered text messages: Will was trying to wrestle a gun away from his friend and was shot accidentally during the struggle. The other boy dead of a self-inflicted gun wound right after. She started to tell us about the other boy and a note recovered at the scene, but began to cry so hard that she could no longer speak, her shoulders shaking with the force of her sobs.

I'd never felt the desire to love someone, physically love someone by kissing and holding them, as I did in that moment. Her grief tore me apart, and I wanted to be the one to help her through it. It felt unfair and so wrong—I didn't want to leave her. I wanted to wrap her up in my arms, tell her it would be all right, and then I wanted to make it right.

I looked down at Tess's head nestled into the crook of my arm and her body wrapped around mine.

I don't want to hurt you.

But I know I'm going to.

* * *

ANNA

Dylan lifted me up and hugged me tight when I tapped his shoulder, pulling his attention away from some intense business call. "Anna Banana. Look at you!"

"You like?" I asked, shaking out my newly colored locks.

After my Friday classes were done, I went to some edgy salon with a cult-like following in South Boston. I told the colorist I wanted something in the auburn family, but that she could basically do what she pleased. The result was my favorite color job to date: auburn with some very subtle golden streaks framing my face and random cherry red strands mixed in underneath.

I had a good feeling about the colorist from the second I walked into the shop. Her head was recently shaved, with her scant, quarter-inch buzz dusted a bright violet. She wasn't cheap either, which for some reason I also admired. It's like she knew she was good so she expected to be well compensated. It definitely took balls to charge Newbury Street prices in that part of the city.

"You know what? I should probably be telling you that you look best au natural, but this," Dylan turned me from side to side, "suits you."

"I needed a change."

"Anything wrong?"

"Nothing wrong exactly, just...I don't know."

"Mom said your roommate is *fabulous*," he stated, comically channeling his inner Margot. But he was concerned, fishing for what it was that had me so unsettled.

"I can't wait until you and Kasia meet Fiona, she's the best. Oh, and she's your biggest fan."

"Yeah?" he asked, confused.

"The hockey tickets. She's a fanatic."

"I'm glad they're being used. Warn her, though, that I'm coming for the playoff games and she's not sitting on my lap."

"You might have to wrestle her for them."

"I'll leave that to Kasia." He paused for a moment. "I feel weird handing my keys over to you. It's like I'm saying I'm on board with you and your boy toy shagging at my place, and that's just wrong on so many levels."

I burst out laughing. "There will be no shagging, Dylan. That, I can guarantee." He raised his eyebrows. "Yeah, breaking up is hard to do."

He winced. "Ouch. Does he have any idea?"

"Afraid not."

"May the force be with you," he said as he dangled the keys over my open palm. "Are you going to be all right alone with him?"

I rolled my eyes. "Seriously? This is Jonathan we're talking about."

"I don't care who we're talking about. I want you to call me tonight and again tomorrow morning. And you better pick up when I call you, understand? I'll have my doorman upstairs in two seconds flat with the spare key if you don't."

I threw my head back, exasperated. "I. Will. Be. Fine."

"Love you," he said, looking worried as he made his way towards the first class boarding counter.

"Thanks, Dylan. I'll call you later. Safe flight and tell Kasia I'll see her soon, ok?"

"All right."

I sank into the back seat of the car Dylan had waiting to take me from the airport back to his Chicago apartment. When I pulled up outside of the building, Jonathan was already there waiting for me. *Lord help me.*

"Anna!" He held his arms open as I made my way towards him, wracked with guilt. After hugging me he pulled back holding onto my shoulders, taking me in. "It's really good to see you. And I like the hair," he said, smiling as he admired my new look. Then he leaned back in and bent his head down for a kiss, and it took everything I had in me not to pull away. I was miserable in that kiss.

He kissed me again as soon as we were in the apartment, but I broke away after a moment, trying not to make it obvious. "Tell me about school, Jonathan. How's it been?"

"I'm happy for the most part. I miss you, but I like it." He studied my face, and I couldn't even venture a guess as to what he saw there. I felt twitchy and anxious and sad. "I'm glad you wanted to see me, Anna, but I feel like something's wrong. I felt it when you called the other night, and I'm pretty sure of it now."

I sank down onto the couch and hung my head. I told myself it was like ripping off a bandage: the faster I did it the better it would be for both of us.

"I don't think I've ever been good enough for you. I've always thought you deserved better." He sat down next to me and took my hand but said nothing. "You've always been so good to me. And I'm...I could never. I think I'm as cold as ice."

"You're not cold, Anna. You've just...You've been through hell."

"And you got me through it. Everything over the past couple of years...You saved me. I should be able to be everything to you, give you everything back, but I can't. Do you understand, Jonathan? I think something's missing between us. Something is wrong with me that I don't feel—"

He put his hand on my knee to stop me. "You will. It's just that you don't feel that way about me."

"But I do love you, Jonathan."

"I know, but you don't *love* me. I'm not so innocent in all this. I knew it wasn't the same for you, but I loved you so much, felt so much for you, that I wouldn't let you go even though I've been living my life."

"Living your life. What does that mean?"

"Nothing."

"Are you seeing someone? Have you met someone at school?"

"No...Yes." He let out a tired breath. "There's no one special but I haven't been one hundred percent faithful." He took both of my hands in his. "I'm really sorry."

I wasn't even angry. I was, after all, talking to my closest friend. He was never a lover. I never felt a burning passion or desire for him.

"I don't blame you. You're an eighteen year-old guy and you've been dating a frigid bitch for the past two years." I laughed when I said that last line.

He shook his head and smiled at me. "You're not a bitch."

We both burst out laughing then, finally acknowledging how ridiculous it was that we'd been dating for a really, really long time and had never done the deed.

I shook my head. "I don't know why I'm this way." I'd gone from laughing to wiping at stray tears in the span of thirty seconds. "What's wrong with me?"

He wrapped an arm around my shoulders and pulled me in close. "There's nothing wrong with you. You're perfect. You weren't ready and I would never push you." I laid my head against his strong chest then, my breath staggered, holding back the sobs that were coming. "One day you're going to meet someone, and with him it's going to be different. I'll hate the guy, but you're going to be in love with him. It's going to be all right."

"I feel terrible, like I've held you back for the past two years."

"Not one minute of the past *four* years that we've been close has been a waste for me, Anna. Not one minute."

We talked for hours, and wound up curling up together on the couch. I fell asleep in his arms, as I had so many nights before.

I hoped what he said was true. I'd come close with Jonathan, tried to force myself to just go through with it and take the next step, but I always pulled back, was always coming up with some excuse. I was convinced that there was, in fact, something very wrong with me.

It was awkward at first that next morning. I made coffee while he ran down to the corner to some patisserie that was supposed to have the best croissants in Chicago. When he came back, we sat across from one another at the kitchen table, sipping our coffees and devouring the pastries. It sucked. Feeling stiff and uncomfortable in the presence of someone you were so close to is just about the worst feeling ever.

Jonathan finally broke the silence, tilting my chin up so that I had to look at him. "Please don't feel bad. I don't want you walking out of here today thinking that you've hurt me or that you've done something wrong, understand?" He was being too good to me, letting me off easy. "We're always going to be friends." Before he left, he turned back to me and said, "I'll always be here for you, Anna."

I was on a plane heading back to Boston by mid-afternoon on Saturday. I was utterly wiped out, a boneless sort of tired. I practically had to peel myself out of my seat when the plane landed, and my head slumped against the window as soon as I got into the cab heading back to campus.

Saturday at dusk, the campus was stirring to life. Groups of people were hanging out on the lawn, laughing and buzzing with the anticipation of what the night could bring.

My room was empty when I let myself in. I knew Fiona and the rest of them would be at the hockey game, and then they'd all head to whatever parties were raging afterwards.

I wondered how the two lovebirds were doing. Terrence tried to be casual about it Thursday morning during class, complaining that he'd be on his own this weekend, that all of his friends were whipped. "Brandon's always with Victoria lately, Colin's hooking up with Lauren, and Declan's going to be missing in action with his girl in town."

I did my best to keep a casual smile on my face, but damn, it hurt. So that night during our run, I was resentful when Declan wanted to talk about it, to exchange details about our significant others. Was he looking to warn me? And why would he do that? To make sure that I steered clear? I didn't want to hear anything about this girl he was in love with. The thought of Declan being in love with someone else? There were no words to adequately describe the pain it caused me.

After I unpacked, I stood under the hot stream of the shower for a long time. I tried to think of something, anything else, but couldn't stop picturing Declan with his hands and lips on this mystery girl. Did his kisses feel as good as the ones he gave me? Did she shiver when he so much as put his hand on her shoulder?

I sank into bed and pulled out my worn copy of *The Outsiders*, Will's all-time favorite book. I started from the beginning, even though I could pretty much recite it word for word. Before my parents sold the house, I'd packed all of his favorites to take along with me. Looking over the highlights and doodles and the folded-down corners, I was content in the knowledge that Will's hands touched those very same pages. After a little while, when my eyes got heavy and I rested the closed book on my chest, I imagined Will falling asleep in the exact same way.

I was in a sound sleep, book on my chest, hair still wrapped in a towel fashioned as a turban, when Fiona came stumbling in with some guy in tow. They laughed as they fell into a heap on her bed. I was about to make my presence known when Fiona said, "I used to think Declan was one of the good guys, but he's soooo not. I know he's your friend, Terrence, but *he* is an ass."

One of the good guys? Fiona was tipsy. And from the sound of it, Terrence was not particularly interested in talking about Declan. At the moment it sounded as if he was nibbling on some part of Fiona.

"And you know what the worst part is?"

God, she sounded whiny.

Terrence murmured, "What, baby?"

Baby? He barely knew her. I was just about two seconds away from barfing.

"The *worst* part is that his girlfriend is nice *and* she's pretty."

Shoes were coming off and clothes were hitting the floor. I was seriously hoping I was smack-dab in the middle of a nightmare.

"Why is that bad?"

"Well, 'cause I wanted to be able to tell Anna that she's a homely bitch…That's why."

Terrence was still going about his business with Fiona, but he came up for air to say, "He's got it tough, right? He's fucking one girl while he's leading another one on."

"Yep...I hate him."

What to do? I wanted out of that room but didn't want them to notice me. *She's pretty. She's nice.* I didn't want to think about Declan or that girl, or think about the two of them together.

I heard Terrence say, "Anna should—" before I stuck my fingers in my ears. I couldn't listen to any more. I decided to bolt, figuring they were probably so drunk they wouldn't even remember seeing me. I went straight to Danielle and Lauren's room, knocking loudly until Danielle opened up. She was out tonight, but since that bad experience with Frank, she'd been taking it easy with the drinking, always remaining in control.

"Brutal," she said after I told her everything. "I saw them together, Anna. I didn't realize that you had feelings for him. I mean, I've seen you two walking together, hanging out between classes and all, but I didn't know it was anything more."

"It's not," I said firmly. "He has a girlfriend and we're just friends."

She shrugged and smiled, unconvinced but supportive. "Lauren isn't coming home, so crash here. She's with Colin again."

I was grateful for the bed even though I knew sleep wouldn't come easily tonight.

Chapter Eight

DECLAN

I approached her tentatively Monday night, bracing myself for an icy reception, but she just smiled and said, "I was wondering if you were coming along. I thought the cold might be too much for you tonight."

It *was* cold outside, but it was nothing to someone like me, a guy who spent most of his waking hours on the ice. I'm thinking Anna knew that.

She looked adorable, with her red nose and her braids peeking out from underneath her knit skullcap. She pulled her sleeves down over her hands and gestured to the road. "Let's get going before my muscles tighten up."

We ran in silence. I didn't really know what to say. I wanted to know where she'd been over the weekend, but I was afraid she'd tell me she was here all along—that she'd been at the party watching me hold hands and occasionally peck my girlfriend on the cheek. I was pretty certain Fiona would have told Anna about her encounter with Tess, but if she did, Anna sure wasn't letting on.

The wind whipped up even more by the time we returned, and Anna's hands were curled into tight, uncomfortable looking fists. I walked her to the back door, which had become our custom, and then took her hands and rubbed them in mine. She smiled and said, "I need to go buy some gloves tomorrow," as she pulled her hands back. "See you, Declan."

I walked back to my place with my head hung low. She was distant and it hurt. I was desperate to be around her even though I knew what I was doing was wrong.

With Tess, it was as if she was out of sight, out of mind. And this time she wouldn't be coming back for three weeks. She had tests and papers due, and I had away games on the weekends for the most part. How did that make me feel? I felt free.

So I made any excuse to see Anna, pushing my way back in even though she pushed back. I never missed our nightly runs—would have hobbled alongside her with a cast on my leg if I had to. And I pretty much had her schedule memorized, so I could bump into her at least once or twice a day. I knew when she ate, where her classes were, when and where she studied in the library. She was trying to protect herself by keeping some distance between us, but I knew she was losing that battle, same as me.

I plopped down across from her in the cafeteria with an overloaded tray of food. "Hey, Red, does this remind you of one day long ago?"

When she smiled at me, her warmth and tenderness melted me to the core. "Is this where I'm supposed to say that I doubt you can put away that much food?"

I nodded. "Then you decide you're starving and go get yourself something to eat. How do you sit in here just reading a book with the smell of all this," I paused to take a long orgasmic whiff of my fried chicken, "surrounding you?"

"Come to think of it, I *am* starving. I'll be right back."

I was waiting for her, happy as pig in shit, when a cloying voice broke into my thoughts. "Wow. It takes a lot to fuel this body, huh?"

Charlotte sat down facing me, her legs straddling the bench, her hand running up and down my arm from elbow to shoulder.

Anna plunked her tray down across from mine a few seconds later. "I think I've lost my appetite."

Charlotte's gaze whipped up. She looked Anna over for a long moment. "Declan, you're being rude. Introduce us."

"Charlotte, this is Anna. Anna, uh, meet Charlotte." I couldn't mask my annoyance. She was acting bossy, and more important, she was interrupting my time with Anna.

Eyes wide, Charlotte looked to me. "Anna?" She looked like the cat that ate the canary. Damn, I forgot. She saw those scribbles in my notebook a few weeks ago.

"Anna is an old friend." The words came out flat because they were a lie. We weren't just friends then, and simple friendship was definitely not what I felt for Anna now. I looked over to see her staring down at her plate.

"So then you must know Tess."

Anna looked up. "No, I don't," she answered evenly.

"I'm confused. How did you two meet?" Charlotte asked, picking at what she had to have known was a sore subject.

Anna looked as annoyed as I felt. "Long story," she said in an offhanded way.

"I just *love* long stories."

Anna scooped a giant spoonful of mashed potatoes into her mouth, chewed and swallowed, deliberately taking her time. Tension mounting, Anna looked right at Charlotte and said, "You may like hearing them but I don't like telling them."

Charlotte fixed Anna with a death glare. "She's charming, Declan."

"I'm not charming. And I'm not going to pretend I like you 'cause I don't," Anna said, shrugging her shoulders.

"What is your problem, psycho?"

"*My* problem? I don't have one. *I* don't get off on embarrassing other girls in public, by calling other girls sluts. That's *your* problem, though, isn't it?"

Charlotte looked as if she'd been slapped. I felt just the slightest bit bad for her until she stood up, looking down her nose at Anna when she said to me, "Tess is a class act. I don't know what you're doing slumming with...this." Then she leaned down to catch Anna's eye. "Sweet hair, Raggedy Ann."

Loud enough for Charlotte to hear, Anna called out, "What a nice girl," heavy on the sarcasm.

"That was a little harsh."

"You're referring to her, right?"

"You were both—"

She shook her head, cutting me off with a bitter laugh. "Maybe you don't know me as well as you think you do, Declan. Maybe I'm not so nice."

Anna pushed her tray forward so that it slammed into mine. She stood up and tried to pull her bag up onto her shoulder, but it got caught on the edge of the bench and lurched her backwards. Frustrated, she had to turn back my way to unhook it. That's when I saw the tear running down her bright red cheek.

I stood up and reached over to take her hand. I wanted her to stay, wanted to fix what had just happened.

She pulled her hand back. "No!" Lowering her voice, she said, "Just let me go."

Quarter after and there was still no sign of her. I waited a while, even though I knew if she wasn't there at ten on the nose then she wouldn't be coming. So I went to her.

Fiona opened the door, eyeing me as if she couldn't decide whether to be mad at me or not.

"Is Anna here?"

"She's out running. I figured she was with you."

"Nope. I guess she took a different route."

"Don't mess with her, Declan. Don't be selfish."

"I'm trying. I'm trying to stay away but I can't."

When Fiona looked over my shoulder I turned to see Anna standing in the doorway. Pretty sure she'd just heard my confession.

"I'll be back later," Fiona said as she scooped up her laptop and a few textbooks. She stopped to exchange a look with Anna before she slid past us both.

"I was worried when you didn't show up."

She peeled off her top layer and tossed it over a chair. "Turn around, Declan." I turned, edgy and tense in the ensuing silence. I listened to her breaths as they slowed and evened out, heard her toe off her shoes, strained to hear as each piece of fabric was removed and tossed aside. Breathing in deep to calm my nerves, I got the vanilla scent she always gave off mixed with the earthy tang of sweat. "Wait here if you want to talk."

I didn't move from my spot in the center of her room until I heard the slap of her flip flops on the tile floor and the door close behind her. It was the first time I was ever in her room. I should have just sat on the bed and waited for her to finish her shower, but I couldn't waste the opportunity. I studied everything I could see: the posters hanging on her side of the room, the books on her desk and the pictures. I looked for a picture of her man, but only saw a few pictures of Anna with her friends, and one of her with another girl and an older boy who looked too much like her not to be related. I thought for a second that it was Will in the picture, but it couldn't be; the photo was too recent. I saw another frame tucked into a corner, and knew right away this had to be him. He looked to be around my age, maybe a little younger. Standing there in his football uniform, he was smiling as if the person taking the picture had just said something really funny. When the glass caught the reflection of the light in the room, you could see small fingerprints on its surface. I imagined Anna holding the frame, touching every inch of his face. I hurt for her, knowing just how much she loved him.

Her books were all ones I thought were more suited for boys than girls: *The Outsiders, Call of the Wild, Lord of the Flies.* For some reason that made me smile, but then I shook my head, knowing I was easily impressed when it came to Anna. A shelf full of nursery rhymes or conspiracy theory books would have led me to the conclusion that she was way more enlightened and cooler than the rest of us. As for the posters, bands I'd never heard of with trippy cover art provided the color, and were interspersed with black and whites of bridges and buildings. I could only identify the Chrysler Building and the Brooklyn Bridge. I couldn't help but smile taking it all in.

"That's Dylan."

I was looking at the pictures again when she came back into the room. I turned to see her standing there, face flushed pink from the run, wet hair combed and braided over one shoulder, dressed in pajama pants and a snug t-shirt. She brushed past me to put her shower basket away and then sat down on her bed.

"Did I ever tell you about him?" she asked, snapping me out of my dreamy stupor.

"He's your cousin, right?"

"Yes, and I live with his parents, Vince and Margot. That one was taken this summer when we were out at the Vineyard. That's his girl-friend, Kasia."

"She's pretty."

Anna cocked an eyebrow. "That's like saying Swiss chocolate tastes decent. Kasia's drop-dead gorgeous and she's as nice as she is beautiful."

I put the picture down and took a seat across from her on Fiona's bed.

"So, do you hate me?"

"Why would I hate you? Oh yeah, because you insinuated that I'm as mean and spiteful as that witch?"

"Wasn't my intention, but yeah, that."

"She did something really awful to Danielle."

"I know. I was there."

Her eyes went wide. "And you're *friends* with her?" She shook her head. "Why'd you just sit there like you lost your tongue while she kept picking away at me?"

"I don't have a good excuse. I...I felt guilty." She was waiting on me for an explanation. "Something happened a few weeks ago and Charlotte was putting the pieces of the puzzle together. She knows."

She slapped her palms on her comforter, frustrated. "She knows what?"

"She knows how I feel about you."

"Well then enlighten me. How do you feel?"

"Anna." Her name was a plea. I couldn't take the distance anymore, the physical distance or the dance she and I were doing around each other. I moved to stand in front of her and pulled her up to her feet. "Why should I stay away from you? After all this time, I don't want to be right next to you and not be with you."

Her hands were on my chest, the fabric of my shirt fisted in them. "This hurts too much. I don't want to think about you with her. I don't even know her but I hate her. I don't want to hear her name, I don't want to know what she looks like..." Her voice broke when she whispered, "You love her."

I didn't even feel guilty when I said, "I don't love her...Not that way," because here, standing right in front of me, so close that her breath felt warm against my chest, was the person I loved so hard and so deep that I couldn't stop myself.

I wanted. I wanted. I wanted.

I wanted to hold her hand walking through campus, I wanted to introduce her to everyone as my girlfriend, I wanted to dance and goof around with her, have my arm slung around *her* shoulders hanging out at those parties in the woods. And at this very moment I wanted to pull her in even closer, wanted to feel her body skin on skin, wanted to kiss her and claim her.

ANNA

"Do you think I want to imagine you," he whispered as he gently tugged the top over my head, "kissing *him*?" He tossed my shirt onto the floor, then sucked in a breath when he laid his hands along the sides of my breasts. He moved slowly, inching along my skin down to my waist, then onto the curve of my hips. He locked eyes with me when he slowly pushed the fabric of my drawstring pants down until they slipped off, pooling at my feet.

I knew I should have been pushing him away, but oh my Lord. His hands, big and calloused, passed over my skin leaving me lazy and warm and wanting. With his eyes fixed on the swell of my breasts, he fingered the lace strap on my shoulder with one hand while the other gripped the flesh on my hip. He spoke my name before angling his head down to kiss me.

And frigid bitch no more.

With Declan's mouth on mine, I wasn't thinking, worrying or second guessing like I always did. When I hooked one leg around him, his hand slid lower to cup my bottom and squeeze as he drew me in closer. He turned and sat himself back onto my bed with me in his lap. He kissed me like he was desperate, groaning as he strained against me, pushing up as he pulled me down. Some tripwire I never knew existed had me moving with him, heat and desire pooling in me like a physical ache. If he asked, if he just would have tried, I know I would have let him.

I felt drunk and foggy, so when he let out a frustrated breath, rested his head against my chest and apologized, I couldn't make sense of it.

"I'm sorry."

It was the worst possible thing he could say.

"I'm not," I whispered in a choked voice. I wasn't sorry. I should have been, but I wasn't.

He didn't belong to me anymore, I knew that. And although I tried to live my life without judging others, I always thought people who cheated—well, there was no acceptable excuse. But how could I regret something I'd been dreaming about and wanting so badly? I'd never felt this way, or wanted anyone the way I wanted him.

"Why is the timing always wrong?"

"The timing? What do you mean?" he asked absently.

My braid had come loose and he was running his fingers through my hair, his eyes set on the swell of my breasts where the strands ended.

I was fifteen again, both scared and excited by his attention. I touched my finger to his chin. "You seem particularly fascinated with the view down there."

His laugh was soft. "I'm comparing the view now with that sweet picture in my mind from three years ago."

"And?"

"Oh my lassie," he whispered, affecting his best Scottish accent as he traced one finger across the top of one breast and then the other. "Oh how you've grown."

I laughed but there was a sad note to it. He looked up at me, serious again. "What did you mean about timing?"

I rolled off his lap and laid back against my pillows. Still dressed only in my underwear, I liked how his eyes raked over me from top to bottom; it made me feel powerful in this situation over which I had no control.

"We met when we were too young. Now we meet again and the timing still isn't right."

Declan leaned over and placed one chaste kiss on my forehead. Then he grabbed my clothes off the floor and handed them back to me. I slid the top over my head and put the pants back on too. When

I was dressed, he joined me on the bed, both of us on our backs looking up at the ceiling. It reminded me of lying on the dock all those years ago.

"We were meant to meet again...I know that." He rolled over onto his side facing me. "I don't want to stay away. I can't." I nodded and he smiled, breathing in deep. He kissed my forehead again and then sat up. "We'll figure this out, Anna."

Chapter Nine

ANNA

One week passed, two weeks, three. It's amazing what can happen, how things can change in such a short span of time.

We were together every day at some point. He'd plop down with us girls at lunch, he'd walk me to class, or he'd text me with some stupid pretense that I could see right through. Declan would ask for my class notes—we had no classes together. He'd ask me to tutor him in Spanish—I studied French. My personal favorite? He'd ask me to help him do laundry—I'd patently refuse. We'd typically wind up in his room, talking and then making out on his bed, nothing more.

I wanted more.

There were things I did with Jonathan just because it was expected. It wasn't out of desire. With Declan, though, I found myself looking at him, wondering what it would be like, imagining it. Wanting to lick and touch every inch of his body, to make him feel so good that he'd be moaning my name.

My name, not hers.

I'd sit in class thinking about him, sometimes having to jolt myself out of a state when I realized I'd just flung my head back, eyes closed, imagining his hand moving between my legs. Having to pass off this crazy lust as nodding off in class, the way your head jerks when you wake suddenly. The feeling had settled as a kind of wretched ache in my body.

I didn't tell him about breaking up with Jonathan. He never asked, and I didn't want my newly single status to be the thing that persuaded Declan. I wanted him to feel as certain about me as I did about him—committed enough to know there was no one else he could be with.

Was I upset that he didn't break it off with her that night, the night he said he couldn't stay away from me? Disappointed, pained, wounded—every one of those words fit. I truly believed we were meant to be together. Didn't he feel the same? Maybe I wasn't being fair. After all, I wasn't exactly all in with Jonathan to begin with. I was never head over heels. I admitted sadly that it must be different for Declan. And worse still, I knew that by continuing to see him I was lowering myself and committing the worst possible breach of girl code: *Thou shall not take another girl's boyfriend.*

So I didn't talk about Jonathan but he sure did talk about Tess. It hurt to listen. Felt like a knife wound every time he spoke her name. But that was part of who Declan and I were together. When one of us needed to talk, the other one listened.

Tess came into his life when things were dark and she made him happy again. I envied her that. Tess was his first. I envied her that. Tess needed him, needed him so much that it didn't feel right anymore. She wouldn't take a break-up well. He worried about her.

God, I envied her that.

* * *

DECLAN

I wouldn't slow down enough to stand back and take an objective look at what was going on. If I did, I'd have to acknowledge how fucked up my life had become. In the moment, from close range, all I could see and all I could feel was Anna.

I was in love with her.

I faked my way through phone calls with Tess. The guilt didn't gnaw at me like it should have. I didn't want to stop what I was doing. I didn't want to deprive myself of one minute with Anna.

I went to classes, studied and practiced with more drive and energy than ever before. I laughed with my friends, hung out with Anna at parties, at my dorm, at hers.

I liked spending time in Anna's room with her and Fiona, even more so when Fiona was out. We'd listen to music and she'd tease me about my limited knowledge on the subject. I'd act interested when she introduced me to a slew of bands I'd never heard of: Tame Impala, Cage the Elephant, The Strokes. I liked the music and all, but I'd have been just as content listening to Pavarotti sing heavy metal, just as long as I was lying in bed next to her.

Brandon, Colin, Jimmy, Terrence—they were her friends too. Anna could hold her own sitting in my room surrounded by those obnoxious guys, and they thought she was great. She became friends with Victoria and Melissa too. She wouldn't give Paige or Charlotte the time of day, though, so she'd generally sit with her crew in the cafeteria and then at some point I'd leave my group to go over and sit by her.

We weren't all out in the open, but you'd have to be blind not to figure out what was going on between us. In public I'd fight to contain myself, but whenever I had the opportunity I'd pull her behind the stacks in the library or drag her into an empty classroom, unable to keep my hands and lips off hers.

Time is funny. Everything changed between us in those days and weeks that followed, or I should say, things went back to the way they were so long ago.

I literally had a bounce in my step, and probably looked like a nut walking around with a smile plastered on my face twenty-four-seven. Every thought was centered around Anna. Her smile. Her goofy laugh. The way she smelled, and the taste of salt on her skin after we came back and collapsed on my bed after our runs. The way she kissed me, soft lips passing over mine. Or the way her arms would drape around my neck, giving my hands access to the curves of her body. Being with her felt good and right. I was happy—the kind of happiness that makes you feel invincible.

Another weird thing about time? It flies when you're having fun.

Chapter Ten

DECLAN

Tess was coming, and as the weekend drew closer I started to feel as if I was coming apart at the seams. I ripped into Frank over some stupid, harmless comment he made about Fiona's breasts, and I found myself smacking the side of the ATM machine outside of the bookstore, hard and repeatedly, when my card didn't work one afternoon.

The day before she was due, I got into a fight with one of my teammates after he checked me into the boards. It was my fault. My head wasn't on straight and I'd left myself open for the hit. He didn't even hit me that hard. It's just that I was a powder keg ready to go off.

Our team captain, Ryan Walker, laid into me after practice. "As your captain I should be trying to find out what's going on with you, but right now I'm too fucking angry to care. First off, you're a freshman and Gallagher's a junior. I don't care if he checked your ass right up into the stands, *you* are in the wrong. Get your shit together and stop acting like a dick, Banks, or you won't be getting any ice time. It's that simple."

I tried to talk to Gallagher after practice, but by the time Walker finished ripping me a new one he was gone. Truth is, I never liked Chris Gallagher, so knowing I had to apologize to him was a fitting way to end my craptastic day. The guy was cocky, rude and he pulled some sneaky moves on the ice—underhanded moves that could land his opponents in the hospital. But Walker was right. I was out of line.

Brandon was outside the locker room waiting for me. He didn't say a word until we were sitting in a booth, waiting for our burgers at an off-campus place with Victoria.

"You're a fucking mess."

"But it's a mess I made myself, right?"

Victoria's expression was sympathetic. "Yeah, a hot mess." She looked at Brandon and then back to me. "Not looking to add any more drama to the situation, but Anna told me she has one extra ticket and asked if I wanted to sit up close with her and Fiona tomorrow. She's coming to your game."

"You know what's crazy?" I asked them. "I *want* her to be there. I want to look up and see *her* there."

Victoria said, "Then I guess I'm missing something."

Brandon added, "Don't take this the wrong way, but you're always laughing when you're with Anna. You seem happier when you're with her."

That wasn't entirely true, the always laughing part. Anna was one of the few people I could really talk to, and no topic was off-limits between us. I mean, I'd openly cried in front of the girl. But I knew what Brandon was saying. I was happy. I was fucking ecstatic when I was with Anna.

"I'm not *un*happy with Tess, you know." For some reason that I couldn't exactly pinpoint, I felt like I had to defend that relationship too.

Victoria put her hand on top of mine. "We're not putting Tess down. It's just hard not to make comparisons. You and Anna seem good for one another, that's all. And Declan, we're kind of worried about you."

"Yeah," Brandon said. "What the fuck are you gonna do this weekend? Have you talked it over with Anna?"

"Not really. She knows Tess is coming...I'm sure of it. I mean it's not exactly a secret. But what can I possibly say to her? 'Hey, do you mind laying low for the next forty-eight hours?' Anyway, Anna isn't about to go making a scene or anything. She's got a boyfriend too. It's not like I'm the only one sneaking around here."

Victoria shot Brandon a look before she said, "I think you're wrong about that. Colleen told me Anna broke up with her boyfriend."

"When?"

"I'm not sure exactly, but she made it sound like it was a while ago."

"No," I said, shaking my head. "She would have told me."

Anna wouldn't keep that to herself, would she? She really never did talk about the guy, though. Jonathan. His name hadn't come up in a long-ass time. Fuck. I'd been going on and on about my relationship woes while Anna just sat there and listened. A sickening sense of clarity came over me.

I put a twenty on the table. "I'm heading back."

After I made a pit stop at Chris Gallagher's place, ate crow and apologized, I headed straight for Anna.

"What's up? Are you ready for tomorrow? My brother said the goalie for UNH is like a brick wall. Nothing gets by the guy."

"Yeah, I hear the same." I was trying to be polite but I wasn't in the mood for small talk. "Fiona, I need to talk to her. Where is she?"

"She's on her way to some art exhibit at the Gardner Museum with a few people from her class. It's for an assignment but she mentioned getting something to eat with them afterwards. She won't be back for a while."

"Do you know where it is?"

"Why? You gonna go hunt her down, Declan?" She shook her head. "No, I don't know where it is." Fiona's expression was changing before my eyes. She looked cordial enough when she opened the door, but now she looked like she wanted to damage my face. "She already knows, if that's what you came here to tell her. The whole freaking dorm knows that your babe is in town for the weekend."

I was standing by her desk, looking at her pictures, scanning the cards and papers, searching for some evidence of her boyfriend.

"I don't think you're a bad guy, so don't take this the wrong way. I don't think it's *just* that you want to have your cake and eat it too, but that *is* what you're doing. You're holding Anna back. She could be dating anyone. Owen? The guy who picked her up tonight? He's totally into her. It was written all over his face." She let out a cheerless laugh when she added, "Even your boy Terrence. He hooked up with *me* even though I know that little creep is really crushing on Anna." She poked my shoulder hard. "Seriously, what are your intentions here?"

My intentions? It was like listening to an overprotective father instead of an eighteen year-old girl. But what Fiona was saying was true and it wasn't funny. I had nothing to say in my own defense, so I stuck with the truth. "I care about her, Fiona. I'm trying to fix this."

I walked around campus in the dark for the next two hours. Spent that time role-playing the conversation I needed to have with Tess and thinking about Anna.

Tess had no idea what was coming, and I felt lower than dirt knowing I was about to crush her. How would she react? I wished she was the type of girl who'd scream, curse, slap my face and tell me off. I'd consider that a blessing. But I knew Tess. I could already picture her crumpled up on the floor crying. Knew she'd make me feel like I was hurting her in the worst possible way, killing her. I was angry at her then, resentful of the vice-like hold she had on me.

And how would Anna react if she saw me with Tess? I didn't want to hurt her. Still couldn't believe she broke up with her boyfriend to be with me. That guy was her rock, the one who'd gotten her through some of the worst times in her life. And she left him for me. It made me feel good—I won, right? But it made my heart sink at that same time.

I was going to have to take whatever came my way. It was time to pay for my crimes.

* * *

ANNA

Owen was pulling the full court press. He was a junior, very good looking, polite I guess, and he had a decent sense of humor. He was laser-focused on me the entire night, though, and it was getting exhausting. I could tell from his face that he was disappointed when I made a quick exit after dinner, using an upset stomach as a lame excuse. He really wasn't a bad guy. In fact, under different circumstances, like maybe if I'd never crossed paths with Declan Banks, I probably would have been into him. It was me. I was agitated and nervous.

The thought of coming face to face with this girl had me tied up in knots. I knew I could easily avoid the situation. I could go home this weekend, let Margot and Uncle Vince fuss over me. I could spend the weekend eating gourmet food, shopping with a woman whose credit card knew no limits, and I could lounge around in my well-appointed, oh so comfy room. But no, I had to see her. I had to see *them* with my own eyes.

That old saying about not being able to look away from a car wreck? I knew a head-on crash was coming, knew I was going to suffer the force of the impact, and still, I couldn't look away. I didn't just plan to stay on campus. No, I also made plans to sit my ass in those rink-side seats, so close that I could see the beads of sweat dripping from his brow.

I imagined he would be sweating.

Fiona had broached the subject tentatively a few weeks ago, after his girlfriend's last visit. I wanted to ask her, wanted to get every last detail, but I held back with an iron clad will.

By Monday, Fiona was the one ready to burst. "I had an interesting night on Saturday."

Really? I felt like asking what was so interesting about letting Terrence feel you up. I took a deep breath. "Good for you."

"When exactly did you get back, anyway?"

"Saturday, late afternoon."

She cocked her head to the side. "I didn't see you?"

"No, I don't think you or Terrence noticed my presence."

She threw herself back on the bed. "Ugh...Please tell me you weren't here the entire time."

"Nope. I bailed after the opening remarks."

"Want to refresh my memory?"

"Certainly. Declan's a dick. He's leading Anna on. He's fucking someone else. According to you, that someone else is gorgeous and," I looked up at her and made a cutesy face laced with as much venom as I could muster, "she's *sooo* nice."

"Shit, Anna. I'm sorry." She paused, her expression thoughtful before she went on. "I don't think I'd say *gorgeous,* but she's not exactly unfortunate looking either. I think you're bullshitting me about the *so* nice part too. She was neither here nor there. Not a bitch but not super friendly either. But that's not fair. We didn't talk for long, so I can't really give an accurate assessment of the girl's personality."

"I'm not mad at you, Fiona. You know that."

"Are you mad about Terrence?"

"Are you high? Why would I be mad? I like Terrence for you. He's really nice."

"He is nice but that was a one-and-done. I think we make better friends."

"Why?"

"Um, maybe because he likes to talk about you just a little too much for my taste." She laughed. "I'm not mad at *you* either, bitch. It was just a little ridiculous, you know?"

After a minute I asked, "What was she like? Really, you can tell me."

Fiona sat next to me on the bed and put her arm around my shoulders. "I spoke to them for a total of two minutes, tops. Maybe I shouldn't have gone over to introduce myself, but I'm sorry, there's a part of me that wanted to see him squirm."

"I'm not with him, Fiona."

"But you kinda are. I mean, the way he looks at you?" She let out a soft laugh. "He looked like he was about to crap his pants when he saw me walking towards them."

I didn't want to know but I had to ask, "What is he like when he's with her?"

"He was holding her hand. They seemed close, you know? But I wouldn't say they have a light and easy relationship. He looked a little tense and so did she."

So I felt the need to make sure Fiona wouldn't be taking the law into her own hands this weekend. If she was bent out of shape the last time Declan had his girlfriend here for a visit, *when he and I hadn't even kissed*, I worried this time she'd do something dramatic, like call him out in public. I knew that although she really liked Declan as a person, she was none too happy about what had been going on these past few weeks.

"Fiona?"

"Yes, dearest," she said as she walked in the door, tossing me a brownie before flopping onto her bed.

I looked at the brownie, smiling as I unwrapped it. "How cute, you think I need some love even *before* I get my heart crushed. You," I said, pointing at her, "are a good friend."

"I know it."

"I'm going to be all right, Fiona." I could tell by her look that she wasn't buying it, so I went with the direct approach. "Promise me you won't say anything to him?"

"Too late for that. I told him what I thought about this whole situation last night. He came by looking for you."

"What happened?"

"I don't want you to get hurt, Anna, and that's where this is all heading. He didn't say much. He knows what he's doing is wrong. I mean, did he even *tell* you that she's coming?"

"No."

"That's probably why he was so desperate to know where you were last night. He's panicking, knowing he's about to be in the center of a giant clusterfuck."

"He knows I'm not going to make a scene."

She threw her head back in frustration. "I kind of wish you would."

"No, I won't do that. It's bad enough that I'm going to the game like some pathetic fucking voyeur. I just...I can't help it. I need to see her."

"Well, I'll be right there with you. And don't worry, I'll keep my mouth shut. I promise."

Chapter Eleven

ANNA

The arena was packed. We were playing the team that beat us last year in the semifinals, so this was a grudge match. Fiona filled us in on each player's stats, the ongoing rivalry between our schools, and the sordid gossip surrounding the opposing coaches—apparently there was a George Harrison-Eric Clapton sort of love triangle way back when.

For once I was grateful for Fiona's tendency to ramble on and on about all things hockey. Victoria was sitting with us. And while I considered her to be a friend, she was Brandon's girlfriend so we couldn't speak freely in front of her. Sitting her between Colleen and Fiona, two veritable chatterboxes, took the focus off me. I didn't have it in me to be a stimulating conversationalist tonight.

A lot of UNH fans made the trip down, so when their team came out onto the ice they were met with foot stomps and cheers. One player seemed cockier than the rest, skating backwards, looking up into the crowd and basking in the attention. When he skated by us a second time, he came to a sudden stop. Ice sprayed off the blade of

137

his skate as he lifted his helmet and mouthed my name. It took me a second to put a name to that face—Shane. I could hardly believe it. I remembered Shane and Declan talking about hockey back at camp, but didn't realize or imagine that one day they'd be playing against each other.

"Shane!" I pointed towards our team's bench and said, "Declan's playing," hoping he could at least read my lips.

"I know," he said, and then he smiled as he pretended to check someone into the boards. "Meet me after," he mouthed the words as he pointed towards the locker room. I nodded, knowing full well what I was doing.

"Can you explain *this* to me?" Fiona feigned annoyance. "How does someone who claims to know *nothing* about hockey, claim no *interest* in hockey whatsoever, have hockey players stopping mid-skate to say hello to her on multiple occasions?"

"Yeah," Victoria chimed in. "Who was that?"

"Shane Garrison. We went to camp together a long time ago."

"Holy shit, was this like a grief camp for beautiful people?" Fiona asked, laughing.

"What's grief camp?" Victoria asked but then quickly corrected herself. "Sorry. I mean, that sounds personal."

"It's all right, Victoria. My brother was killed, Shane lost some of his close friends in a car accident, and you know Declan lost his mother, right?"

"The last part I knew, yeah." She paused, brow furrowed like she was working something out. "So you all met there? You've known Declan for that long?"

"A little over three years, but we lost touch for a long time. I was surprised when we ran into each other on campus. Shocked, really."

"Brandon told me about that. Crazy, right?"

"Crazy," I repeated, thinking that crazy was a good way to describe me given the chain of events I'd just set into motion.

Catching up with Shane outside of the locker room? I wanted to catch up with him, sure, but I also wanted an excuse to be there. I wanted—no, scratch that—I *had* to bear witness.

I was driving full speed towards a head-on collision with Declan. And with her.

* * *

DECLAN

"Damn, Banks, that was some game. How many goals you got for the season so far?"

"Four?"

"Don't say it like a question. You know you remember each and every one of those four goals." Shane clapped me on the back. "It's impressive for a freshman. Be proud."

"I can't believe I'm talking to you right now, Shane."

"You're hurting my feelings. I guess you haven't been following my career, while I, on the other hand, have been looking forward to playing you all season. Your name is making the rounds, Declan."

"I don't know about that."

"Aw, he's bashful," Brandon teased, bumping my shoulder hard. "I'm Brandon, by the way."

"Shane Garrison."

"Good game, Shane. Declan didn't make it past you too easily," Brandon smirked, "but he *did* get by you."

"That he did."

"Maybe someday, if I *ever* get to play, I'll get by you too."

Brandon couldn't shake it. He was bitter. He wasn't necessarily mad at me, but he was resentful that I got ice time and he didn't.

"If it makes you feel any better, I got zero minutes freshman year and a total of twelve minutes sophomore year. Things didn't start looking up for me until junior year."

"No fucking way." Brandon threw his head back in frustration.

"If I have to sit most of next year too, I'm transferring. I'll be a starter for University of Honolulu."

Shane turned his attention back to me. "I saw Anna! I couldn't believe it when I spotted her. Is she here visiting you?"

Brandon let out a half cough, half laugh. "Yeah, Declan, is she here for a visit?"

I shot him a look before answering, "She goes to school here. I didn't know it until I ran into her a few weeks ago."

"You're blowing my mind. What a weird fucking coincidence. So are you with her?"

Tess threw her arms around my neck a split-second later. "Great game, baby!"

I kissed her cheek and hugged her close, but had a pit in my stomach the size of the Grand Canyon. "I want you to meet an old friend of mine. Shane, this is my girlfriend, Tess. Tess, Shane Garrison."

"Hi, Shane."

Shane looked back to me before offering Tess a half-hearted smile. "Nice to meet you."

"What are you doing tonight? Can you come and hang out with us?" I asked.

"Uh, yeah. I'm friends with Walker and a few of the other guys on your team. I'm going to their party in—"

"Turner Hall?"

He nodded. "And I'm meeting up with Anna." He looked past me then, lips quirking up in a happy smile. "Hey! I still can't believe I spotted you up in the stands. Tonight's a regular blast from the past." He moved past me to pick Anna up and spin her around—a little too friendly, I thought.

"Shane," I called out, interrupting their reunion, "are you still with Jessica?" It was stupid of me. I didn't think before I said it.

He shot me a look, like he was disappointed and mocking me at the same time. Was I that easy to read? "Still with Jess," he said as he set Anna back down.

Anna didn't look my way once. She was doing it for me, giving nothing away, I guessed. I was grateful, but it felt like a kick to the gut at the same time.

As more of the players came out, a few of Shane's teammates started buzzing around Anna and her friends, introducing themselves. Victoria left them and walked over to wrap her arms around Brandon.

"Where were you sitting? I was looking for you," Tess said.

Victoria smiled. "Just sitting in a different section, a little closer to the action. It was a great game, right?"

Tess got up on her toes and tilted her head up to kiss my cheek. "It *was* a great game."

"Come on," Brandon said, "let's head out."

Walker's party was now the last place on earth I wanted to be, but there I was, pouring myself a beer as my stomach threatened to revolt.

Anna shouldn't be here.

That's what was running through my head. You'd think it was because her presence considerably upped the odds of an awkward confrontation, but that wasn't it. I know it makes me an ass to even think it, but I wanted Anna to be at home, away from the guys who were eyeing her up, talking to her and making her smile.

I spent most of the night in a corner of the living room with a few of my teammates, along with Tess and Victoria. Fiona came over to talk, but Anna stayed on the opposite side of the common area with Colleen, Lauren and a few other girls from their hall. Shane was by her side most of the time but made his way towards me when he saw Tess and Vic go for the bathroom.

"So, looks like you've gotten yourself into a situation."

"What did Anna say?"

"Not much. I'm not book smart, but even a moron like me can

see what's going on."

"I've been with Tess for two years. That first day I saw Anna on campus..." I took a long pull on my beer, still trying and failing to process how I felt. "Everything changed."

"And now?"

I shook my head in defeat as Tess made her way back towards us.

"Shane, did you and Declan meet at hockey camp or did you play against each other in high school?"

"Camp."

"Where did Jessica wind up going to school?" I asked.

"Princeton." He beamed with pride when he said it.

"So," Tess said, "you date a genius?"

"Someone has to know how to manage all that NHL money I'm going to be making."

"How's that going?" I asked, curious as to how that all worked.

"I've got some interest, but I'm finishing my last year of school. I'm not the sure thing that you seem to be."

Tess smiled, looking back over her shoulder and up at me. "You hear that?" She turned back to Shane. "He acts like he has to have a sensible career all lined up. Like the NHL is only a pipe dream."

"That's because Declan's smart."

"He's going to make it," she said, taking my hand and wrapping it around her front so that she was snug against me.

I felt the color drain from my face when I looked past Shane to see Fiona and Anna looking right at me. Her expression was flat, unreadable. When some guy from Shane's team handed Anna a cup, she turned her attention back to him, forcing a smile.

I leaned down and whispered in Tess's ear, "I gotta take a leak. Be right back."

After coming out of the bathroom, I made my way back around the other side of the room. I stopped when I got near Anna and said, "You shouldn't take an open cup from a guy you don't know."

Someone watching wouldn't have even thought we were talking.

I wasn't looking directly at her, and she didn't even raise her head when she shot back, "Thanks for the advice."

"Don't trust any of these guys," I warned as I kept moving past her.

"Don't trust any guys, got it."

I deserved that. "Anna, you know I'm dying here, right?"

"Don't worry. I won't blow your cover."

A few minutes after I got back to my spot with Tess, I nearly choked on a sip of my beer when Fiona, Colleen and Anna started making their way towards us.

Colleen was staring at me and Tess, while Anna was looking at the ceiling, her fingernails, at anything other than us. Fiona was the only one to speak. "We're heading out. It was nice to see you again, Tess."

"You too, Fiona."

Tess's eyes followed when Shane tapped Anna's shoulder and took her aside. He was whispering in her ear and she was nodding. The two of them hugged tight and then she left with Colleen, Fiona and Lauren following behind.

"Who was that girl with Shane?"

"Anna."

"She's pretty."

Thank God for Brandon. He butted in, asking me about our practice schedule. When I answered, Tess groaned, "Eleven o'clock?"

I was used to being on the ice at five in the morning, so an eleven o'clock practice seemed like a gift. And the timing was perfect as far as I was concerned. Quick breakfast, Tess on a bus heading back to Maine by ten, and then life would go back to normal.

"Maybe I'll head back Monday morning instead. I don't have class until the afternoon."

"Sounds good," I said, trying to fake some enthusiasm as my heart sank.

There would be no lazy Sunday afternoon, no Sunday night

studying at the library with Anna. But who was I kidding? Anna wouldn't be on speaking terms with me after this weekend, let alone be willing to let me feel her up in the dark corners of the library.

Tess wasted no time when we got back to the room. I could barely get through it. I felt like crap. Guilty, ashamed, used—you name it. But I did do it, which says a lot about me, and none of it good.

My mind was racing. So many things I wanted to say to Tess. If I had any balls, I would have told her how much I cared about her, how I didn't want to hurt her, but how I wanted to experience this new chapter of my life on my own.

I didn't have any balls.

She stayed Sunday. At her insistence, we parked ourselves outside while Frank and a few of the other guys played basketball. At one point she moved closer, sat in my lap and kissed me. She was never much for public displays of affection before, but now she wasn't coming up for air, oblivious to anyone watching the show. Then Tess said she wanted to eat in the cafeteria with my friends when I offered dinner in town that night. Tess was making her presence here known, staking her claim.

Either my timing was for shit or the universe was looking to kick me in the nuts. I purposely stalled until after six, figuring Anna would be done with dinner and already on her way to the library. I spent every Sunday with the girl, so I knew her routine. But no, Anna was sitting just a few tables over from my group when we locked eyes. When she saw me sit down with Tess at the long table where the boys, Melissa, Charlotte, and Paige were already seated, Anna got up to leave. She looked lifeless.

She had to be hurting. If the situation was reversed, there's no way I'd be able to sit and watch her with some other guy. It would kill me. I also knew I'd never let her do that to me. I would have walked right up to her and called her out in front of her man, let the chips fall where they may. Me, me, me—my wants, my needs, me first. I felt physically sick watching her silently take what I was all but shoving down her throat.

Charlotte, looking to get back at Anna after their last run-in, made a point of calling out, "Hey Anna, come hang out. Why you leaving so soon?"

A few heads swung in my direction, but Brandon and Victoria distracted Tess, drawing her into conversation. I leveled my gaze at Charlotte and told her to shut up. I didn't say it out loud because I was a fucking coward, but she could read my lips. I saw Melissa grab her arm in anger as Colin called her a bitch under his breath.

Anna was gone by the time I looked up, but I saw Colin jogging out the door, no doubt trying to catch up with her. He was a far better man than I was.

Tonight, I thought. *Tonight I have to put an end to this.* "Tess, let's go. I don't feel like eating this crap."

I guess my tone didn't leave any room for discussion because Tess followed along without protest. She took my hand and stroked my forearm with her other hand, huddled in close as we walked towards the campus bus stop.

"You weren't joking when you said you wanted Chinese, huh?"

My smile was weak. "Sometimes that whole group thing...I just need to be away from it."

"I totally get that. You know, Declan, this is probably all temporary for you anyway. You could go for the draft after this season maybe...Next season at the latest."

"Why would I do that? I want my degree."

"I'm not saying *never* finish college. I'm just saying that you could go back after."

When the bus pulled up we took two seats in the back. "I'm asking you again, why would I want to do that?"

"I'd say it's pretty obvious. You should go pro sooner rather than later. We could have financial security. What if you get injured now? What happens then?"

I dropped her hand and lowered my head, resting it against the seat in front of me, drained. "Then I'd get a job in the field that I earn my degree in, Tess. I'm not just good for hockey."

"I didn't mean that."

I still wasn't looking at her. "I think you did. And I don't want to think about financial stability right now. Fuck...I'm eighteen years old."

She sat in silence but I could feel the storm brewing inside of her. She practically hissed, "That's because you *never* have to worry. It must be nice to know you can charge whatever you want on daddy's credit card whenever you feel like it."

I looked to her. "Why should I have to make decisions about my entire life right now?"

"Declan," she said, turning her head to look out the window. "I'm not trying to make decisions for you. But I do think about the future. I just always imagined it would be you and me. Together. Married. Family. There's no one else for me."

I grabbed her hands in mine, bracing for the fallout. I was about to go for it, to use those bullshit lines that guys always use but in my case were so true: *I need to take a break...It's me, not you...There are some things I need to figure out on my own.*

But she beat me to it.

She whipped back to face me. "I thought I was pregnant a few weeks ago." She looked angry in response to my reaction, which I could only imagine was a look of pure terror. "Yeah, I was scared to death too. That's why I wouldn't let you touch me during that last visit. And when I saw how happy you are here," she waved her hand around, "in your *new* life, I was scared. I didn't want you to be mad or disappointed in me. I didn't want you to feel like you were missing out, stuck with me and our...our baby. I didn't know what to do. I was so relieved that it didn't come to that, Declan. I was relieved for *your* sake more than mine. So don't tell me that I don't think about what you need, ok? All I do is think about you and care about you."

"I'm sorry, Tess."

She leaned into me and cried. "I love you. If you don't want to play hockey, go pro or whatever, then don't. I don't want you to feel like I'm pushing you."

"I just want to be eighteen, you know?"

She nodded against my chest. A minute later she asked, "Declan, if I was…What would we have done?"

"I would have taken care of us, Tess. You know that."

That night, she wanted me again. Told me she loved me again and again.

I said it back to her.

* * *

ANNA

"You want my advice?" Without waiting for a response, Shane said, "You're making it too easy for him. He's crazy about you.….It's written all over his face. He wanted to kill me when I hugged you before, and he's been looking over here all crazy-eyes whenever another guy so much as talks to you." He leaned in and whispered, "But you're here, just *waiting*. Fuck him, Anna. Don't wait."

"I don't know what I'm doing, Shane. I feel like a fool."

"I'm not telling you to hook up with some random guy just for the sake of making him jealous, but if some girl was leading me around by *my* dick, that's what I'd do to her. You're too good for that, though, and you could get yourself into trouble that way. Just don't let him think you're down with this. Don't let him think he can have her and have you too."

I walked out of the party with three very quiet girls in tow. Fiona pretty much stabbed the ground-floor button when we got into the elevator. "Well, *he* sucks."

Colleen held my hand. "Are you all right?"

"I'm ok."

"Then I'm sick to my stomach *for* you," Lauren said.

"I can't believe I went there. I actually chose to torture myself. Something is seriously wrong with me."

"Anyone in your shoes would have done the same," Colleen said.

Lauren nodded. "My morbid curiosity definitely would have won out."

Fiona took my other hand. "So now that you know, what will you do?"

I looked to her and forced a smile. "I know you want to hear some badass girl power crap right now, but if I'm being honest, I just don't know. I want to hear it from him. I need to know how he feels about me."

That was Saturday night. By Monday morning I could hardly get out of bed. I felt like I was unravelling.

She had her ass planted in his lap, practically grinding against him out in broad fucking daylight on Sunday afternoon.

When I stood there taking in the scene like a dumbstruck fool, Colleen prodded me from behind like a warden would her prisoner. "Keep moving, eyes ahead, keep moving."

I had no appetite on Sunday night, but went to the cafeteria at Fiona's insistence. There was no escaping the happy couple.

It burned.

Seeing Declan with his arm around that girl was bad enough, but the bubbly way that Brandon, Victoria, Terrence, Melissa and Frank interacted with her was another slap in the face. She was accepted, wanted—same way I felt when I was with them. Clearly I was not their friend. I was just the girl on Declan's arm for the time being. And now that someone else had taken up residence in that spot, it was *that* girl they were looking to welcome. A backstabbing Judas, each and every one of them.

The icing on the cake? When that bitch Charlotte called out to me, I froze. It was like I was on the set of one of those angst-filled teen movies where the mean girl taunts the freaky social outcast in public.

I was the outsider, the freak.

My eyes actually hurt, and they had to be red-rimmed and swollen Monday morning when there was a knock at my door. I was still in bed when I should have been in class.

Fiona didn't push when I told her I wasn't getting up. She just ran back with a muffin and juice before she went to class without another word. The girl was up for sainthood.

I wanted to see him but dreaded what was coming. I wanted him to crawl to me, to explain himself, to beg for my forgiveness and perform some act of penance. I wanted him to reassure me that it was *me* he wanted. Me. But I despised this weak side of myself. I didn't want to give him the satisfaction, didn't want him to know he had the power to do this to me.

His eyes went wide when he caught sight of my face. Guess I looked *really* hot.

"You didn't go to class."

"You're perceptive." I got back under my comforter and rolled onto my side away from him.

"Are you sick or something?" He sounded awkward and uncomfortable.

"Are you kidding?"

Was I sick? Was he actually going with the amnesia approach, pretending the weekend never happened? Or was he going to blow it off, minimize it, smooth everything over? *No big deal...She was here, now she's gone...We're good, right?*

"Just get out, Declan."

He came closer and sat on the edge of my bed. Just the feel of his weight sinking the mattress hurt me deep in my chest.

"I know how badly I'm fucking up. Three times this weekend, Anna. I tried. She says things. I just...I couldn't bring myself to do it."

"Then don't," I said flatly. "Maybe you don't want to break up with her. I have no claim on you and you have no claim on me. Maybe what we were…Maybe I was just a distraction, someone who was around when she wasn't."

"Anna," he moved the arm that was draped over my face to shield my eyes, "don't talk about us in the past tense."

"Fuck off."

He sighed and then asked, "Why didn't you tell me you broke up with your boyfriend?"

Was this guy serious? He actually had the nerve to look annoyed.

"Why should it matter?"

"It does."

I laughed in his face. "Why? Did it make you feel better about what you were doing?" I stared at the ceiling, trying to quell the rage and the sadness swirling inside of me. "I broke up with Jonathan because I'm not a liar. I don't treat people that way. What you do with Tess…" I paused because saying that girl's name made me choke up, and I did *not* want to cry. "How you live your life isn't for me to decide. And from now on, I want you out of my life. You obviously don't care about me. I guess I was too dense to figure it out before, but you made everything crystal clear this weekend."

He put his hand on the blanket over my foot, rubbing it for a second before I kicked his hand away.

"C'mon, hear me out, Anna."

His soothing tone grated on me, unleashing the hurt, embarrassment and fury that had been building up steadily over the past forty-eight hours. Now I was on a roll.

"You two looked so cute together, sticking your tongues down each other's throats in front of everyone. Is that how you hicks do it up in Cape Elizabeth? You should have just fucked her on the grass in front of everyone Sunday afternoon while you were at it. That would have been hilarious."

With the venom I was spewing I shouldn't have been expecting the storybook ending, the one where Declan declares his undying love for me. Yeah, that *so* didn't happen.

After a few moments of dead silence, I mumbled, "Please leave, Declan. Please just get out."

I covered my face with my forearm again so that he couldn't see the tears spilling from the corners of my eyes. I wanted him gone. I fucking hated him in that moment. He kissed my forehead and then I heard the door shut behind him.

I decided to make a day of it.

"Holy crap, you're still in bed? It's five o'clock," Fiona said as she flopped down next to me.

I couldn't help but crack a smile. "I'm actually feeling a little better now. I just had to wallow in it, you know?"

"Totally. I'm the same. When I feel down I go all in. Sad songs, sappy movies, greasy food…I have to immerse myself in it and wait for it to pass. And it always does pass."

"He came over."

"I'm not surprised. I mean, it's obvious that he cares about you… But fuck, you know? Anything earth shattering to report? Did he break up with her?" She didn't look like she was expecting me to say yes.

"No," I said, shaking my head, resigned to the whole shitty situation. "You feel like splitting some wings and a pitcher? That weird little bar off campus that screens old movies on Monday nights is playing Kingpin at seven. Wanna go?"

Fiona got up from the bed and smiled down at me. "Absolutely. I love me some Big Ern. Can I ask the other girls?"

I whipped the covers off and gathered my things for the shower. "Sure. Just warn them that I cannot be held responsible for my actions if anyone so much as speaks his name."

Chapter Twelve

DECLAN

Thanksgiving break was coming up, but to call it a break was misleading. I had practice Wednesday afternoon, practice Friday morning, and a big game against Vermont on Saturday.

Tess wasn't very understanding when I told her I was staying at school instead of taking the three-hour bus ride back to Maine. To me it didn't make sense. My father was probably planning to make a meal out of his Wild Turkey—the booze, not the animal—and Tess's house was not where I wanted to be. Some of the other guys were staying, I explained, and I wanted to show the coach I was here, putting in extra time on the ice and in the weight room.

"Who else is staying on campus?" Skeptical and suspicious, as per her usual. This will be my life, I thought, always having to reassure her.

"Every teammate of mine who doesn't live nearby. Brandon and Walker are staying, and a few of the guys on the basketball team too. You know, the people who *have* to be here."

"I should just head down there and stay with you instead of going home."

"Tess, my practices are long and the game on Saturday is away. You can't ride on the team bus."

She sighed. "Jesus, I'm going to be miserable. Stuck in Cape Elizabeth for four days with my family and no Declan to distract me."

I faked a cheery laugh. "You better not let your sisters hear you talking like that."

"Sometimes I wonder how on earth we're even related. Becky and Deena think Cape Elizabeth is the greatest, the social epicenter of the universe."

"They're in high school. That's how they *should* feel."

"I never did. The only thing that was ever good about that town was you."

"Aw, I'm flattered."

"You should be." After a moment she said, "You know I'll never be able to live there, right? I can't settle down in a small town like that, Declan. It would be the death of me."

"A little dramatic, no?"

"No," she snapped. "Seriously, I'm *never* going back there after college."

"Good to know."

Surprise, surprise. The light, fun conversation lasted all of two minutes before we fell back into our deep, exhausting drag. I felt like baiting her, extolling the many virtues of my home town and then telling her there was nowhere else on earth I'd rather live out the rest of my days.

"Declan," she sighed my name. "I'm just saying that I see us living someplace a little more exciting, like Chicago, LA or New York."

"I'm not looking so far ahead. I just want to be eighteen, remember?"

"Yes, I do recall that conversation. And I want to be in the moment too, but imagining our future together makes me happier than anything else."

"Tess." I swallowed, trying to work up my nerve. "I want to feel free."

Her tone was cautious when she asked, "In what way?"

"Free of worrying about everyone and everything. Free of thinking about what my future holds. Don't you ever meet people at school...Maybe meet people you want to get to know better?"

I was holding my damn breath.

"I have people who express interest in *me*. And I'm human, I look at other guys, but I've never wanted anyone else. I already know in my heart that you're the one. And if I lost you, I'd have nothing. There'd be nothing left."

I was choking on the words pushing up out of my chest, choking on my own silence.

"Declan, are you trying to tell me something?"

"Tess, I love you. I just—"

She cut me off. "I know you love me, and I love you more than anything. I need you, so much. I want to be with you now and every day. There's no one else for me."

Say it! Just say it!

"Tess." She was crying. "Come on, don't do that. Please don't cry."

"You have everything, Declan. I know you don't need me. But I'm different. I feel so down when I'm not with you. Sometimes I worry what I'd do to myself if..."

It wasn't the first time. Those thinly veiled threats did their job, kept me in my place. I'd never forgive myself if she harmed herself because of something I did. I couldn't live with the guilt. So I spent the last few minutes of that conversation calming her down, promising that I'd come home on Thursday and take the bus back first thing Friday morning.

I steered clear of Anna in the days leading up to break, and she certainly wasn't looking for me. I deserved ten times worse than the few nasty things she'd said to me last week. Playing the part of Tess's boyfriend while she was forced to look on—what the fuck was I thinking? I was a coward and a bastard, the lowest of the low. Couldn't even face myself in the mirror.

I looked out my window every night at ten o'clock, but didn't see her making her way out towards the road. The past few days had been rainy with a biting wind. The miserable weather fit my mood.

I wanted to see her—do more than see her—but I lost the right to anything where she was concerned. If I couldn't be all in with Anna then I'd have to suffer the loss of her.

I couldn't have it both ways.

* * *

ANNA

I could feel his eyes on me. Maybe I was imagining it, but I had the distinct feeling that I was being watched.

The driver hopped out of the sleek black Mercedes, bowing his head as he took my bag and opened the door for me. I cringed, praying that Declan, or anyone else for that matter, hadn't just witnessed that scene.

I wasn't necessarily embarrassed by the perks my aunt and uncle's wealth provided, it's just that I preferred to fly under the radar. People were prone to act weird or treat me differently once they found out about my family.

My father, despite having no head for business, held some corporate VP position. He talked himself up like he was a quick-thinking, decision-making industry titan, when in reality he was much like the vice president of a country—a figurehead with no real responsibility. Every single thing he had was a direct result of his sister's marriage to Vince Cole. Uncle Vince made sure that my father was always employed and well compensated. The Clarkes lived very nicely as a result, but the Cole family inhabited an entirely different stratosphere.

Uncle Vince ran one of the largest multi-national corporations in the world. My cousin Dylan was now second in line, his father's right-hand man. One day he would take the reins and assume control over Cole Industries. They had private planes, chauffeur-driven cars, a chef who followed them to any one of the several residences they owned, housekeepers, personal shoppers—you get the idea.

Living with them afforded me access to all of this. It was nice, don't get me wrong, but that kind of wealth comes with its share of drawbacks. The security guards, the household staff manning every square inch of the house, people pandering to you when you don't even know them—it could be unnerving. Dylan grew up to be guarded, always wary of people wanting to be associated with him because of his name and his money. Before he met Kasia, I don't think he ever looked at a woman without suspicion. He was never sure if they liked him for the person he was, or if they were just in it for access to the Cole Industries lifestyle.

I turned to look as we pulled away from the curb just as the lamp switched off on Declan's desk and his room went dark.

Chapter Thirteen

ANNA

Family holidays have been trippy since Will died, and this one was shaping up to be as dysfunctional as ever.

Right off the bat, my father informed me I'd be meeting his new main squeeze. He was bringing her to Thanksgiving dinner at Margot and Vince's. I was *super* excited for that. Then I was spending Saturday with my mother. Last year the woman jetted off to a spa in Arizona with her boyfriend and didn't bother to check in once over the holiday, so receiving a phone call *and* an invitation? I was momentarily speechless. I was tempted to decline, but I didn't. Mom sounded sincere on the phone and I guess I'm a bit of a sucker.

Who could have predicted that by the end of the weekend I'd be feeling so positively blissed out? After slogging through what was the hands-down most awful week of my life—or as my girl Fiona had dubbed it: Tessaggedon—I suppose I was in dire need of a break and some positive vibes.

My father was on his best behavior on Thanksgiving Day, and his girlfriend was actually normal. She wasn't the Botox-enhanced, fake-titted gold-digger I was expecting to meet. No, Sheila was tasteful, articulate and...nice.

Margot came and sat on my bed that night to dish. "I didn't think she was entirely awful. Her highlights didn't look natural, but aside from needing a new colorist, I thought she was ok."

"I know...Weird, right? I liked her, and I think I liked my father better because he was with her."

Margot looked far away. "Todd has always been...I don't know how to say it. I just always felt like he needed me to look out for him. And he needed a wife who could be a help to him, to support him. It's not your mother's fault, it's just that maybe they were too much alike to be good for one another."

"Both immature, both selfish, both needy?"

"Something like that," she said, smiling. "So what are we doing tomorrow? I feel cheated. I only have you to myself for one day."

"Spa, bookstore, dinner at La Viola?"

"Perfect." She leaned over and kissed me goodnight. "I've missed having you home, Anna."

The next day Margot and I had facials, mani-pedis and massages. In between treatments, Margot sipped her mineral water thoughtfully as I told her everything. She wasn't surprised about the breakup with Jonathan and she smiled when I described Declan.

"There's more," she said. "You sound like you care deeply for him but you're sad. You should be happy when you're in love, Anna."

Unlike my friends, who think they know it all and enjoy telling me *exactly* what I should do, Margot didn't give me any advice.

"You poor thing. Thinking about someone you love with someone else, wondering if they care about that other woman...It's like having your own heart torn in two."

It hurt to hear Margot commiserate with me because it sounded like she was speaking from experience. I loved my uncle, but knowing him well, I didn't doubt it.

La Viola was the kind of mom-and-pop joint where you could feel comfortable in jeans while enjoying a fifty-dollar bottle of Chianti with your overpriced baked clams. And I'll admit, those garlicky little clams sent me straight to Nirvana. It was expensive, like every place in this town, but it was the place you went to when you wanted to let your hair down.

Margot and I had just been seated. I was starving, anxious for the server to bring our bread, when I felt a hand on my shoulder. I turned up to see a girl wearing her wait staff uniform. Her face looked familiar but I couldn't place it.

Margot greeted the girl with a warm smile and the sort of tenderness she didn't bestow on many people. "Hello, dear."

"Hello, Mrs. Cole. How are you?" Before waiting for a reply she looked back to me and said, "Anna, I hardly recognized you. You look so much older. Are you in college now?"

"Yes. I'm sorry, I—"

She touched her chest. "Carolyn. It's been years. I was friends with Will and with...Drew."

The lightbulb came on. Carolyn was Drew's girlfriend. The girl who broke up with him just two weeks before. He was so distraught —couldn't cope, couldn't live. I closed my eyes and felt Margot take my hand.

"How have you been, Carolyn?" I managed, recovering.

She shrugged her shoulders and smiled. "I'm doing all right. I transferred to Fairfield. I'm living at home for now." She paused, looking over at Margot briefly before saying, "Anna, I'd really love to catch up with you if you have any time this weekend."

I was silent for a moment but quickly came to the conclusion that I really did want to talk to this girl. Carolyn seemed like she had something she wanted to get off her chest, and I was still hungry to learn every detail about that night, as painful as it might be.

"I'd like that. Can you meet for coffee tomorrow morning? I'm due at my mother's by noon."

We set our plans and then another girl came over to take our order.

"Well, that was interesting," Margot offered.

"You seem like you know her pretty well, Margot."

Margot dipped her bread in the oil, then studied some cheesy Venetian gondola mural in a way that was uncharacteristically evasive. "This is Dylan's favorite place, too. I'm practically a regular."

We sat in silence until Margot reached across again and gave my hand a reassuring squeeze. "Carolyn is a nice girl and I feel for her. Her mother told me she had quite a rough time during her first semester at Penn. She had to come home."

Carolyn was at a corner table when I walked in, talking to a waitress at the cute French pastry shop off Main Street she'd suggested.

"Anna," she greeted me, smiling as I approached. She looked back to the server. "Tori, do you remember Will's little sister, Anna Clarke?"

"Oh my God! You probably didn't even know me in high school, but I remember you. I remember," she laughed, "being obsessed with all things Will Clarke related. I think I started scribbling Mrs. Tori Clarke in my notebook in fourth grade. How are you?"

It was beyond odd, speaking with people who dropped my brother's name so easily—and in happy conversation, no less. It made me smile.

"I do remember you. Tori Williams, right? You were the star player on the volleyball team."

"Yes, but my setting and spiking days are pretty much over now. High school is one thing...I was a big fish in a small pond. The girls who play in college are either super talented or they're Amazons. I tried out for the team, but yeah, that didn't work out. Hey, do you know we have a friend in common? Jeremy Rivers comes in here pretty often."

"Really? I'm going to text him right now and tell him I'm here. I haven't seen him since the summer."

"I didn't know you were friends with Jeremy." Carolyn sounded surprised.

"Yeah. He was really good to me after, uh, everything."

Carolyn nodded and Tori changed the subject, taking our order before leaving us.

"I'm glad you agreed to meet me, Anna. I was kind of afraid to ask you last night."

I shook my head to reassure her. "I'm so glad you did. It's like I still feel the need to hear every detail...Learn anything I can about that night."

Carolyn sat on that for a moment before she said, "I don't think about the actual event. I was always obsessed with trying to piece together what led up to it."

"I can understand that."

"You know," she said, "I've always felt the need to tell you that I'm sorry. I feel so terrible that Will died that night." She reached up and pinched the bridge of her nose, trying to stop the tears from coming. "I mean, I feel sad for Drew also, but Will...He had nothing to do with it."

"How were you, um, after? Margot told me—"

"I was a mess. And your aunt is a seriously wonderful lady. She came to see me right after I came home from school, did you know that?" I shook my head. "Yeah, she's been very good to me." She took a deep breath, settling into her story. "My parents pulled me out of school senior year. I'd already been accepted at U Penn, so I did the last few weeks of classes with a tutor at home. I couldn't leave the house. I thought people were looking at me everywhere I went, and I was sure everyone hated me. I was the cold bitch who'd driven Drew to it. And according to half of the senior class, it was as if I'd pulled the trigger and killed Will myself. Two of the nicest, most popular boys in our class were dead because of me." She shook her head. "I don't know why I thought I'd be able to handle going away to school. My poor roommate. She knew within a week that she was living with a seriously unbalanced individual. I put my fist through a window one Saturday night in early September. I was taken away in an ambulance and spent some time at," she waggled her eyebrows and smiled weakly, "a facility."

I took her hand as Tori laid our coffees and croissants on the table without a word. Carolyn smiled at me. "I'm so much better now, Anna, but it was a long road. I was confused and angry for so long."

"Me too. I blamed everyone and I was so, so angry."

"I'm sure you blamed me."

"You and everyone else," I said, shaking my head. "I hated Drew's dad for having a gun in the house in the first place. I was mad at my parents for...Well, for a lot of things. I was even mad at Will, if you can believe that. I was so damn mad at him for going over there that night."

"I was too," she said, smiling as she brushed at a tear on her cheek.

"I'm better now too, Carolyn. It still hurts like hell some days, but now I know that sometimes things just happen and we have no control over them. Only Drew made that night happen, no one else. You should be able to be seventeen years old and decide that you don't want to date a boy anymore. I don't think anything was your fault. I don't even blame Drew anymore. God, I just...I miss him."

* * *

DECLAN

I was cursing Tess as I sat cramped in that Greyhound bus on Thanksgiving morning. Without a car, the two-hour trip stretched to just under four. Stiff from practice the day before and unable to sleep, I came off the bus only to see that Tess hadn't even bothered to pick me up at the station. Instead of calling her, I went straight to my house.

I texted my dad the day before to tell him I'd be in town, and he called me back right away. I groaned when I saw his number, but I answered. Something was up. He'd been reaching out and calling me at least once a week for the past three weeks. The conversations were always stilted and awkward as shit.

"I'm glad you're coming home. I'm cooking."

I felt like asking why, but as usual, I decided not to bother with the questions. Cook for the two of us, why go through the trouble? But when I walked in the door, I saw the reason for my dad's efforts. A petite, dark-haired woman was arranging a vase full of flowers on the dining room table. The table was set with my mother's fancy dishes.

"That's my mother's china," I said as I dropped my bag on the floor.

"It's such a beautiful pattern." She walked towards me smiling. "You must be Declan. I'm Diana, a friend of your father's."

"Uh, hi. He didn't tell me about you."

"Well, I feel like I know everything about you. Your father talks about you nonstop. I've even become a bit of a hockey fan because he's always watching your games."

"Really?"

I felt like I was in some kind of warped alternate reality. I wasn't entirely sure my father even knew my middle name, let alone any actual details about my life. With that, he came walking into the room and smiled, surprised when he saw me talking to his woman.

He looked good, better than he had in years. His skin and eyes looked bright and clear. He stood up straight, not stooped over like usual. Maybe he was getting laid, I thought bitterly.

"Hi, Declan." He came over and hugged me stiffly. "I see you've met Diana."

"Yes."

I smiled at her. I don't know what it was about her, but despite the urge I had to push my father away, I liked Diana.

She broke in to ease the uncomfortable silence. "Dinner is ready. We were just waiting on you. Is your girlfriend coming?"

"Um, let's eat without her. I'll head over to her place later."

My phone was on vibrate. I could feel it buzzing and then pinging with incoming texts throughout the meal, but I ignored her.

I actually enjoyed their company at dinner. Diana did most of the talking, telling me about her two sons, one who played basketball at UMaine, and the other, an accountant working in New York City. She prompted my dad to add to the conversation when she told me about the recent trip they'd taken to go hiking at Loon Mountain. My dad spoke, awkwardly at first and then more relaxed as the meal wore on. He stuck to more comfortable topics, like hockey. And he definitely had been watching my games, as he recounted all of my best plays of the season so far.

I found myself saying, "Why don't you two come down for a game soon. The tickets I get for family are pretty decent."

My dad swallowed and looked to Diana, who was holding his hand. "I'd really love that, Son."

Diana smiled at my father and then me. "I can't wait, Declan."

As I was driving over to Tess's later that afternoon, I realized there was no bottle of wine on the table during dinner. My father didn't have booze on his breath either.

Interesting.

Tess's sisters practically tackled me when I walked in the door. Deena and Becky were twins, freshmen in high school. They were like two crazy firecrackers, always up for some fun, and they drove Tess bananas. I think she would have preferred being an only child because, unlike me, she didn't know how lonely it could be.

"Get off of him, you two!"

"Deena, Becky...How's it going? Do you like high school so far?"

"Love it!" Becky squealed. "I'm playing volleyball and—"

"I'm running cross country."

"Any boyfriends?"

"No," they said in unison, disappointed.

"Don't put any ideas in their heads, Declan," Tess's dad said as he came in and shook my hand. "How are you? I've been following the games, like everyone else in this town. You're the big talk in the Oak Diner. You've even made *me* into a minor celebrity."

I always liked him. He was a nice guy. Her mom was pretty nice, too. She was into appearances a little too much for my taste, but she was all right. She came into the living room with Tess trailing behind and hugged me. "So glad you're home, Declan. How is first semester going?"

"So far, so good. It's a little tough juggling classwork on top of my hockey schedule, but so far I'm doing all right."

Everyone in the family greeted me warmly except for my girlfriend. She was sporting a pissy expression, standing a few feet away from me with her arms crossed in front of her. "Glad you decided to grace us with your presence. We ate already."

"But we waited for you to have desert," Becky broke in.

Before knocking on the door I'd checked my phone. Twelve missed calls and four text messages.

Where are you?

Did you even come back today?

A phone call would be nice.

Where are you????

"I went home first. I ate with my father."

"Why?"

"Because he asked me to."

"It's five o'clock, Declan. You could have picked up the phone, you know."

With that, I noticed that one by one, the rest of the family was retreating back into the kitchen. Everyone knew to run for cover when Hurricane Tess was about to hit.

"Yeah, well I spent nearly four hours on a bus today. Then I had to *hitch* a ride to my house. My travel itinerary ate up a lot of my day."

"Are you staying tonight?" she asked.

"I'm staying but I have to catch the bus at nine."

"Nine o'clock?" she whined.

"I told you I'd be coming home and turning right back around. I have mandatory practice tomorrow and then the Vermont game on Saturday."

Her expression was softer when she asked, "Can we go back to your place after dessert? I need some time alone with you."

"My father has company."

"You're kidding me, right?"

"No. A lady friend, in fact."

She wrinkled her nose. "For real? Doesn't that piss you off?"

"Should it? It's been almost four years. He looked happy and it was actually a little better between us."

"Really?" She looked unconvinced.

"He looked good and he wasn't drinking."

She stepped in closer and rubbed a hand along my shoulder. "That's great, Declan. I'm glad."

She sat on the couch and patted the seat next to her. Her sisters were in the kitchen helping their mom with the dessert while her dad was outside getting more firewood. We were alone. Tess leaned in and kissed me, stroking my face and then lowering her hand to stroke my thigh. I put my hand on hers to stop her.

"What is it? What's wrong with you?"

"Nothing. I'm just sore and tired from being on that bus all day."

"Come on," she said, leading me outside, grabbing two sweatshirts off the hooks by the door.

We walked down the street to a park by the elementary school. She guided me to a swing and then sat on my lap, facing me. She took my face in her hands and spoke between kisses. "My parents said I could ask for one big thing or a bunch of smaller things for Christmas. I asked my mom if my big thing could be a trip. Like a spring break trip with you after the season is over, somewhere warm. Our March breaks overlap."

She was making plans three months in advance?

"Your parents will be all right with you staying in a hotel room with me?"

I was skeptical, and also hoping that the answer was no.

"My mom is fine with it. She just won't tell my father that I'm going with you. He'll think I'm going with friends. You, me in a skimpy bikini, the ocean, a hotel room with a king-size bed..."

I can't imagine that I looked too excited.

"And if *you* happen to be wondering what to get me for Christmas, I would be *very* excited to open a box with a new Vuitton bag inside. I'll send you a link to the exact one that I want, all right?"

I felt like I had a brick on my chest. After smiling my way through desert and gritting my teeth while Tess spent the better part of the evening scrolling through vacation websites, I made my way home. I was so damn relieved to be alone again.

Before going to bed, I took a quick look at the text she sent me with a link to the Christmas present she'd all but demanded. Six hundred dollars. Who does that? But I guess I couldn't blame her. Other girls had that kind of stuff and Tess just wanted to be like everyone else.

I tried to go back, to remember what it was like when I first met Tess. I know I was crazy about her, wanted to spend every free minute of every day with her, but I just couldn't rekindle those feelings.

I cared about her, and I knew she loved me. But when I pictured this future of ours that she was always talking about, I didn't see a happy couple.

Sitting on that bus the next morning I was the polar opposite of happy, but I didn't see any way out.

Chapter Fourteen

DECLAN

Anna passed right by me on her way to class. She met my eyes and smiled, never breaking her stride. A few hours later I saw her sitting with two guys and another girl in the library, in the section where I used to corner her and kiss her. When I approached and said hello, she looked up and smiled politely before returning to her conversation.

The last time I saw Anna, she'd been her version of mean. She was looking to hurt me back, when nothing short of a knife wound to the chest could inflict the kind of pain I'd caused by parading Tess around in front of her. But now she was impassive, cool and detached. I preferred the Anna who bitched me out. This Anna was scary.

The next day I saw her in the bookstore so I tried again. "How was your break?"

"Oh...Hi." Her expression was tight. "It was really good. Yours?"

"It was ok."

"I heard you guys beat Vermont. Fiona said that was a big win."

"Yeah."

"I've gotta get to class. It was nice to see you, Declan."

She was treating me like a distant acquaintance, telling me to fuck off in her own passive aggressive way.

"Yeah...Nice to see you, too."

My hand aching, I glanced down to see the pen I was holding now clutched in a white-knuckle grip. When I looked back up she was glaring at me.

"What do you want? Want me to give you a big wet kiss hello? Want me to ask all about you weekend? Ok, I'm game." She switched over to some super-pumped cheerleader voice to mock me. "How was your Thanksgiving, Declan? How's Tess? How many times did you fuck her this weekend?" She shook her head in disgust before turning to go.

I followed her out and watched her walk the length of the campus green, telling myself the entire time that she wasn't mine to look at. She wasn't mine to miss.

I spent a lot of time in the weight room and more time running the streets of Boston. I meant for the workouts to be a distraction, time to tune out and not think, but I found myself brooding over the whole fucked-up situation the entire time. My feet pounded the pavement hard, running at a pace that drained me, and after count-less reps, I'd drop the weights to the ground with a loud, angry crash —poor form in the gym but I didn't care.

She wasn't mine, but I still couldn't get her out of my head or my heart.

* * *

ANNA

"So, was Mama well behaved?"

"I heard her say to my father, 'What's gotten into her, Max?' So yeah, Mama needs some time to get used to the new, outspoken me, but she'll deal. I always walk around grinding my teeth, swallowing the words I really want to say. For once I spoke honestly." Fiona bounced on her toes. "It felt so… freeing!"

I hugged her. "That's terrific."

"How was your family bonding time?"

"Well, everyone has a new boyfriend or a new girlfriend except for me." I nodded when Fiona laughed. "My father brought a date to Thanksgiving dinner and I actually liked her. With her around, he wasn't as much of a tool as he usually is."

"And mother dearest?"

"That was interesting. We spent Saturday afternoon together at her place. She made a nice lunch for us and we talked. Oh, and the weirdest part? She was entirely substance free. I can guarantee there were no happy pills involved." Fiona frowned. "Really, I mean it was good. She told me she's dating someone who lives in town, an attorney. I can't explain it, but I didn't feel as angry as I usually do when I'm around her. Do you think it's because I'm getting older?"

"It could be them. Maybe they're behaving better, more like adults. And how are you doing with the whole Declan situation?"

"Hurts like hell but I think I'm finally seeing the light. He's not mine, he's hers."

"What are you going to do?"

"Keep my distance. Hopefully that whole out of sight, out of mind thing works."

"I'll keep you occupied. I'm even boycotting his hockey games in a show of solidarity."

"No, I don't want you to do that. You can still be friends with him. It's fine with me."

"I'm not feeling very congenial towards him right now."

"He's a good person, Fiona. He needs real friends like you, not people who stroke his ego like Paige and Charlotte."

"That's definitely not the only thing those two would like to stroke," she said, shaking her head in disgust.

I had no ill will towards Declan. Even though *I hate him, I hate him, I hate him* ran through my mind at fairly regular intervals, I knew I didn't really have any hate in my heart for him. No, I loved him. I'd never want anything for him but good things. But I couldn't be around him, at least not anytime soon. Everything was still too raw.

I managed to keep my wits about me when he showed up at the library and when he pretended to run into me on the way to class, but when he followed me into the bookstore I basically lost my shit.

Before coming back from Connecticut I made a pact with myself. Swore I wouldn't be weak, swore that I'd say hello, smile and act like I was just fine. I wanted to come off as strong, even though his betrayal had all but sucked the air from my lungs and gutted me.

And he acted like such a jerk, all disappointed that I wasn't falling right back into step. Did Declan expect me to keep carrying on like his girl, like his close friend, after he'd made it painfully clear that I was neither one of those things?

Was he becoming one of those guys, the star athlete who starts getting caught up in all the adoration and attention? Did he actually think I'd be looking to line up so he could dish out some more abuse? If so, the boy was delusional.

I was moving on, even if it killed me.

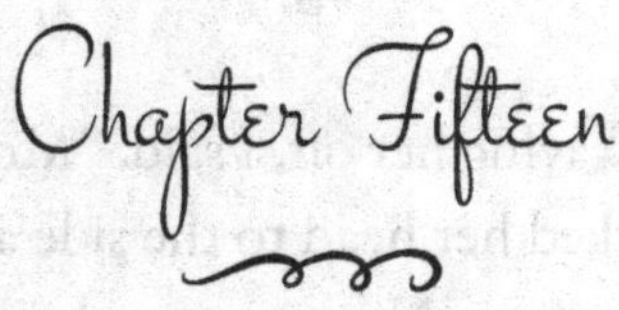

Chapter Fifteen

ANNA

Those few weeks leading up Christmas break were busy. I had work to catch up on and then final exams were breathing down my neck. The parties, however, did not die down.

Now that the cold had set in, the woods were out of the question so we generally hit house parties thrown by the upperclassmen. Two weeks in, I finally ran into him. I made sure to stay on the opposite side of the large common room, as far away from Declan and his friends as humanly possible.

When he waved I waved back, but that was it. It's the saddest thing, being formal and polite with someone you were once so close to, with someone you've shared your deepest thoughts and most intimate secrets.

When I felt a tap on my shoulder I braced myself, expecting for it to be him. Danielle and Lauren were looking over my shoulder, Lauren angry while Danielle had gone white as a sheet.

"I see you took my advice."

After gritting my teeth, I whipped around and said, "I would *never* take advice from you, Charlotte. For one, I hear you're an imbecile who only got into this school because you're a legacy, and two, I think you're morally bankrupt."

She rolled her eyes. "Your *hair*. I was talking about your hair, Anna. Too bad for you, though. Seems like Declan goes for brunettes."

"Are you done?" Waving her off, I said, "Move along."

"Almost." She cocked her head to the side and gave her rendition of a sympathetic expression. No surprise, she couldn't pull it off. "I almost feel bad for you. It had to hurt, seeing Declan whispering in her ear, kissing her, knowing he was making sweet love to his woman each and every night." She smiled and shrugged. "He used you."

"I think you should shut the fuck up." Danielle then proceeded to toss a full beer right in Charlotte's face.

Charlotte looked furious and ready to pounce. She was practically foaming at the mouth, especially when a few guys standing behind her started outright cackling. I was fighting to keep from laughing myself, taking in her beet-red cheeks and the hair that was now wet and matted to one side of her head. Her hand shot up to smack Danielle's face, but Lauren blocked her.

"No cat fights, ladies."

Charlotte glared at Danielle. "I'd watch my back if I were you."

"Ooh," Danielle teased, "I'm so scared."

After she stomped off, Danielle turned to us wide-eyed, her breaths shallow and rapid. "I can't believe I just did that."

"She had it coming," Lauren reassured her. A moment later she added, "Good, I just saw Charlotte leave. I was *so* not into having a retaliation beer dumped on me tonight. Now that the wicked witch is gone, let's have some fun."

A group of about eight of us from our dorm spent the next two hours dancing and doing the occasional shot. I was having a great time. I didn't know if Declan was still at the party, and for the first time in a long while, I didn't care one way or the other. I felt free and happy, dancing, singing along to my favorites and laughing with my friends. Guys were coming up to dance with us, but I wasn't interested in anyone until much later in the night when I'd had too much to drink.

He caught my arm when I stumbled. "Thanks."

"You steady now, Anna?"

"Do I know you? I mean, should I know your name?"

He had a nice smile. "I'm Chris Gallagher. We haven't met, but I've been asking around about you. I've seen you on campus. Hope you're not offended."

"I'm not offended."

The music was loud, so when he spoke he was leaning down over me, talking right into my ear. And then when I'd answer him, he'd lower his face to mine so he could hear me better, I guessed. He was a big guy, built just like Declan.

He danced with me and my friends. He wasn't coming on too strong but I knew he was interested. Was I interested? I don't know. He smelled *really* good, and I was feeling loose, relaxed and happy. When he put his hands on my waist and the music slowed, I didn't stop him, but when he went to kiss me, I turned away on impulse.

"Sorry, Anna, that was too fast. You're just really beautiful, that's all."

I smiled at Chris because that was a seriously sweet thing to say, but when I looked up I locked eyes with Declan, who was staring me down and looking positively livid.

So that's how it is? You can dish it out but you can't take it? Well take this, Declan.

I pulled Chris's head down to mine, then kissed him and kissed him *good*. And to say Chris was receptive was an understatement. He pulled me in so close that I could feel him hard against my stomach.

I pressed my hands against his chest. "We're good. It's ok," he whispered in my ear as he backed away a few inches.

Tap, tap, tap on my shoulder. And they weren't gentle taps,

either. "Can I talk to you for a minute?" Declan was now standing behind me.

Chris said, "What's up, Banks?" as he leveled Declan with a look that was borderline aggressive.

"Nothing, just need a word with Anna."

I looked over my shoulder, dismissing him. "I'm all right."

He took my elbow and whispered in my ear, "Don't, Anna."

I jerked my arm away from him. "Leave me alone."

"Are you deaf? She said to leave her alone, Banks. I suggest you do that."

Now he was facing off with Chris. "Watch yourself, Gallagher." Chris laughed in his face and then Declan looked back to me, disgusted. "Do whatever you want, Anna."

One of Chris's friends came by with another tray of shots. I took one, he took two. The amber liquid felt hot as it made its way into my system. We started dancing again, but I was starting to feel like the room was spinning.

"Come on. I'm taking you home."

The cool air felt great as we made our way outside. Chris scooped me up, carrying me as we walked back towards campus. He was big and strong. It felt nice, and I was too tired to walk all the way back.

He made a turn off the main street.

"My dorm isn't this way."

He said, "My place is."

"I think I should go back to Loyola."

"Shh, you're tired. My place is closer."

"No, I want to go back. I think I'm gonna be sick."

"I'll take care of you, baby."

"Put her down." It was Declan's voice.

"Oh Lord. Banks, get the fuck out of here before I beat the shit out of you, all right?"

"You're not taking her home, Chris. She's not for you."

"She's with me, so head on home, frosh, before I make you regret this."

"Everyone knows how it is with you. You take girls home when they can't even walk. That's how you like them."

I was lightheaded. It took some effort to focus on Chris's face when he looked to me, smiling when he said, "He's full of shit, Anna. I'm gonna put you down for a second so I can take care of this, ok?"

I nodded. When he put me down, I think I stumbled a few feet back and wound up perched on someone's stoop. I couldn't stand on my own, and watching Declan and Chris go at it was making my head spin even more. They were tackling and punching, two giants beating one another to a pulp. Declan had the advantage, not in size but in sobriety. When Chris crumpled to the floor, Declan came over to me, eyes set to kill. He picked me up and threw me over his shoulder, groaning under the strain of my weight and the injuries he'd sustained during the fight.

"Declan," I whispered. I wanted to tell him to put me down, that I was going to puke, but he cut me off.

"Shut the fuck up, Anna."

He walked the rest of the way in silence. I could hear him suck in a gasp every time he readjusted me on his shoulder as we made our way up the hill towards the dorms. At some point I fell asleep.

The next thing I remember, Declan was holding my hair back as I puked up everything—every single drink.

My head felt like it was being cinched in a vise. Worst hangover in the history of hangovers.

"Well, look who's up."

"When did I get home?"

Fiona handed me an aspirin and a bottle of water. "I got in after you. Declan had you all tucked in by the time I got here."

"Oh shit."

It was all coming back to me. I peeked under the covers to look at my clothes. I wasn't wearing a bra, just a tank top and my underwear. My hair was in a ponytail. My clothes from the night before were tied up in a plastic grocery bag next to my bed.

"What did he say, Fiona?"

"Just that you'd had too much to drink. He made me promise to stay up with you in case you threw up again."

I was biting back tears. "That's all?"

"Yeah, that's all." She let out a deep breath. "But when I walked in, Anna, he was sitting on your bed staring at you, running his fingers through your hair. I felt like I'd barged in on something personal. It made me so...sad for him. And he looked like crap. Was he in a fight? When I asked him, he blew me off."

"Yeah, he had a fight."

"Maybe Christmas break is coming at a good time," she said as she grabbed some quarters. "I'm going to get you a ginger ale. Be right back."

I spent the day in bed, sleeping and recovering. I wanted to talk to him. I wanted to know if he was all right and I wanted to thank him for getting me home safely last night, but I just couldn't bring myself to do it.

* * *

DECLAN

Not a word from Anna since Saturday.

Her memory of that night was probably spotty at best, but I'm sure Fiona told Anna that I brought her home. Did she know that I'd undressed her, too? Hoped she wasn't mad about that. I had no choice but to change that shirt, and the wet bra had to come off as well. I closed my eyes as I stripped off her puke-stained clothes, all except for one nanosecond. And I'm a freaking pig, because I

180

couldn't imagine her in that moment without getting hard these past two days.

As I was cleaning her off with a washcloth, she looked at me sadly and said, "Maybe I should play the damsel in distress more often. Maybe then you'd want to take care of *me*." She cried before falling asleep not sixty seconds later. I felt like the worst kind of person, hating myself for what I'd done to her.

Tuesday I found myself searching the library, floor by floor. She was in her usual spot: up on the top floor in a remote corner. She liked to curl up in those soft upholstered chairs instead of studying at the tables with everyone else.

Anna looked small and sad today, sitting with her knees tucked into her chest and her nose in a book. I took a deep breath and walked over, dropped my backpack and flopped into the chair opposite hers.

"Want to talk about what happened?"

She had dark circles under her eyes and she looked pale. One corner of her mouth curved up into a smile when her eyes met mine. "I suppose I owe you a thank you. So thank you, Declan."

"Don't say thank you, just don't do that again."

"I already wrote *I will not get totally wasted and hook up with potential rapists* one hundred times on the blackboard, sir. I'm good." After a minute, she asked, "Were you ok after the fight?" She reached over tentatively and touched the faded bruise on my jaw.

"I'm fine."

I couldn't help but put my hand over hers where it rested on my cheek. I'd been missing her so badly and craved any sort of touch or contact.

"Danielle told me that guy Chris has a terrible reputation." She slid her hand back and clasped both hands in her lap, looking down. "I'm grateful that you didn't let him take me home."

"I've heard some crazy shit about him. I'd never let him get his hands on you, Anna."

She let out a breath and her shoulders slumped.

After a minute of silence, which for some odd reason never felt uncomfortable when I was with her, I asked, "Do you talk to your parents much anymore?"

Her head jerked up. "Where did that come from?"

"I was just wondering. With my dad...It was weird this Thanksgiving."

"Well, yeah. I've always been on speaking terms with them, but I haven't *enjoyed* speaking with them until recently. Maybe things are better because I don't live with them anymore. Neither one is ever going to win parent of the year, but there has been some improvement."

"That's good."

"It is. Sometimes my instinct is to push them away, reject them when they try to make an effort. Especially my mother. But I figure that if I smack her hand away every time she reaches out, then I'm no better than she is."

We sat in silence again for a few moments before she asked, "So what happened with your dad?"

"My father had his girlfriend at the house when I came home for Thanksgiving." When I looked up Anna was smiling. "I was annoyed that I liked her so much. It made it hard to hate on my dad. And he was sober. I haven't seen him completely sober since before my mom died."

"Wow." She reached for my hand and held it, rubbing her thumb along the back of it. "Same with my mother. It's easy for me to be mad at her when she's popping those stupid pills, but she was sober over break, too. I didn't ask, because we've never once talked about her addiction issues." She let out a cheerless laugh. "How dysfunctional is that? But anyway, when I see her making an effort, it's easier to have some forgiveness in my heart for her." She eased back in her chair, and I was grateful because she looked liked she was comfortable, like maybe she wanted me to stay. "So tell me about your dad's new babe. What's she like?"

"His lady love?" I laughed, waggling my eyebrows. "I shouldn't make fun. Her name is Diana, and I don't know…She's nice and she's easy to talk to. They even came down to my game this past Saturday. We met up and talked for a few minutes afterwards, but then they wanted to take me to dinner…" I trailed off, shaking my head. "I made up an excuse. That would have been way too much bonding time, and I'm just not there yet."

"One step at a time, right? Maybe it's the same for us as it is for them. They have their twelve steps to sobriety or whatever, and we have our steps to take. It takes time to forgive. I've been working on forgiving at least a dozen people since Will died."

"Who do I have to forgive besides my father?"

"I don't know…Forgive yourself? You couldn't save her. Seems like you feel responsible for her and for everyone else in your life." She leaned over and squeezed my knee gently. "And maybe you need to forgive her."

"My mother?"

"Maybe. Forgive her for leaving you, even if that's not what she meant to do." That was a lot to take in, but Anna was oblivious to my inner freak-out. "I never understood why you were so certain it was a suicide. Isn't it possible that it was an accident?"

"Taking pills and downing vodka can't be an accident."

"Yeah, but if I remember what you told me correctly, she didn't drink the *entire* bottle or take *all* the pills. And she didn't leave a note. Everyone leaves a note."

"Is that a fact, Clarke? I think you've been watching too much Law and Order."

There was no one like her. I couldn't have this kind of conversation with anyone on earth except Anna, where the saddest topics were punctuated with laughter. When she stopped laughing, I asked, "Did your brother's friend leave a note?"

"Yes. Matter of fact, it was addressed to me. The detective made me read it the next morning to help them piece everything together."

I could see the memory had upset her. I was damn near shaking when I reached over slowly and guided her into my lap. "Please let me," I whispered in her ear when I felt her resist. She settled into me then, her head on my chest, her arms wrapped around my neck, my arms wrapped around her. "I know I should keep my mouth shut, but I'm so fucking lonely without you."

She nodded, and then neither of us moved for a long while. I was taking pleasure in the feel of her body against mine, hoping that she felt it too, that she needed me in her life as much as I needed her. I could have stayed in that same position, holding her for days. But then Anna shifted. She kissed my cheek and whispered, "I should go, Declan."

I sat there for a while, thinking about Anna and mulling over everything she'd said. It was my least favorite time of year, just two days until the twenty-second. Was it possible that my mother didn't mean to do it? That it was an accident? I'd never been angry with her, never blamed her. I only blamed myself and my father. But sitting there alone, I found myself talking to her in a way that was different from all the other times before. I asked her how she could do it, how she could leave me knowing I'd have no one. And I asked her the one question that would torment me for the rest of my life: Why?

I taped myself up before practice and told Coach I was getting over a stomach virus to get out of doing the full physical workout. I suspected that I'd either fractured or badly bruised a rib...or two or three. I was still sore as hell from tangling with Gallagher. I figured as long as I avoided being checked for the next week or so, I'd be fine.

I thought I'd have hell to pay from my teammates when they found out about the fight, but the only dirty looks I got were from him. I wasn't looking for us to be friends so I really didn't give a shit about that.

As I repeatedly hit shots past the back-up goalie manning the net, I thought about my mother. I always thought about her on this day, this crappy day people call an anniversary. It should have a different name.

In years past I'd remember certain things, the best days, and I'd just miss her in general. But today was different. I had nagging thoughts, questions I wanted answered. Was there a note, and if not, what did the absence of a note mean? Did my mother leave one that we just never found? Doubtful, as I'd torn their room apart on more than one occasion looking for clues. Did my father find a note that he kept from me? I was lying on my bed after dinner on Thursday night thinking about it some more.

Most of my friends were getting ready to go out—one last hurrah now that their finals were over. Some of us had our last final tomorrow. That was me, but it was just a matter of handing in a paper. Even though my work was done and sitting neatly on my desk, there was no way I was going out. I had a short practice scheduled for tomorrow, the last one before breaking until the day after New Year's. And while that would usually be enough to keep me in, I had different reasons. This day wrecked me every year, so the idea of having a few drinks, laughing and shooting the shit just didn't appeal to me.

It was weird to be away from home on this day, without the physical reminders of her—the scents, sights and rooms that brought me back to that moment. I thought maybe it wouldn't hit me as hard this year for that reason, but it did.

Three soft knocks on my door brought me back to the present.

She looked shy and uncertain standing in the hallway. "Hi."

"Come on in."

"I was debating back and forth all day whether or not I should come and see you." When I cocked a questioning look her way, she said, "I imagine today is hard for you. I don't know if talking about it hurts or if it's good for you."

Anna remembered. I pinched the bridge of my nose, tried to tamp down the emotions. I never brought it up in conversation, hadn't mentioned the date since we were at Heart Songs, but she remembered. I was surprised in that moment to realize that I knew Will's date too: March twentieth. The ties that bound us together were odd and unusual and a comfort.

"I'm glad you came."

"What have you been doing all day?"

"I finished my paper early, and since then I've been laying low. Just been thinking for the past few hours."

She smiled as she flopped onto my bed, arms crossed behind her head. "I'll just think with you."

I nudged her over with my hip to make some room for myself and crossed my arms behind my head just like her. It felt so unbelievably good.

"So, do you have any rituals or anything?"

I let out a breath and acknowledged how right this felt. It was another thing, a question that no one but Anna would ask.

"I went to the early Mass, lit a candle for my mom, then pancakes."

"Pancakes?"

"Yeah, she used to make them every Saturday and Sunday morning when I got back from practice. She'd drink her coffee and we'd talk while I ate. It was our thing."

Her eyes crinkled at the corners when she smiled. "That's a nice memory." A minute later she asked, "Where did you go? I hope you didn't go to the cafeteria. Their pancakes are awful."

"No, I went to that diner across from the chapel. The pancakes aren't as good as hers, but whatever, they were decent. When I'm at home I go to the same little place. It's like a shack down by the beach that's open year-round. They have great waffles, but I don't really like the pancakes there either. My mother had this old cast iron pan that just made them taste, I don't know, different."

"That's how it should be. They shouldn't taste better anywhere else, right?"

"I never thought about it before, but yeah, I think delicious pancakes would be disappointing." I tapped a finger to her nose. "What do you do on March twentieth?"

I wanted her to know that I remembered too, and she looked surprised but happy. "I like going to the cemetery." Her smile dropped. "Do you think that's creepy?"

"No. I don't really do it, but it's like a mausoleum place...There's no headstone or anything. It feels impersonal and cold where she is, so I don't go there."

"I like going to Will's grave. I like brushing the leaves away, tidying up, putting fresh flowers in front. And it makes me happy to see that other people have been there, too. Will had so many friends. There might be a little stuffed animal, some flowers that have dried out, or a rock set along the top of the headstone. Sometimes people leave more personal things, like a varsity letter. Oh, and one time I found a note that just said: *I'll always love you, Will*. I wonder who left that." After a moment she added, "It's good to know that people still think about him."

"What else do you do?"

"Margot and Vince come with me, and Dylan if he's home, and afterwards we eat lunch at this place Malcolm's. It was Will's favorite. They have the best onion rings on the planet. So we have cheese-burgers and onion rings in his honor."

"I like that."

We laid there side by side, each lost in our own thoughts. I can't describe how good it felt. How right and natural it felt to be beside her.

"I've been thinking about what you said...About a note." She leaned up on her elbow to look at me, waiting. "What if it *was* an accident? Why would my mother do that? Was she trying to punish my dad?"

"What do you mean?"

"Punish him for ignoring her? For not being a good husband? If that's the case then it's a little hard to accept, you know? I always thought she was innocent in this."

She didn't say anything, just laid back down again. And even that was perfect. I didn't need advice, didn't need an answer. Sometimes I just needed a sounding board and she knew that.

"Remember I was telling you about Drew's note? How the police made me read it?"

"Yeah?"

"When I was home over Thanksgiving break, Drew's ex-girlfriend asked me to get together with her. This girl, Carolyn, she wanted to apologize to me." Shaking her head, she said, "That's crazy. What did she do wrong? She was seventeen and she broke up with her boyfriend...Big deal. He was crushed when they broke up, but what Drew did is on Drew, no one else. And I don't think Drew did it with the intention of punishing Carolyn, but he *did* punish her. She's been through hell the past three years."

She took in a shaky breath and spoke slowly. "I blamed everyone at first, but now I know that it doesn't do any good to point my finger at anyone, not even Drew. God, I loved Drew. He was like a brother to me. Not like Will, of course, but he was a close second. So I can't blame Drew or hate him because I loved him. I guess what I'm trying to say is that when it's all said and done, it's everyone's fault and no one's fault, and it doesn't matter either way."

Everything she said was sinking in but making my head spin at the same time. Was I going to be like this girl Carolyn if I broke up with Tess? The one left suffering, wracked with guilt? And my mother. Jesus, did she just do that just to get back at my dad? I was lost in thought when Anna poked my side and said, "Are you all right?"

"Shit!" I pressed on the spot, wincing. She'd nudged me right in the ribs.

She jerked her hand back, but a moment later she reached over and gently lifted the hem of my t-shirt up, gasping when she saw the tape. "You're hurt." She rolled onto her back again and covered her eyes with her forearm. "I'm so sorry, Declan."

"Hey," I said, grimacing as I attempted to roll over onto my side towards her. "Hey," I repeated, lifting her forearm up to see tears welling in her eyes. "It's nothing but a bruise, Anna. I would have broken every single one of ribs to keep you away from him, ok?"

She reached up cautiously, her hands cradling my face. "I don't know what I'm doing anymore. I know that I love you, and not being with you hurts so much. But I feel like a fool."

"Don't say that. I want *you*, and I promise I'm going to make this right. You mean everything to me."

Her hands dropped back to her sides. She slowly pushed up and eased herself around me before standing up. "Declan, it's ok. I won't hate you or anything. I never will. But please, don't say things you don't mean and don't make promises you won't keep."

I grabbed her hips and pulled her back to me, dragging her into my lap and bracing my arms around her so that she couldn't move. "Don't tell me what I feel, all right? Don't act like you know how it is for me. I haven't been in love with Tess for a long time. I *am* in love with you. I think about you all the fucking time. About how good talking to you makes me feel, about how happy I am when I'm with you, about how much I want to touch you, be with you."

"I want to be with you too," she whispered as she rested her head back against my chest.

"In every way, Anna. I want to show you how much I love you in every way."

She arched back when I kissed her neck, giving me access, and then took each of my hands in one of hers, moving them under her shirt and guiding me to her breasts. She let out a soft, sweet whimper when I touched her, and I knew she could feel my body, feel how much I wanted her.

What we did, it wasn't wrong. That girl was already in my blood, coursing through my veins. I'd never felt closer to anyone before in my life.

Nothing could convince me that being with Anna was wrong.

Chapter Sixteen

ANNA

People are different at night.

They let their guard down, say things they wouldn't normally say out loud. They like dark corners, to be out of sight when they do dirty deeds.

Everything is different in the harsh light of day.

So all the things he said last night, the *No one else but you*, the *It's never felt so good*, the *I love you* whispered over and over—what did it all mean?

I'm not putting it all on him. I was a willing participant. I felt powerful knowing I could make his body react to me in that way. I liked the feeling, the heaviness in my breasts and the wet, achy want in my core. I wanted him to touch me and I wanted him deep inside of me.

Curled up together afterward, he said there was no one else but me. When he cleaned us up and noticed the faint streaks of blood, he pulled me close to him and told me that I was his. Before we drifted off to sleep, he told me he'd love me forever.

"I'll love you forever, Anna."

I woke to pounding on the door and Declan's body turning stiff and rigid as a board next to mine.

"Oh shit," he whispered.

"Declan, open the door!"

The voice didn't sound familiar, but from his reaction I knew it had to be Tess screeching on the other side of that door.

I could hear Brandon with her now. "Tess, what's the matter?"

"Where *is* he?"

"Calm down, he's probably sleeping with his earbuds in. Tell me what's going on."

I kept my eyes closed. "Anna," he whispered, barely audible. Nudging me, he pleaded, "Wake up, Anna."

"Declan!" I pictured a swirling flock of angry crows outside that door, caw, caw, cawing. She kicked at the door twice, punctuating each word when she cried, "Wake up!"

I opened my eyes to look at Declan, who looked like he was staring down the barrel of a shotgun. More afraid of the banshee on the other side of the door than of me, I gathered.

"Hey, I'm so sorry but can you go?" he whispered and then looked in the direction of his window.

I bolted upright in bed. "Oh my God, I'm so stupid." I grabbed for my clothes, now scattered all over. "I'm so stupid," I repeated as I struggled to get my shirt on over my head.

"No!" he whispered.

Excuse me, make that lip-synched.

"I cannot believe you." Now *I* was whispering. I should have been screaming at the top of my lungs.

The knocking stopped, and Tess's shrill cries from before morphed into a mournful wail, each word choked and dripping wet. "You're in there...I can hear you."

"What are you doing, Tess?" Brandon was starting to sound a

little frantic himself. "Get off the floor. He's not in there. He's probably getting breakfast already. He's always up early."

I pushed past Declan and opened the window. I was climbing out a fucking window. Who was I?

He grabbed my wrist. "Anna."

I jerked my arm back. "*Don't* touch me. I'm such an ass. I can't believe *that* was my first time and I'm always going to remember it because the guy wanted me to slink away the next morning like some slut, like his dirty little secret."

He hopped out after me as Tess ramped it back up to a shriek from the other side of the door.

"No, you don't understand."

He wouldn't let go of me until I slapped his face with my other hand. I'd never slapped anyone before. There was a sharp, cracking sound, and I must have packed some power because it left a bright red mark on his cheek. It should have felt satisfying but it didn't.

I was thankful Fiona was out when I opened my door. The number of times she'd helped me nurse a broken heart over Declan was borderline embarrassing at that point.

I cried in the shower, wanted the hot water to wash away every memory of him. In his arms I felt safe and special, precious and loved. But nothing about it was special. I needed to wash myself clean, scrub his rotten, putrid scent off of me.

Wrapped in my towel, I ignored Jimmy knocking and calling out to me. When he didn't let up after a few minutes, I answered him but didn't open the door. I was so beaten down that speech was an effort.

"Please go away, Jimmy."

He slid a folded up piece of paper under the door and said, "It's from him, Anna."

Anna I'm so sorry.
I love you.
Please forgive me-D

The hastily scribbled note had the same rushed but neat penmanship that Drew's had. The words were identical. The bloody fingerprints were the only thing missing.

I don't remember calling Margot, but remember her soothing words and something about Vince being in Boston. I vaguely recall Uncle Vince gathering me up in his arms and hurrying me downstairs with Fiona shooing away anyone who came near or asked a question.

It felt like falling off a cliff into a pitch-dark, bottomless void.

The next morning I woke up in my bedroom back home wondering how I'd gotten there.

* * *

DECLAN

Not even halfway through my freshman year of college, but look at me. Grades were better than decent, snagged a promising spot on my division one hockey team, and I'd learned to lie like a CIA operative.

After a few deep cleansing breaths, I let myself in through Terrence's window to borrow some sneakers, sweats and a baseball cap, and then made my way back into the dorm through the front door.

Hey, what are you doing here? Yeah, I just got back from breakfast. Right. *Get your story straight, Banks.*

Brandon and Jimmy's door was open, so I knew Tess was probably in there. And yep, she jumped up and charged towards me when I went to open my door. "Declan!"

I did the whole shocked and surprised act. Don't know if I pulled it off, just know that I felt like a dishonest prick.

It was obvious she'd been crying. Brandon was standing behind her, eyebrows raised as if to say, "You're fucked." Jimmy was standing behind her too. His look said, "You're an asshole."

"I was just grabbing breakfast. What are you doing here so early? Why didn't you call?"

She threw her arms around my neck and started bawling, barely able to get the words out when she said, "I had to tell you in person. It's terrible."

My throat went dry and the only sound I could hear was a whoosh, whoosh sort of pounding in my ears. *Please God*, I prayed, *don't let her be pregnant*. Ignoring Brandon and Jimmy, I walked her back across the hall and closed my door behind us. She fell into me, clutching at my shirt. "Tess, calm down." I rubbed one hand up and down her back, growing more tense with every moment that passed without an explanation. "What's the matter?"

"It's my father. He-he-he got lay-lay-laid off." She raised her voice. "Forget Christmas presents, forget spring break, forget even getting a *used* car so that I can get around that crappy, spread out for miles campus."

"He lost his job?" She wiped her wet nose on my shirt and nodded. "Shit, that sucks. Your poor dad."

"I'm so *sick* of it! Living in that tiny house, always having to cut back and settle for less."

I backed up a step, and the hands that were just holding Tess dropped down to my sides. I didn't want to argue with her right now, but the girl had no perspective.

"Your father does good by you. He works his ass off, provides you with nice clothes, a roof over your head, a college education…You *know* it was a struggle to let you room and board on campus when you could have easily commuted, but he made that happen. Cut him some slack."

"Easy for—"

"Me to say? I'm gonna stop you right there. I haven't had a happy Christmas memory in four years, Tess. No tree, no decorations, no fucking holiday cheer. And no presents for Christmas *or* my birthday. And by the way, thanks for checking in on me yesterday to see how I was doing on my mom's anniversary."

The nerve of me to be mad at her after what I'd been up to, but I *was* mad. "Stop acting like it's the end of the world. Your father will get another job. You won't starve. And here's a novel idea...You can get a part-time job and take care of yourself, Tess."

She looked as if I'd slapped her. The bit about my mother wasn't really fair, but I was sick of the constant *woe is me* act. And I was angry at her for making me fuck things up with Anna again. Yeah, that was ridiculous on my part and totally unfair. Tess wasn't guilty of messing up anything—all of it was one hundred percent on me.

"You're right," she whispered. "I'm sorry, Declan." She pulled a tissue from her purse and wiped at her eyes and nose. "I'll wait until you're done with practice. I took my mom's car so I'll drive you back home."

I rested my forehead against hers, tired and sad. "Maybe it doesn't seem like it right now, but you're stronger than you think. Everything is going to be all right, Tess."

It was like I was juggling two sets of emotions, two women and two lives. I wanted to shore Tess up, prepare her for what I was about to tell her, and at the same time I was itching to peel her off of me and run to Anna. I wanted to beg Anna to hang in there just a little bit longer, to trust me, to wait for me. I felt trapped.

Her stomach let out a loud rumble. "Did you eat?" I asked.

"No, I left at six-thirty this morning. I'm starving, actually."

"Let's go eat. I'll take you to the diner."

"I thought you already ate."

More lies, coming right up. It was scary how easily they rolled off my tongue.

"I did, but the cafeteria food isn't great. I could go for a cheddar bacon omelette. More energy for practice."

"Ok."

"I'll be right back. Just want to tell Brandon we're going out and that I'll be back in time for practice."

Tess was walking around the room, straightening up in a way that looked like she was snooping. If she found a pair of women's underwear then so be it. I was fucked, one way or the other.

"Gimme a notebook," I said to Jimmy as I raced into their room.

Brandon came up close behind me as I was scribbling out a note. "She heard you two, Declan."

"I don't think so."

He pushed my shoulder, knocking the pen from my hand. "I heard Anna's voice clear as day, so Tess did too. If she's acting like she didn't hear you with a girl and she's pretending that shit didn't happen, then that's fucked up on an entirely different level."

I ripped the page out of the notebook and folded it up. "Can you give this to her?"

Brandon backed away from me, palms up. "No fucking way. I'm not getting in the middle of this mess anymore."

"Seriously? You won't do this for me?"

"No," he said, arms folded across his chest.

"Jimmy?"

"I'll do it." He didn't look thrilled about it, though.

A few minutes later, Tess and I were making our way towards her car in the lot between my dorm and Anna's. *Why couldn't she have parked on the back road.* Tess was practically jogging trying to keep pace alongside me, and when she went to take my hand I moved it before she could grab hold. I just wanted to get the hell out of there.

There was a massive SUV with tinted-out windows in the lot. Some beefy looking bodyguard-type dressed in an expensive suit was standing outside the vehicle. The way he stood with one hand resting on his hip implied the presence of a gun clipped to his waistband.

Tess smirked. "Which rich brat does he belong to?"

"I don't know. Yeah, the whole bodyguard thing is a little excessive."

With that, I saw a tall, well-dressed man heading for the car taking long strides, his arms huddled around someone he looked to be holding up. Fiona was walking alongside them, trying to keep pace.

Fuck.

"Where are you going?" I heard Tess call after me.

"What's going on?" I said as I rushed over. "Anna?"

"*You*," Fiona stabbed a finger in my chest, "stay away from her."

I went to move past Fiona but the bodyguard stiff-armed me, knocking the wind right out of me. The other man put her in the car, closed the door and then rounded on me.

Looking at Fiona and then back to me, he asked, "Is he the one who wrote the note? Is that your idea of a sick joke?"

"What are you talking about?" I asked, catching my breath. By then, a small crowd had gathered. "Sir, I don't understand."

He was shaking with rage. "Don't you *ever* step foot within a mile of my niece again or you'll live to regret it. Do you understand?"

He got into the car without waiting for a response. The bodyguard closed the door behind him, gave me a quick but menacing stare down, then got in the car and drove off.

I stood in that same spot, too stunned to move. Fiona walked back down the hill with Victoria, Jimmy and Brandon, leaving me without a word. Tess was sitting on the ground about five feet away from me with her mouth hanging open and tears spilling down her face. One guy I didn't know was saying something stupid about how cool it was that I'd been bitched out by *the* Vince Cole, likening it to getting a verbal ass-kicking from Bill Gates. A girl next to him joked that I probably just blew my chance of getting hired by Cole Industries after graduation.

I walked over to Tess and reached a hand down to help her up. "I'm so sorry."

"Tell me exactly what it is that you're sorry for, Declan."

I could see Charlotte, Paige and a few other girls standing at the base of the hill, watching me and Tess, loving the drama. I probably should have waited until we were alone to hash this out, but the gig was up.

"I cheated on you."

"With that girl. With Anna."

Brandon was right, Tess already knew.

"Let's go home. We need to talk."

I texted my coach, telling him I had a family emergency and would be missing practice. He texted back: Unacceptable. I wrote again, telling him I would be back on campus by three o'clock today. It was ten now. Two and a half hours up to Cape Elizabeth, two and a half hours back, half an hour to talk.

As I turned the key in the ignition, another text came in, from Jimmy this time.

Something about a suicide note and her brother????

What the hell did that mean? And that man I now knew to be her uncle said something about *my* note? I shot Anna a quick text. I had to, even though Tess was no more than two feet away from me.

Are u ok? Worried about u.

Tess and I drove in silence for the first two hours. She was looking out the window most of the time but would periodically glance over in my direction. She was waiting on me to say something. And while I had a hundred different thoughts racing through my head, I didn't know where to begin.

"I cheated on you too, Declan."

I shook my head, never taking my eyes off the road. "Seriously, Tess?"

"Someone from school. It was over as soon as it started. It was a mistake."

I wasn't angry at her for the cheating, but I *was* angry. Her unwillingness to let go, the way she shut me down every time I tried to talk to her about our relationship, keeping me on a leash and threatening me, hinting at what might happen if I left her—I had a lot of reasons to be angry.

I was stewing silently as Tess fidgeted, growing more uncomfortable the closer we got to home. We were just about a mile from her house when she said, "My point, Declan, is that I forgive you. Please forgive me. Let's move on." She took a deep breath. "Anna never happened as far as I'm concerned."

"No." I wasn't participating in this bullshit anymore. "She happened, just like you felt something for the guy you were with."

"I don't feel *anything* for anyone but *you*!" Her voice was shaking. "Don't do this, Declan. I can't, I can't...I don't know what I'll do if—"

I slammed on the breaks. "Stop!" I screamed. "Stop it! *Don't* threaten me. Don't make me feel like I'll be responsible if you hurt yourself. Fuck, Tess! How can you say shit like this to me after what my mother did? How can you fucking do it?"

Her lips were trembling and her face had gone pale. I looked at her, waiting for her to say something, anything, but she just turned away and stared straight ahead. I felt used up and dog-tired, my body slumped over, head resting against the steering wheel. After a minute, I let out a breath and pulled off the shoulder back onto the road, driving slowly. When we got to her house, I went to grab her bag from the back but she got to it first. I got out after her, following her up the front steps.

Tess spun on me. "Where are you going? Just leave!"

Her father came out onto the porch looking between the two of us. "Tess and I broke up. I'm worried about her, sir."

"Shut up, Declan!" When I took a step closer, she looked up at the sky and yelled, "You've *got* to be kidding me!"

I ignored her. "She's said some things in the past that make me worry about her. I just wanted you to know."

"What things?" He looked to Tess.

She lifted her chin and sneered, "The big hockey star, thinks he's all that. Please, I'm not going to *hurt* myself over you."

"I'm sorry, Tess."

"I *hate* you!" she called after me as I walked down the path leading back to the main road. "Merry fucking Christmas! I hate you, I hate you, I *hate* you!"

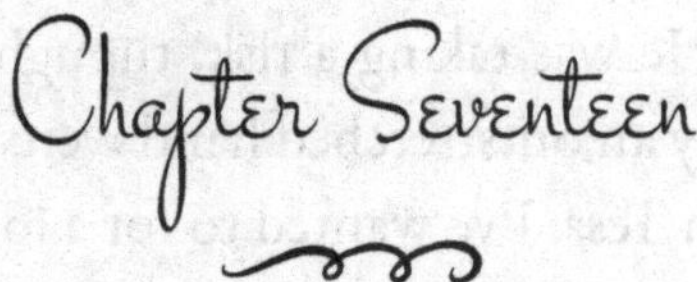

Chapter Seventeen

DECLAN

I fished my phone out of my pocket and dialed a number I rarely called. He pulled up alongside me five minutes later.

"Thanks, Dad. Listen, can I drop you off back at the house? It's a long story, but I have to head back down to Boston or else my coach is going to bench me. He's probably already benched me." I muttered that last line to myself.

"If you don't mind, I'll drive you down. I'm picking something up on Newbury Street that I ordered a few weeks ago. I'll drop you off at campus and then get you on my way back."

"All right." I was too keyed up to even protest the idea of being cooped up in a car with him for five hours.

After fifteen minutes of silence, he asked, "I'm assuming your answer to the question, 'Is everything ok?' would be a no."

"Good guess."

He looked out the window and took a deep breath. I sensed he was gathering his courage, gearing up to say something. I silently prayed that he'd just leave me be, but no such luck.

"I know I was never the one you came to for advice or for help. I know I wasn't the best father. But if you need to talk...If you want to, I'm here. That's all."

I looked over, took him in. My instinct was to give him the silent treatment—that was my go to. In its own way, it was more powerful than angry words. He was taking a risk, though, and Anna's words about smacking away an outstretched hand were ringing in my ear.

"I broke up with Tess. I've wanted to for a long time, I guess, but everything came to a head today."

He nodded. "She's angry about it."

"Outraged, pissed, furious...She makes me feel so goddamn guilty all the time."

"Guilty?"

"Yeah, like I'm abandoning her, you know? It feels like a choke hold. And now that I have broken up with her, I feel so bad about it, about hurting her."

"But you're not in love with her."

"No." I was laying it all out there today. "I'm, uh, in love with someone else."

He nodded. "She makes you happy, this other girl?"

"Yeah, really happy. But I think I've managed to screw everything up on that end, too."

"Love, especially at your age, has to make you happy. You have to choose happiness, Declan."

Whatever, old man.

I turned my head and stared out the window. About ten minutes later my dad said, "It's no secret your mother and I weren't happy." He looked to me. "And I take responsibility for that. I was angry for most of our marriage and I took it out on her. If I wasn't physically absent from our home, I kept myself at a distance emotionally. I punished her."

My blood was boiling. "You were an asshole. You were a terrible husband and shit for a father."

He kept his eyes on the road, and I watched as he swallowed and nodded his head. "I deserve that."

I noticed, not looking away as I usually did, that my father's face had changed. The gray hair that used to show just at his temples was now sprinkled throughout. There were creases and wrinkles that I'd never noticed before. There were good changes too, though. His eyes were clear, and his skin now had the color of someone who strolled the beach daily and rode his mountain bike on the weekends.

I guess he took the fact that I was still looking at him as a sign that I was still interested in what he had to say. I actually was.

"Declan, I was a young man once, too. And I...Well, life threw me a few curveballs that changed things, changed me. I don't necessarily expect you to understand or forgive me, but believe me when I say that the decisions you make at your age can affect you for years to come. So choose wisely. Choose happiness."

"Stop being so fucking cryptic. What happened between you and Mom? Why was she so unhappy...Unhappy enough to do *that*?"

He looked to me, swallowing his unease before fixing his eyes back on the road. "Your mother was best friends with my high school sweetheart, Maryann. Your mom was beautiful, funny and kind, but Maryann? Well, we were two pieces of a puzzle that just simply fit together. She was meant for me." One corner of his mouth turned up, and I had to fight the urge to slap that smile right off his face. "I could spend every minute of every day with her and never get bored. She made me laugh every single day, but I also knew I could tell her anything without fear of judgment, and it was the same for her."

He cleared his throat. "I made a terrible mistake one night. It was just after we'd graduated. There was drinking, a bunch of us were down at the beach for a bonfire. Maryann had been gone for two weeks, staying with her dying grandmother in northern Maine." He paused before he said, "I was with your mother."

I let that sink in for a bit and then gripped both sides of my head with my hands. "She got pregnant...with me."

My father said nothing for a long minute, and his silence was confirmation of what I now knew to be true.

"I was eighteen and felt like my world had been blown apart. The day I was supposed to be catching a train to Boston to start college wound up being my wedding day."

"Boo fucking hoo." Seething with rage, I took a deep breath and pushed it down because I wanted him to go on. I was so sick and tired of being in the dark. "What happened to the girl?"

"Maryann? She was crushed. You know, betrayed by her boyfriend and her best friend. Maryann left for school in Boston, just like we'd planned, but I stayed behind. We were planning to start our life together that fall, but everything fell apart. She met someone else eventually. Married him. She lives in Marlborough now. Her children are younger, of course."

"Do you keep in touch with her?"

"No, she never spoke to me again. Someone told her what happened the day she got back. I tried calling, I showed up at her house, I took a beating from her brothers that was well deserved. Back in the early days I though about her all the time. Constantly thought about what life would have been like. The great what if."

"Must have been shitty for Mom," I remarked bitterly.

"It was. I think she always had feelings for me, even before that night, but I had nothing but resentment for her. I felt I'd been trapped and," he held up his hand to stop me before I spoke, "yes, that's crap. For a man, the responsibility lies with him. That's the fact. I was the one who was wrong. I gave in to some fleeting temptation. I was angry at your mother when it was my fault, no one else's."

"Did Mom leave a note?"

He looked confused for a second until he realized what I was asking.

"There was no note. She'd asked me to come home, to go pick out the tree as a family." He looked over at me. "I'm sorry, Declan. I really am. I should have been so many more things to you and to her.

That day, I didn't come home. I was my usual, resentful, bitter self. She wanted me there, and for that reason alone I wouldn't come."

"Why didn't you just divorce her? She could have met someone who made her happy."

"I wanted to. I brought it up a hundred times. But I couldn't get the words out of my mouth before she'd threaten me."

"I'm sure she didn't use *me* as a threat. Didn't seem like you would have cared if she took me away and you never got to see me again."

His hands gripped the steering wheel. "That's not true, although I've given you every reason to think that it is. It's not true, Declan."

"It doesn't hurt anymore, Dad. I really don't give a shit so don't worry about it. I just want to know about Mom."

He sighed. "I care about you a great deal. And I'm sorry you had to grow up like that, with two parents who just coexisted. It was so hard when you were little. We fought constantly. She'd accuse me of calling Maryann, of seeing her secretly. There were days I was afraid to leave for work. She'd threaten to hurt herself, and you…You were just a baby." He was shaking his head. "Everything was my fault. And while I accept that, I resented the way she held everything over my head. I felt so goddamn trapped."

"You were afraid to leave for work? I hardly ever remember you being home."

"Time passed but things between your mother and I never improved. I started drinking a lot more, and then it just became easier to check out, to stay away."

When he went to say something else, I interrupted, "Dad, let's just drive for a while." I'd reached my limit.

When we pulled up outside of the arena, my father asked, "Are you all right? With hearing all that, I mean." I was exhausted, the cumulative effects of the day's events bearing down on me. When I nodded he said, "I'll be no more than an hour, Declan. I'll be here waiting for you."

. . .

I should have been nervous going in to talk to Coach, but my hockey career was the last thing on my mind at the moment. Still, respect for the coaching staff was something learned in pee-wee league, so I didn't take it lightly.

"Coach?"

"Banks. Have a seat."

I took it as a good sign that he didn't look angry. "Coach, I'm very sorry for missing practice today, I—"

"I have no time for bullshit, Banks. Did you have a legitimate emergency?"

"Yes, sir."

"Do you have anything else you want to tell me?"

I paused. "Last week I didn't have a stomach virus. I needed to take it easy at practice because I bruised my ribs in a fight."

He looked up and nodded. "Is this going to affect the team?"

"No, sir."

"Did you have your ribs looked at, or did you diagnose yourself?"

"Um, I just...They don't hurt so bad so I figured nothing was broken."

He steepled his fingers under his chin and studied me. "Banks, you're a good kid. I've known that since day one. But you've gotta keep your head on straight. You're the one...The one the scouts are already coming to see. They'll be blowing smoke up your ass about turning pro early, and if you start taking that shit to heart, start thinking you're above the routines and the rules of this team, then I'll show you the door. I'll cut you loose right now. I care more about respect, commitment and teamwork than I do about winning. Am I making myself clear?"

"Absolutely, Coach."

"Good. Now go see Mitch. Make sure those ribs are healing

properly. You're starting against UMass when we come back from break. I want you ready, son."

"How did it go?"

"Good."

I wanted to smile because I was so relieved, but now that I was back in the car with my father, all the shit from before was coming back at me and fucking with my head.

"When do you have to be back down for practice?"

"I get a week. I'm due back on New Year's Day. First practice on January second, game at UMass on the seventh, and, um, I'm starting."

"That's good." He smiled at me. "It's the opposite of being benched."

About half an hour into the ride back home he said, "Declan, the point of me telling you all that before was just so you'd understand how sorry I am. I've needed to apologize to you. I'm sorry it's taken this long, and I'm sorry I needed someone else to show me how to do the most basic things when it comes to being a parent...Things as simple as talking to my son and making an effort."

"Diana?"

"Yes."

Again, my urge was to shoot something back about not wasting his time, that he'd missed his chance, that I was too old, too far past the point of needing any parenting. But I made a conscious effort to talk, even though it hurt, physically hurt to show him kindness.

"She seems like she's good for you. You look better."

"She is good for me. Sounds crazy, but sometimes I don't even *want* anything this good. I feel like I don't deserve her or deserve to be happy. Needing people, it makes you feel weak sometimes."

I shrugged. "Not if you both need each other."

He nodded then and swallowed. I'm sure this level of heart-to-heart was a lot on him, too. We rode the rest of the way in silence. My thoughts were drifting from my mother, to memories of my parents together, to Tess, and then always circling back to Anna.

I'd called her three times since leaving campus this morning, and every time the call went straight to voicemail.

I'd start to say something, but then stop midway through my awkward, stuttering apology and opt to re-record over it. I didn't want to tell her over the phone anyway. I had to see her in person, get down on my knees and plead with her to believe me when I said that I loved her and there was no one else. *You're the only one.* She needed to know, she needed to believe it.

It would stand to reason that one of the wealthiest families in the country wouldn't have their address listed. I searched every avenue of the internet I could think of, but still came up empty. Out of options, I scrolled through my contacts and landed on the name of someone who most *definitely* did not want to speak to me.

"Hey, Fiona. Sorry for calling so late."

"Save the pleasantries, Declan. And it is late, you moron, so—"

"Please don't hang up," I pleaded. "This morning was a fucking disaster. I was going to break it off with Tess as soon as I got home, but then...Well, you already know what happened. Everything just blew up. But I did break up with her, Fiona. I broke up with Tess."

"Are you looking for a pat on the back or something? You only grew a set of balls *after* you were caught. All this time, deep down I really thought you were a stand-up guy, but you're not."

Her words hurt me deep, and for the most part, I agreed with her. "Just give me her address. I really need to see her."

She didn't speak for nearly a minute, but then gave in and rattled off the address. Before Fiona hung up on me, she said, "I wouldn't go there expecting a warm reception."

. . .

I was on a mission, walking out of the house by eight the next morning, but stopped in my tracks when I saw Tess standing in my driveway. She was leaning against her parents' car, dressed in only jeans and a t-shirt. December in Maine isn't t-shirt weather, even for me.

"Tess," I said, taking off my sweatshirt and handing it to her, "put this on." She took it and held it to her face, taking in the scent before she pulled it over her head.

"Declan," she croaked and then shook her head, looking down at the ground where she was absently kicking pebbles.

I moved closer and put my hand on her shoulder. I felt terrible but resolute at the same time, strong in the belief that I was making the right decision. No matter what happened with Anna, I didn't want what I had with Tess anymore.

"It's going to be all right. You may not believe me, but this has nothing to do with her or anyone else."

"She's beautiful *and* she's rich, Declan. I get it."

"Should I be insulted? What exactly do you *get*, Tess?"

"I can't compete."

"Like I said, this doesn't come down to Anna. I need to do this. It might make me sound like a selfish prick, but I don't want to feel responsible right now, responsible for anyone."

"So that's it? Everything we were and now we're just done? I'm nothing to you?"

"You'll never be nothing. I'll always care about you."

"You're killing me, Declan."

"I'm not." She started to cry again. "You're making this so damn hard."

I hated this. Hated to see her sad. Hated knowing that I was the one who did this to her. That resolve I had a few minutes ago was crumbling until she said, "You think you're so special, right? Don't you wonder why she isn't scheming her way into any of your friends' beds? Why she's so hell bent on taking you away from me? That rich, privileged bitch....Anna *Cole*," she sneered when she said the wrong last name, "wouldn't care a thing about you if you weren't on your way to the pros, Declan."

"I'm done," I said as I walked around her and got into my car, slamming the door behind me. She was walking towards me when I peeled the car into reverse and turned out of the driveway.

I knew exactly who wouldn't be happy unless I was raking in the money and basking in the glory of a pro hockey contract. Tess never realized how transparent she could be.

It still took me a little over four hours to get to Connecticut, even speeding at the rate that I was.

When my father asked, I told him I wasn't sure about tomorrow. He was invited to Diana's for dinner and would be meeting her two sons for the first time. I think he was hoping I'd be there as a buffer. With any luck I figured I'd be spending Christmas with Anna. Without said luck, I'd be poor company for anyone else.

I turned when I saw her house number on the stone pillars, not realizing I still had nearly a half-mile drive ahead of me. When I got out of my car, the massive double doors opened and a guy a few years older than me stepped outside. It was her cousin, Dylan, and he didn't look friendly.

"You must be Declan." When I nodded, he looked me up and down before dismissing me. "She doesn't want to see you."

"I don't want to upset her, but could you just tell her that I'm here?"

"Nah, don't think so."

"You don't understand what happened. I never would have written that note if I knew—"

His laugh had a nasty edge. "I don't think anyone's *that* sadistic. I think that was just one very messed up coincidence. The exact same words, signed with a D. If a forensic handwriting specialist saw it, they'd swear Drew wrote it himself. Only things missing were the blood and bits of grey matter." He swallowed and looked away for a moment. "Like I said, she doesn't want to see you."

"Please, I just need to talk to her."

Dylan's attention shifted to a truck pulling up the circular driveway. A big guy, slightly taller than me and built like a lumberjack got out. Dylan's expression did a complete one-eighty.

"Jeremy, it's been a long time." They shook hands while I stood there like the odd man out. "How are you?"

"Never better."

"That's what I hear. See if you have some time to give our guy an estimate on what we discussed over the summer."

"I'm on it. Is she home?"

"Yeah, Anna's upstairs. She's been waiting for you."

The guy gave me a smile and a head nod as he passed by, taking the steps two at a time and fist bumping Dylan on his way on the door. Who the fuck was he? *Jeremy, Jeremy*. Right, the guy who let her hide out when she was jail bait.

Dylan watched as Jeremy walked inside, then fixed me with a look that was at once bored and irritated.

I stood my ground. "I'm not leaving until I see her."

He crossed his arms over his chest. "Whatever you've got to say, she's not ready to hear it. Anna needs to be with us, with family around her. So just do yourself a favor and go home...I won't ask you twice."

I dug the small box out of my pocket and handed it to Dylan. "Will you at least give this to her?"

He took it, and then he closed the door in my face.

ANNA

"Jeremy!"

"Anna," he said, looking at me with the warmth and kindness of a true friend. He looked down then and his eyes popped open. "Where are your clothes?"

"Oh my God, you prude, I was just at a yoga class."

Big giant lie. I was wearing tiny black spandex shorts—like barely covering my ass cheeks tiny—and a tight, white tank that did little to mask the shape of my breasts.

I was lost.

I was gone, and the girl who had taken my place wanted this. I felt angry, sexy, powerful and weak. If it came without romantic love, without affection, then so be it. I needed it—lips on mine, stubble raking over my skin, the tug on my hair, the weight of a body pressing down on my own.

Jeremy shrugged his shoulders and collapsed onto one of the oversized bean bag chairs. "So, how's college life?"

"Eh, it has its ups and downs like everything else. I missed seeing you over Thanksgiving break."

"I love being my own boss and everything, running the show, you know? The only downside is that when something goes wrong, it's on me. I was stuck in Stamford, up to my ass in cable and wires that entire weekend."

We spent the next twenty minutes just catching up, me sitting across from him on the floor with my back against the foot of my bed. He said at one point, "There was some guy here when I pulled up. Dylan looked like he wasn't too happy with him. Younger, like around your age."

I nodded and looked away as I willed the tears to stay inside. "Maybe it was someone from school that I really don't want to see."

"Got it, but are you all right?" he asked, reaching over to touch his rough, callused hand to my cheek. "You can talk to me, Anna."

I closed my hand over his and then slowly moved to him and crawled onto his lap so that I was sitting astride him. He leaned back a bit, surprised, and held my hips with both hands to prevent me from getting any closer.

"No," I whimpered. "Don't push me away, please."

He moved one hand back up to my cheek. "What is it? What's the matter?"

Avoiding his eyes, I inched up closer, settled myself lower. I could feel him growing huge and hard, the thin fabric of my barely-there shorts providing no barrier whatsoever. My head fell back on an exhale. God, I wanted this.

"Anna, what the hell are you doing?" he said as he grabbed my chin and forced me to look at him.

"I've missed you, Jeremy. I want you," I pretty much begged.

His hands moved up slowly from my waist to the sides of my breasts, but then he stopped abruptly. He whispered my name, shaking his head as he motioned for me to move back. But I wasn't having it. I ran my fingers through his hair and grabbed hold as I moved in to kiss him deep. Jeremy took my shoulders and forced me back, his stare cold and accusing.

"Is this what you want?" He gripped both of my hips, pulling me down as he rocked up, pushing hard against me three or four times. "You want me to stick my dick in you, Anna? You want me to use you, hurt you? And you want to use *me* like I'm nothing, like I have no soul?"

I scampered back, crashing into the bed frame opposite him. I covered my face with shaking hands, but could sense Jeremy standing up and moving towards the door. I looked up to see him turned away from me, his hand on the doorknob. His voice cracked when he said, "Do you know how many rich, older women have propositioned me like I'm some dude for hire in a toolbelt? How many girls came at me in high school? Girls who wanted to date the bad boy...Maybe looking to get back at their daddies, or maybe just to say to their friends that they took a walk on the wild side? I'd fuck 'em and I'd tell myself I was having the last laugh, but I knew I was being used. They didn't give a shit about me. They would never lower themselves to be with someone like me."

"Don't say that."

"I know that's not how it is with you." He came back and sank down next to me on the floor. "But you don't want *me*, Anna. You're hurt and you're asking for more pain. Don't do it."

"Too late for that."

He pulled me in and kissed the top of my head. "Can you please put some clothes on so we can talk? I'm strong, but you have a woman's body now, understand?"

When I was securely covered in sweats and a hoodie, I sat on my bed next to him. "I slept with that boy you saw downstairs." When he didn't say anything, I said, "He was my first."

"Wow. All that time with Boy Wonder and you two never did it?"

"No," I said, smiling. "I'm a freak."

"I take back the Boy Wonder crap. I have nothing against

Jonathan. He was always good to you. I always got the feeling he wasn't too fond of me, though."

"He thought I had a thing for you. And given that he was probably frustrated with some aspects of our relationship..." I shrugged.

"Got it. So you met a guy at school, became a woman." He held his hands up defensively, laughing when I went to swat him. "So what went wrong?"

"He had a girlfriend at home. I heard he broke up with her yesterday, but I know it's only because he got caught. She showed up on campus and I was in his room."

"Ooh. Was there a brawl? Did she come at you?"

"No. A friend told me that she definitely heard our voices, so she knew, but I was gone by then because he, he...He asked me to sneak out his window. It's on the ground floor. I felt like...That was the morning after we'd been...And he...I felt so dirty."

I couldn't talk, get a full breath in, or stop the tears.

"What a piece of shit."

"It gets worse," I sobbed.

He was rubbing my back. "Whenever you're ready, honey."

"He sent one of his friends over with a note for me. He didn't even break away from her for the one fucking minute it would have taken to see me in person. The note, Jeremy, was exactly what Drew wrote to me after he shot Will."

"Wait...What?"

"Word for word. Same paper ripped out of a spiral notebook. Similar handwriting. It freaked me out. I think I basically went catatonic. I don't remember much past that point except that Uncle Vince came and got me."

"That *had* to just be a weird, fucked up coincidence."

"I know it was. It's not the note, it's knowing that I can still spiral out of control like that. It's been nearly four years. You think I'd be better, be able to control myself. Not freak out and lose it in public, or attempt to sexually assault my good friends," I said, poking him in the ribs. "My life feels upside down again, Jeremy."

"Do you love him?"

"Yeah, I do."

He took a deep breath. "We all make mistakes, Anna. Every guy fucks it up sometimes. But make sure this guy deserves you. You have to be number one, no excuses."

We sat for a few more minutes before he told me he had to go. "When do you head back to school?"

"I've got a few weeks."

"All right, before break ends you're coming out with me and Carolyn."

"Oh yeah, sorry about that. You told me you had a new girlfriend and I still tried to maul you." I couldn't help but laugh when I added, "That was a new low for me."

"No worries."

"Her name is Carolyn?"

"You know her. It's Carolyn Harris."

I smiled. "Wow. When did you two start up?"

"I've known her since we were kids, but this is pretty recent. Carolyn told me she saw you over Thanksgiving."

"I'm so glad she reached out to me. And I'm really happy for you, Jeremy. She seems great."

"Yeah, she is." Jeremy paused before saying, "Carolyn makes me feel things. She's not like a...What did you used to call Jonathan? A comfy sweater?"

"Your point?"

"Comfy sweaters are nice, they're easy. But they don't make you feel anything. Feeling everything...It can hurt."

I was living proof of that. Declan made everything hurt.

When Jeremy turned to leave I called after him, "We're ok? What happened—"

He held up his hand to stop me. "It's cool, Anna. What happened here today is between us."

I did a lot of thinking over the break.

I didn't return any of Declan's calls but did text him back a few days after Christmas, basically just to ask him to stop contacting me for now. I was civil, told him we'd talk when we got back to campus in a few weeks. He wrote back once more asking if Dylan had given me the gift. I answered yes, but that I hadn't opened it yet.

I couldn't bring myself to unwrap the small box. It's like it was radioactive or something, like it had the potential to destroy me. I shoved it far back into my desk drawer, out of sight.

Christmas Day itself wasn't the happiest affair. I spent the morning with my mother, feeling guilty when I left to go back home, knowing that she wasn't seeing her boyfriend until the next day when they were flying off to Nevis for the week. Typical Mother, she had the nerve to look pouty and hurt when I left, even though she had basically left me alone for the majority of my childhood.

Back at the Coles, the air was slightly more festive and bright, but I was mopey. My father was running his mouth like a sloppy fool after guzzling four glasses of wine before dinner even hit the table. His new girlfriend looked appropriately appalled, so I figured I wouldn't be seeing her at our next family gathering. Even Kasia and Dylan seemed to be on edge around one another. Margot fluttered around, entertaining the guests, which included a few European business associates. With everyone mired in their own misery and Margot occupied in her attempts to make everything fabulous, no one noticed when I snuck upstairs right after dinner.

I spent the better part of that night thinking. Did I miss him? With every fiber of my being, yes. But Shane and Jeremy were right. I had to be the only one—no excuses. I couldn't shake the feeling that if Tess hadn't caught him in the act, he might have kept this shitty charade going at my expense.

When Victoria came by and told me Tess heard us arguing in the room, I was glad. Now, though, it made me question everything. Maybe that's the only reason they broke up. Maybe she broke up with him. Maybe he still really loved her.

I believed him when he said he loved me, I did, but I didn't have faith that he was devoted to the idea of the two of us together, no one else. I also couldn't shake the feeling of shame and fury that came over me every time I thought about him gesturing towards the window, asking me to leave. All the sweet bullshit he whispered in my ear that night would never change the fact that Declan had asked me to sneak out like his mistress the next morning, like the piece of ass he had to keep hidden from the wife.

I came to a conclusion: I needed to focus on myself and I had to be alone to do it. Being wrapped up in all this Declan drama over the past few months had made me lose sight of my goals.

That shit stops today.

Over the next three weeks, I ran every day to clear my head. I increased my distance and my speed, moving my runs from slow and contemplative to a more competitive pace. The physical workouts were good for me—I needed all the endorphins I could get.

I started researching summer internships, toying with the idea of staying in Boston or New York if I was lucky enough to find a firm willing to take on a first-year undergraduate with absolutely no experience.

After telling Dylan about my plans, he arranged for me to meet Kate Donovan, his friend Darcy's sister-in-law. Kate, an up and coming architect based in Manhattan, and her husband, a well-established general contractor, had built a small but successful firm together. They were in the middle of a massive project, remodeling a boutique hotel in Soho.

I expected to just meet her briefly that day, but Kate had something else in store. I was handed a hard hat at nine a.m. and didn't stop until we broke for lunch at two. In five hours I got more of an education than I had in an entire semester. It was the most exciting day I'd had in months and it renewed my passion for design.

Kate and I talked nonstop over lunch about everything from design elements to building department issues. She suggested that I apply for the summer program offered at The Cooper Union and laid out some ideas for the portfolio I would need to present.

As the waiter cleared our plates, Kate said offhandedly, "If you're willing to come to New York for the summer, I'd love to take you on. You could be part-time with me if Cooper Union works out, full-time if it doesn't."

"Are you serious?"

"Absolutely."

"Don't you want to, you know, see my work?"

She smiled. "I already have. With this job *and* a baby, I have no time to play tour guide on my job sites. I invited you here today because I've already seen your freehand work. I had Dylan bring some of your sketchbooks over. I want you with us this summer because you have talent. Also, I do think you'll learn a hell of a lot more with us than you would at some stuffy firm like Easterman or Stern. Being based on-site and seeing how the plans you develop come to life through the construction phase is *really* learning. It will be a true working experience for you. Think about it."

"I will...I mean I have. If you're serious then I want it."

"Great! So get to work on that portfolio. But don't be too disappointed if you don't get Cooper Union, Anna. I got accepted entering my senior year. There were some younger students there but it was mostly upperclassmen. It's definitely worth a shot, though." She looked at her watch. "Crap, it's three-thirty already. I've got to run. Darcy's been babysitting all day and she's probably exhausted."

Kate handed me a card with her cell phone number scribbled alongside the firm's number and email address, and then she was out the door. I sat there for another fifteen minutes, sipping my tea, basking in the feeling of being excited for the future and feeling proud. Kate saw my sketches and believed I had talent.

There was more to life than boy drama. I had talent and I was going places. *I don't need anyone but me.* The thought made me feel powerful and free, and maybe just the tiniest bit sad.

I spent every day between Christmas and New Year's researching the requirements for that summer program online, trying to get an idea of what to include in the portfolio I'd be submitting with my application. I decided on one urban design that would incorporate landscape, transportation and urban renewal elements into the plan, one floor plan for a home that focused on sustainability, and then one design that I hoped would make me stand out. I decided to use the plans I drew up for the interior cabin of a sailboat Uncle Vince had built for Dylan last year. The original design was pretty amateurish, but it was fundamentally good and I could easily tweak it to make it more professional. I had until February first to submit my application, so I had my work cut out for me if I was going to have most of it completed before returning to school.

With the exception of New Year's Eve, I spent every day during the rest of the break locked in my room working. I stood firm when Margot and Vince tried to strong arm me into coming down to Palm Beach for a week. I'd subjected myself to that scene once before and had since decided that hobnobbing with a bunch of entitled prep school brats was not for me.

Margot relented, only because she could see that I was hard at work and excited about this project, rather than sitting at home wallowing in despair. Instead, she arranged for a very swanky dinner to be served on New Year's Eve. I invited some old friends and all of my dorm mates who lived within a reasonable distance to come spend the night with me.

In addition to Fiona, Danielle, Lauren and her younger sister, two of my close friends from high school also came, and I was so glad they did.

I remembered thinking I might have made a mistake last summer, deciding to come to Boston alone. I'd come to rely on Jonathan and my girlfriends so much that I worried I wouldn't be able to cope without them. Had it been a rough couple of months? At times, yes, but there were also so many great moments. Looking around the room, I was thankful for all the new friends I now had, friends I might not have made if I didn't branch out on my own and take a risk.

I thought about inviting Victoria because she lived only a few towns over, but I didn't. I was just starting to feel better, and I knew I had to just give the whole Declan thing a rest. At this point, it was better if I didn't have any reminders of Declan or of that last day with him.

So it was a mellow but fun New Year's Eve. There was a good amount of champagne consumed, and we had a lot of laughs.

Dylan called me ten minutes before the ball dropped, and Vince and Margot checked in just after midnight. Jeremy and Carolyn stopped by early that morning to hang out for a while before leaving for his ski house. Jonathan also popped in, and I was happy to hear that everything was going well with him...and his new girlfriend. Even my mother called, with a steel drum band playing in the background when she told me that she loved me.

I had a lot to be thankful for.

Chapter Nineteen

DECLAN

The scouts were at UMass, the scouts were at the Harvard game, the scouts were at our rematch with UNH. Coach called me over after every game. Even though he made his thoughts on going pro early clear, he gave me the courtesy of every opportunity that came my way.

It was a little overwhelming, being told how great you are and having them compare you to some of the people you've idolized your entire life. To be told you dodge checks like Gretsky or can put the puck in the net like Robitielle, LaFleur and Hull, it's hard to keep your head on straight. Coach was good at being the voice of reason, though. He'd ream my ass at practice, calling me out for every misstep. I didn't resent it because he knew how to balance the criticism with encouragement, and I knew that in him I had a true source of support.

Our last game before classes started back up was at UMaine, a sort of homecoming for me. My father and Diana were going to the game, and Diana's younger son was going to be there as a UMaine student rooting against me I'm sure. From what I was hearing, half of my hometown had tickets.

Even Fiona texted me that day, wishing me good luck and warning me not to let her down. I held back from asking about Anna. Every time she came to mind, and it was often, there was a flash of pain. Seeing Fiona's name on my screen brought on that same ache, but it also gave me some hope. If her best friend wasn't cutting me off entirely, then maybe Anna hadn't closed the book on me.

The moment I stepped out onto the ice, I felt this aura, like I was in an entirely different zone. Focused, able to communicate without saying a word to my teammates, leading them. Skating so fast and so hard that my lungs burned and my quads ached, but my energy never waned. Maine was playing to kill and I felt their goons breathing down my neck every minute I was out there, but I was unstoppable that night.

The hat trick was mine, the crowd was behind me, and I owned the night.

It's an odd feeling, being at the center of something with everyone wanting a piece of you. Local reporters had microphones shoved in my face as they rattled off questions, teammates were hollering in my ear, and anyone who walked by felt the need to slap my back in congratulations. The locker room was mayhem, everyone high off the adrenaline of an unexpected win. And we didn't just beat Maine, we'd thrashed them, embarrassed them on their home turf.

Exiting the locker room, I was mobbed with well-wishers. My dad stood off to the side with Diana while I fielded words of congratulations from high school friends and guys from my neighborhood ages thirteen to seventy—people who lived and breathed hockey. And then there were the girls. There were girls from my high school, random girls from UMaine, even Paige and a few of her hometown friends who made the trip all the way from Concord. I knew Fiona was there with her brother and a few other people, but she didn't stick around. She just texted me one simple word: *perfection*.

I was glad Fiona wasn't there to witness that spectacle, because the scene outside the locker room was ridiculous, and moreover, the scene at the house party thrown by one of my teammates was borderline lewd. Every person was passing me shots and the beers were flowing. At midnight I decided to rein myself in so the night didn't get away from me, and I was glad that I did. I put my babysitting skills to good use, stopping Brandon from being dragged into a basement room with two girls who were obviously still in high school, and stopping Paige from leaving with some random douchebag. And that was *after* I'd stopped her from forcibly trying to undo my pants to give me a hand job in the middle of the crowded living room. It was that kind of party.

Walker, oh captain my captain, plopped down next to me at one point and handed me a beer. "This is what it's going to be like, Banks. Better get used to it."

"What's that?"

"I'm pretty sure it's like this every night in the pros. On the road, the women, the adoring fans...Bet it gets crazy."

"What are you planning to do next year, Walker?"

"I've got feelers out, got an agent and all, but I'm not entirely confident at this point. I have an all or nothing attitude about it. I don't want some mid-level league experience like the ECHL. I'd consider playing in Europe for a year or two, but if I'm in the states and it's not NHL, then I'm out of this game."

"Yeah? You could walk away?"

"I have a three-point-eight GPA. I'm a finance major graduating from one of the best undergraduate business programs in the country. I don't see working for some Wall Street firm making a shit load of money as something bad, do you?"

I heard Walker was brilliant, with some kind of encyclopedic memory, but managing a three-eight with our schedule was really impressive. He put my first semester, hard won two-nine to shame.

"No, I guess not."

"Me neither, but I will miss it. I'll miss being on the ice at five in the morning, that peaceful time when no one else is at the rink yet. I'll miss the feeling of robbing some guy of the puck, the breakaways, the sound the puck makes when it slaps off my stick. And I'll miss all of you guys, feeling like I'm the leader of something that's important, you know?"

"I don't know what to do, Walker."

"You're different. I don't know what I'd do if I were in your shoes either. Smart says mature, get more size, develop more as a player, and get yourself a four-year degree to fall back on. But you've got the big guys calling on you. You're not going to be living in motels traveling through the shit leagues. They want you at the show. The money will be there *now*."

Coach asked to meet with me Monday morning back at school. He'd relay all the important information, give me the contacts for the coaches and scouts he'd spoken to. He'd talk me through it, giving me no opinion but an honest idea of the pros and cons. Then it was on me. I needed to make a decision. Even though, technically, I didn't *have* to make any decisions at this point, I felt like I was at a crossroads. I had to get serious, had to choose my path.

I needed to talk to someone.

I needed Anna.

Late Sunday afternoon, I was glad to see the rest of the guys coming in, making their way back after the long winter break. Colin, Jimmy, Terrence and Frank were all in my room, with Frank passing each of us a bottle from a six pack of some Italian beer, Peroni, left over from the big Christmas Eve party at his house.

"I read about it online," Colin said. "Sounds like you were magic on the ice last night."

"I had a good game."

Jimmy pinched a bottle cap between his thumb and forefinger, whipping it in my direction. "Don't be modest, Banks. Brandon said he's never seen you play like that." He laughed as he added, "He said it like he kinda hates you, though. Jealous motherfucker."

Frank chimed in, "He said scouts have been coming to the games. He said they're there for you."

I wasn't comfortable talking about it with them. "I don't know about that. They could be there scouting a bunch of us."

Colin, always the most thoughtful and reasonable one in the group, said, "I don't know. Even if they were dangling that kind of money in front of me, I don't think I'd want that right now."

"Are you fucking crazy, Colin?" Terrence asked, laughing. "You would turn down pro hockey money? Seriously?"

"I'm just saying I might be tempted to wait."

Frank said, "Not me. I'd give my left nut to be a pro athlete."

Eager to take the focus off me, I said, "Walker and I were talking about it after the game last night. He's a senior, so that's what he's been focusing on right now."

Terrence tapped the top of his bottle against mine. "I heard that after-party was out of control."

"What exactly did you hear?" I asked.

"Brandon just said it was basically X-rated, that's all. He's still in bed, hung over. I was waiting for you to fill in the blanks."

"I guess for some people it was crazy."

Frank smirked. "Let me guess. Saint Declan, patron saint of long-term relationships wasn't up for all the down and dirty, right?"

There was more than a hint of contempt in Terrence's voice when he said, "Please, it's not exactly like Banks is the poster boy for monogamy."

I leveled him with a look, then set about gathering my clothes. I was trying to make it look like I was about to do laundry, hoping they'd get the hint and leave. So much for being happy to see them.

"You want my advice?" Frank asked.

"Fuck no."

He was the last person I'd go to for advice about girls, or anything else for that matter. He was the biggest man-whore I knew. After treating Danielle like dirt, he'd been with a string of different girls. Didn't even remember a few of their names.

"Declan, my man," he went on anyway, "you look all torn up even though this should be the best week of your life! You're *the* star on the hockey team and you're a fucking freshman. You won't say it but we *all* know the scouts are there for you, recruiting your ass. And you just got rid of a clingy girl." He held his hands up defensively. "Hot, nice, great, all that...But Tess was holding you back, we all saw that."

"Shut the fuck up, Frank."

He shook his head. "That didn't come out right. I'm just saying, shouldn't you take a break? You're ready to jump right back into something serious with Anna when—"

Terrence interrupted, "You have girls lined up and willing. Maybe you should tap some of that. Have some fun, you know?"

Frank pointed at Terrence. "That's what I'm saying. Why get all into a," he groaned the word, "relationship?" He popped the one last beer in the six pack open. "You have your whole life for that miserable shit."

Frank's advice was terrible, but at least it came from a good place. He truly believed I'd be happier fucking random girls. But with Terrence that shit was self-serving. Who would be there to swoop in and fix Anna's broken heart? *Nice try, asshole.*

"Have you spoken to Anna?" Colin asked.

I shook my head. "Has Lauren said anything?"

"She went to Anna's for New Year's Eve with her sister and a bunch of other girls. She didn't say much...Said Anna seemed better, that's all. Lauren was mostly talking about how sick the house is. I didn't know she was a Cole."

That's because Anna never mentioned it. Not even to me. I knew she lived with her relatives but she failed to mention they were one of the most powerful families in the country.

"Isn't her name Clarke?" Jimmy asked.

"She lives with her aunt and uncle," I answered him quietly.

Terrence asked, "Are her parents dead or something? No," he seemed to remember, shaking his head, "she's mentioned her mother before."

Frank took a long pull off his beer and then smiled. "If I had Vince Cole for an uncle, I'd disown my parents in two seconds flat."

I could feel my face getting hot. I didn't want to be a dick but I'd had enough. "All right, everyone out. I'm heading to the gym."

Sunday night I sat at my desk staring out the window. At ten o'clock sharp I was rewarded with a glimpse of her. She was just a shadow moving in the dark except for the bright reflective strips of fabric snaking down the sides of her running tights. I didn't even think about joining her—knew I wouldn't be welcome. I had to be content watching and waiting.

That gnawing sense of irritation took hold and grew as ten-thirty stretched to ten-forty-five and then to eleven. It was fear, really. My jaw was tight by the time I saw her sprinting her finish down the road. I waited until I saw her coming up the hill before turning off my desk lamp. Did she see the light go out? I wanted her to see, wanted her to know I'd keep watch until I was certain she was safe.

I was strategizing as I stared at the ceiling, unable to sleep. Should I track her down tomorrow? Was that too soon? On the other hand, waiting might give her the idea that I wasn't desperate to see her when I most certainly was.

So even though my first class wasn't until eleven, I got up early and made my way over towards South Campus, where most of the math, technology and art studio classes were held. Majoring in architecture, most of Anna's classes were there. While one side of campus looked staid and Ivy League, this side was more modern. Some buildings were made entirely of glass and steel beams, while contemporary sculptures—some of them really freaking odd—dotted the exteriors and grounds.

Sure enough, I saw her standing outside talking with a few of her classmates. I kept watch from a distance, nearly hidden behind a tree. Some took long drags on their cigarettes as they spoke excitedly to one another. Anna, *sans* cancer stick, rubbed her hands together and smiled after watching her breath turn into a cloud of smoke as she blew out. She was adorable. She was wearing a chunky orange turtleneck sweater over tight, faded jeans that had rips and torn edges. No jacket and holes in her jeans? I mean, she looked good but wasn't she freezing? No, I saw black leggings underneath the jeans that were tucked into her fur-lined boots. Good.

Some guy a full head taller than her, artsy looking in his pea coat and skinny jeans, came up behind her and covered her eyes. She looked alarmed for a split second but then her face broke into a smile when he whispered something in her ear. He dropped his hands from her face and then joined their group of five, talking and laughing. Two girls and three guys. They looked close, like they knew one another well.

Anna once told me about the charrette, the long sessions where her assigned group would meet to labor over design and planning issues as they worked on projects for their integrated design classes. Maybe she'd spent long hours with these people, getting to know details about their lives while they learned about hers.

I felt foolish standing fifty yards away practically stalking her, so I decided to approach. Did it have anything to do with how close that guy was standing next to Anna, or with the way he was now playfully twisting her ponytail? Maybe.

"Hey, Anna."

She turned at the sound of my voice, and her smile morphed into a deer in the headlights look.

"Hi." Long, painfully awkward silence. "Uh, Declan, this is Marielle, Ryan, Jeff and," she gestured to the hair twister, "this is Owen."

Owen. Owen was into her. That was Fiona's take on Owen's feelings. The look he was giving me now only confirmed it. One corner of his mouth was turned up in a smile, a knowing smile. A smile that said: *this girl, this body, this heart—it's all mine.* I wanted to bitch slap that smile right off his arrogant face. He was throwing down the gauntlet.

He playfully tugged on Anna's ponytail again. "C'mon partner, we're gonna be late."

Anna stayed fixed in place, looking at me. I was looking at her. That dipshit Owen stayed too, even though the other three were making their way into the building. I shifted my gaze, shooting him a menacing look. *Run along, asshole,* is what my look said. I don't know if Anna was catching this silent exchange between us, but she ended the stare down when she turned to go and said, "I've really got to get to class, Declan."

Purely to piss me off, I'm sure, Owen put his hand on the small of her back as he opened the door for her and ushered her inside.

* * *

ANNA

I returned to school late Sunday night and wasted no time Monday morning, going straight to see my Intro to Design professor. He wasn't in so I had to cool my jets and wait another day. So I was restless by the time I practically bounced into his office first thing Tuesday morning. He was skeptical when I told him I was applying for the summer program at Cooper Union, telling me I was far too inexperienced. But after looking at the portfolio I'd put together, he agreed to write me a letter of recommendation.

I was all but skipping across campus after that victory, so I didn't even notice him until he was standing right in front of me, blocking my way into my next class.

"Did you just win the lottery or something?" Declan asked, smiling. "You have the biggest, shit-eating grin on your face that I've ever seen."

My heart felt like it was beating out of my chest again. Just the sound of his voice and the sight of him brought on this conflict, this crazy rush of emotion. Yesterday morning when he approached me it was the same—the feeling of being frozen in place, wanting to melt into him, yet hardly even able to form words.

Stay strong, Anna, I thought to myself yesterday. *You need to stay away from him. You have a life outside of him. You have goals, you have important things to accomplish.* This was my mantra.

"Hey," he greeted me again with a sad smile.

God, I wanted to hug him, cry, kiss him and slap his face again, all at once. We stood there awkwardly for a moment before I said, "I'd better go in...Don't want to be late on the first day. See you, Declan."

As I was making my way in, he looked down at his schedule and looked back up to me. "History of the Old Testament?"

Noooo. I didn't want to sit next to him every Tuesday and Thursday morning from ten to eleven-forty-five for the next four months. That definitely didn't fit into my *Steer Clear of Declan* plan.

It must have showed on my face.

"Anna, do you want me to switch out or something? I will, if that's what you want."

I shook my head and gave him a look that said: *Don't be ridiculous*. But if I was to finish that thought, I would have told him not to be ridiculous, that *I'd* be the one switching out of the class.

He followed me in. When I took my seat he paused, probably debating whether or not he should sit next to me. He decided to do it, and I closed my eyes as he settled in. That oh so good and familiar smell invaded my space—some brand of men's deodorant he always wore mixed with his own clean, masculine scent. Being this close to him was painful. I literally ached deep in my chest.

The five minutes that stretched ahead before the official start of class now seemed interminable. I kept looking up at the clock. Damn my obsessive punctuality.

"So how are you?"

A simple, polite question from anyone else, but coming from Declan, it was as loaded as could be.

"I'm good. I've been really busy. I'm applying for this big deal summer program. It's a long shot. I basically have zero chance of making it, but I'm putting together a portfolio anyway."

"Your work is so good, Anna. I'm sure you have way more than just a shot at it."

"Thanks," I said, thinking to myself that he wouldn't know the difference between a truly gifted architect and a crappy one, but that was ok.

His eyes were still fixed on me. I was so damn uncomfortable, especially when he looked at me pointedly and repeated, "But what I meant was, how are you, um, about everything that happened. I—"

The professor, a stern looking older man who turned out to be Father Xavier Delaney, rapped a book on the desk to call the room to order. This wasn't a large class with stadium seating and a few hundred students. No, this was an intimate class of twenty-five or so where, according to Father Delaney, we would discuss the Old Testament in great detail and collaborate with our classmates on projects. He also seemed to be a fan of the Socratic Method, firing questions at you when you least expected it. Declan scribbled in his notebook: *This guy's no joke.* I looked down to read it and stifled a laugh. And as a reward for my impertinence, I got called out.

"Young lady in the wildly patterned, black and cobalt blue dress... What is your name?"

Kasia gave me a closet full of pieces for Christmas, including some knitwear that was, despite this crusty old man's opinion, totally rocking.

The dress hugged my body perfectly, and I had on black tights and some mid-calf, black lace up boots that completed the downtown look. This outfit made me want to dye my hair black when I first looked in the mirror this morning—and I mean that in a good way. The hair dying thing was out for a while, though, since I'd noticed one too many damaged split ends. My hair needed a break from the abuse.

I felt great leaving the dorm with my short black leather jacket and my blond waves tamed into a high knot. I was cold—it was January in Boston after all—but I suffered some frigid legs because I felt good, I felt like an artist. The outfit gave me the confidence I needed to persuade my professor to grant me that recommendation this morning. It screamed ballsy, edgy and creative. So Father X's condescending dig rolled right off me.

"Anna Clarke," I answered.

"Miss Clarke, perhaps you'd like to enlighten us with the names of the first five books of the Old Testament."

I felt like opening with, *What is this, amateur hour?* before I rattled off the names with certainty and a smile, "Genesis, Exodus, Leviticus, Numbers and Deuteronomy."

If he asked me what any of those books signified, I would have been screwed, but memorizing was easy for me and GELDN was just another useless acronym I had stored away in my brain, like SCUBA and ROY G BIV.

He smiled with pursed lips. Round one went to me, but I got the feeling he'd be looking to regain the title soon enough. A class transfer was looking like the smarter option. I had enough on my plate this semester with Advanced Calculus, History of Architecture,

Design Studio Two and an English Literature requirement. I was looking for Theology to be my easy A.

Five minutes later, Declan the Clueless was scribbling another note. Was he *trying* to get me nailed? He wrote: *Can we get lunch together?* When I didn't answer immediately, he nudged me and I looked over, raising my eyebrows in warning. Too late.

"Miss Clarke, what are those five books of the Old Testament called, collectively?"

I held back from rolling my eyes. I felt like telling him he'd have to do better than this. I mean, I'd easily been to twenty or thirty bar and bat mitzvahs over the course of my short life. "The Pentateuch or The Torah."

He wasn't going down without a fight. "And we know what the focus of Genesis and Exodus are, as the names speak for themselves, but can you tell us, Miss Clarke, what are the core principles of Leviticus, Numbers and Deuteronomy?"

I was down for the count. "No, sir, I cannot."

"Very well," he said, obviously pleased with his haughty little self. "I was beginning to think Miss Clarke could teach this class, but obviously she will have to pay close attention just like the rest of you."

By now, other kids in the class were turning around, smiling and smirking. Declan, thank goodness, kept his head down for the remainder of class and didn't pass me any more notes.

After class, he took my free hand and squeezed it before letting go. "Sorry 'bout that."

"Yeah, thanks for that, jerkoff." I couldn't help but laugh as I said, "You think you would have gotten the hint after I got picked on the first time, but noooo."

He was smiling too. "I was starting to think you were some kind of Old Testament whiz kid in there. It was kind of hot, Anna."

I stopped in my tracks and looked at him. "Don't do that. We're not where we were, ok?"

He threw his head back and let out a breath. "Yeah, that's obvious." He looked back at me, frowning. "I guess lunch is a no?"

"I do want to get together and talk sometime, but the deadline for course changes is tomorrow. I don't have the time or the mental fortitude to deal with that dude's crap this semester. I have a tough course load." He was quiet so I said, "It has nothing to do with you, really."

It did, though.

As we walked the length of the quad I began to have this odd feeling, like the air around Declan was somehow different. People were turning to look at him, parting to make way for him as he strode through. Upperclassmen nodded their heads, bumped fists with him, and everyone in general was either saying hello or eyeing him with approval and familiarity.

"What's going on? Did you get voted school president or something? Why is everyone smiling at you? It's weird."

He shrugged. "I had a good game last weekend."

"Oh. That's good."

"Yeah," he said absently.

When I thought about switching my class, I felt sad. The nearly two hours I'd just spent with Declan, just the nearness of him—it felt nice. My body was betraying me already. Sitting with our thighs only inches apart, taking in his scent, hearing him sigh or yawn. I wanted to go back to that place with him, the place where it was good.

The only theology class left was Women in Western Religion. It met at the same time, same days. Goodbye, Father Delaney, goodbye, Declan. I signed the forms reluctantly even though I knew it was for the best.

Dinner? Declan texted a few hours later.

I wrote back: **Can't...have deadline for that application.**

He wrote right back: **Lunch Thurs?**

I did say that we would talk after break, so I answered: **Sure.**

• • •

I took special care getting dressed Thursday morning. I couldn't help myself. I still felt it—the need to be the most beautiful woman Declan ever laid eyes on. Pathetic, I know.

It was damp outside so my hair didn't need much coaxing to fall into loose curls. I wore only lip gloss. He wasn't a big fan of make-up and I really didn't need it anyway; lately my skin always had a nice healthy glow from all the running. I wore a snug navy cami with a red and navy plaid button down shirt over it. I left the top three buttons and the bottom two buttons open. The shirt was fitted in a way that made my breasts look—in my opinion—pretty great. I had on skinny jeans tucked into distressed brown riding boots that came just slightly over the knee in front and laced up the back. They were a Christmas present from Margot and Vince. I didn't care or even want to know what they cost because I loved them. They made my legs look a mile long. I dubbed the look: edgy but innocent farm girl just back from a sexy horseback ride. *I'll never be writing copy for a fashion magazine*, I thought. Long story short, I was pleased. I wanted him drooling over me even if I wasn't entirely sure I wanted to see him.

What did I say about feeling mentally healthy?

With all that looking in the mirror, I was running my version of late and walked in just as class began. There were only two empty seats when I scanned the room, and the one I was gunning for got taken by some guy the moment I turned in that direction. The only other seat was the one behind Declan. I swallowed and made my way up the few steps, hoping my cheeks weren't as red as my shirt.

I was tempted to turn around and run after catching sight of Declan flanked by Paige on one side and her equally charming friend, Cassie, on the other. In front of Declan sat Charlotte and some other girl I didn't know.

What the hell? Why was he here?

It was one of those smaller classrooms set up with tiered seating.

The chairs that were attached to the rounded, classroom-width tables were able to swivel.

Those girls? All of their chairs were swiveled so that they were facing Declan. Taking it in for just a split second, it was clear they were in the middle of a full-on drool fest. Charlotte was smiling and batting her damn eyelashes at him, Paige's hand was resting on his shoulder, her head thrown back as she laughed at whatever inane remark he'd just made. Cassie, meanwhile, was doodling something in his notebook, giggling.

Their heads snapped up once Declan set his eyes on me. I managed a half-smile as I took the seat behind him. He swiveled around and said, "I was glad to see I wasn't the only guy in this class. My schedule is tight so I had to pick the same time slot." Then he mouthed the words, "Is it ok?"

I nodded and gave a him a look that said: *Of course*.

Lie.

I thought it would be tough sitting next to Declan all semester, but this? *This* was the worst case scenario. I wasn't a wuss—not even close—but these chicks brought the mean girl to a whole new level. Watching them flirt with Declan all semester would be hell on earth. I honestly didn't know how I'd manage, but I truly had no choice. The deadline for schedule changes already passed, and I was not going to drop a class that I'd have to make up later because of them. I'd just have to deal.

As the professor sorted through some papers and began handing out course outlines, Paige turned to Declan and said, "Oh my God! That party was *absolutely* nuts last weekend. My friends from home think you and your teammates are like the funnest, craziest guys they've ever partied with."

I hoped for Paige's sake she'd meant to say funniest and it had just come out wrong. *Funnest*, says the college freshman, really? I sat with my sketchbook open and found myself portraying the two of them as cartoon figures: a snarky, devil-horned ogre laughing in the ear of a very guilty-looking, wart-covered toad. The pencil lines were heavy with the force of my anger.

The girl sitting in front with Charlotte obviously hadn't gotten the memo that I was to be treated with disdain. When she caught my eye she smiled and said, "I *love* your boots."

"Oh, thanks," I said, smiling back as I took in Charlotte's annoyed expression.

"I'm Avery, by the way."

"Anna," I answered. "Nice to meet you."

Cassie turned and smiled sweetly. "I like those boots too, Anna. What kind are they?"

"I'm not even sure," I answered absently. I was not telling Cassie the designer's name. First, the thought of any of these girls finding out that my boots cost several hundred dollars or possibly more—a strong likelihood—was embarrassing. Second, I preferred to avoid interaction with Cassie and all of her brethren in general.

Cassie was the most lethal of them all. While Paige and Charlotte were flat out nasty, Cassie was less obvious. A sweet, innocent veneer with a venomous rattlesnake lying in wait to cut you down when she knew no one of import was there to witness.

Cassie helped to organize blood drives and was on the committee for homeless advocacy. People sang her praises: so selfless, so caring. She would recruit the "it" crowd to her causes. I nearly walked out of the last blood drive when I saw them, Cassie draped over Brandon and Charlotte draped over Frank, comforting the boys as they donated. By comforting, I mean they were practically giving them happy-ending rubdowns. If I wasn't B-negative, one of the more rare blood types, I would have bailed.

It was all bullshit. Cassie would be all Mother Teresa one minute, then she'd be laughing behind other girls' backs, making rude gestures about their weight or their clothes. She didn't have me fooled.

I shifted my attention, blocking her out, and listened attentively to determine if attendance was a major factor in our grades. If it wasn't, I would be taking full advantage by skipping class on a regular basis. Whereas I thought Theology would be an easy A, I'd now gladly take the C.

I took my time packing up after class, waiting for the peanut gallery of gaggling females to disperse, but he was standing at the end of the aisle waiting on me. "Where do you want to eat?"

"You know, I don't think I can do that today. I have a lot going on."

I was making my way down the stairs with him trailing, while those four girls were lingering just outside the open classroom doors.

"Anna, come on," he said softly.

"Declan, hurry up," Cassie practically purred. "You know the lines get crazy long in there and you *promised* you'd show me a shortcut for that amortization formula."

Right. The first day of classes and this girl needs a tutor for basic finance? Even I knew that formula. This was laughable.

"I'm not coming," he said to them. "Anna, wait up," he called after me as I strode off.

Still walking, I said, "I told you I can't."

"You mean that you won't."

I stopped and let out a sigh, turning to him. "Just go with *them*, Declan. Your fan club awaits, right? I bet it will be the *funnest* lunch ever."

Sometimes I forgot how big he was. He was towering over me now, his lean but massive frame making me feel as if I was a tiny thing as he leaned into me. My cheeks heated when I noticed his eyes were trained right onto the cleavage I'd foolishly put on display for him today.

"That's what you really want?" he challenged.

"That. Is. What. I. Want," I snapped right back in his face.

"You're jealous," he said, a playful smile lifting one corner of his mouth.

"Not."

"You are and you should be," he said, matter-of-fact.

My cheeks were now on fire. Damn, I was an open book. "Care to explain?"

"You *should* be jealous. Those girls want you to think I was at that party, taking part in everything that went down. And they want you to think I'm into other girls, into them."

We were standing outside an empty classroom. Declan took my hand, led me inside and closed the door before continuing. "If someone said that about you, tried to make me think you were acting wild at a party or you were into some other guy, I'd go ape-shit."

"Don't you see?" I was so damn exasperated and tired from riding this roller coaster. "That's the problem. Until you came along, I'd never lower myself to be someone's second best, someone's back up girl. I can barely even look at you after what you did to me. And after that, after everything that's happened, I still feel jealous! I feel out of control. I don't want to feel like I'm out of control anymore... Like I'm crazy." Declan went to speak but I stopped him. "I should be able to handle those girls. I see how pathetic they are. I know what they're doing. But I'm *not* handling it well. You're not my boyfriend, you *never* were, but still I want to cry, beat your chest, slap your face...Just for being near a girl like that at a party. I don't *want* to feel this way."

He grabbed my shoulders, forcing my gaze upward. "You think I didn't want to choke that fucking jackass Owen the other day? You think I didn't want to bash your friend Jeremy's face in when he walked past me, knowing he was on his way up to your *bedroom*? While I had to just stand there and take it like some goddamn chump? I was so fucking mental I nearly crashed on the way home."

"I don't think we should be around each other for a while," I said, quietly.

He stroked my face with his fingers. "Please don't say that."

"I just..." I hesitated, knowing that what I was about to say, while true, was going to sting. "I don't trust you anymore."

He inhaled and took a step back. After a moment he said, "I haven't given you much of a reason to trust me lately. I know that."

"That's not all of it." I should have just kept my mouth shut, but while I wanted him, there was a part of me that wanted to push him away. Leave me safe from feeling all of this because it was too much. So I pushed. "What I said about being out of control? I...With Jeremy..." His face went white. "Declan, I didn't know you were at my house until after you'd already left. And that day? I was so messed up, so hurt. I wanted someone to take it all away. I begged him to come over." I couldn't look at Declan anymore so I stared at the floor. "I begged him to..."

I thought he'd take a step away, run even, but he took a step towards me instead. He wrapped his arms around me and kissed the top of my head. "It's all right, Anna."

I pushed back against his chest, angry. "How can you say that? I'm telling you that I begged Jeremy to fuck me. Did you hear me?"

"Did he?" he asked through clenched teeth.

I turned to face the wall, leaning my forehead against it, ashamed. "No," I whimpered quietly.

"Is that what you really wanted? Did you want *him*?" he asked, his body close behind mine, towering over me.

"No," I said as I let out a breath.

"Good."

Jesus, it was always the same. Since the day I'd first met him, hearing him say my name made me feel liquid and lazy, like a pool of melted chocolate. And since that night we'd been together, the need my body felt was intense. He wasn't touching me now, but we were so close I could feel the heat emanating from him. I was aware of my chest rising and falling, my breath coming in shallow as he moved in even closer, speaking right into my ear. "Only me." He rested one giant paw on my shoulder and squeezed. "Please, only me."

I turned, ready to surrender, but he was already picking up his backpack and heading for the door. Without looking my way, he stopped and said, "I'll give you time, Anna, all the time that you need. But I'm *not* giving you space."

Just when I thought I was safe, he poked his head back inside and said, "And just for the record, I didn't partake in what was going on at that party, and I'm not into anyone else but you."

I slid down the wall, landing on my ass.

DECLAN

The last month had been, to quote Charles Dickens, the best of times and the worst of times.

On the ice, I could do no wrong. I frustrated the opposition's defense and I was scoring consistently. When we came back from Christmas break, it was as if I'd earned some type of celebrity status. I'd get smiles and pats on the back from people I didn't know, my professors seemed to smile at me more than they did my classmates, and in general, it seemed like a whole lot of people wanted to get to know me.

My meeting with Coach Monday afternoon went as I expected. The NHL draft was more than a possibility for me this coming June. A first round draft pick was a certainty for me if I wanted it. Did I want it?

I walked to class the next morning thinking about the pros and cons. Hockey was my life, my joy, for so many years. Playing in the NHL was what it was all supposed to lead up to. Did I feel old enough, was I ready? And, I thought, I'd miss it here. I'd miss her.

Right at that moment, I looked up to see her walking towards me, a big smile on her face. She was happy to see me? I was confused because yesterday she didn't seem particularly pleased when I showed up outside of her class. When she got closer, though, I noticed that she was smiling to herself. I sobered up realizing she was happy thinking about something or someone else.

I'd spent the past month thinking about that night and about the shit that happened the next morning and in the days after. When I'd lie in bed at night, or sit on the bus as we rode for hours to away games, I'd think back to that night. My dick ached thinking about her, the way she looked naked on my bed, her arms above her head, wrists clasped in one of my hands. The taste of her skin, the taste of her. Her sweet moans as I loved her. Being inside of Anna had wrecked me for anyone else, ever. I was sure of that.

I stood there outside of class smiling because *her* smile was infectious, and when she nearly plowed into me I tried to maintain my smile, even when her expression fell and tightened.

What I wouldn't give to turn back the clock. What I *should* have done that morning was kiss Anna, tell her to stay in my bed and tell her to wait for me. I should have gone out into the hall, gotten Tess and dealt with her straight. But at the time, I felt like I couldn't. I had to bring Tess home that day, *had* to make sure she was safe. And maybe Anna was right. If Tess hadn't caught me, maybe our break-up would have been a long, protracted misery that spanned several weeks. But it wasn't like Anna thought. I had no intention of stringing either of them along. I wanted Anna, of that I was one hundred percent certain. And I knew I'd never so much as kiss Tess again after spending that night with Anna.

But it all went to shit. Certain images were on replay, a continuous looping reel in my mind. Anna's expression right before she'd landed that killer slap—hurt and betrayal that morphed into blazing anger. Her blank, lost look as her uncle led her away. Her uncle and Dylan looking at me as if I was the source of all of Anna's pain. And watching that guy bound up the stairs to her room. He was the one she went to for comfort when it should have been me.

I did what she asked. I'd left her alone for the rest of the break. Now she was back, though, and she *was* going to talk to me. She was going to hear me out.

It seemed like I was taking one step forward most days and then two steps back. That first day in class, I made her smile, made her laugh, but then wrecked it when I got too familiar with her too fast.

I knew Anna—she'd make me work for it. And that was ok. *I'm not going anywhere*, I thought as I claimed the seat next to hers. And what I said to her, that I'd give her time but I wasn't giving her space? I meant that. I didn't care if she was mad that I'd switched into the same Theology class. Didn't feel one bit guilty about conning that old lady in the registrar's office into giving me Anna's schedule. Women in Western Religion? I didn't care what class it was. I wanted to see her and plant my ass in the seat right next to hers... every...single...day.

You can try to shake me off, but I'm not going anywhere.

* * *

ANNA

I have to time this better.

I got to class too early again. I took a seat in the far corner of the room, and when Paige and the rest of them came strutting in they decided to plop down right in front of me. Then some bonehead and his friend took the two available seats right next to me. Declan sashayed in a few minutes after class started. This teacher was a stickler for punctuality, but she let the school's resident hockey god off the hook. Instead of a reprimand for being late, Declan got a big warm smile instead.

Gross.

He looked up and frowned when he saw the seats on either side of me taken. I could see Paige from the corner of my eye, patting the seat next to her while flashing him a big, bright smile. Paige saved a spot for him, how thoughtful.

Cassie acted as if the teacher wasn't mid-lecture when she turned around, all stern and commando-like. "Remember, Declan, nine o'clock tonight at Rusty's. You and Brandon are our ambassadors so we *need* you there."

You're too easy, I felt like telling him. So easy to manipulate, sitting there with your cheeks red again. *Cat got your tongue, Banks?*

I already knew what this was about. Some charity Valentine's Day Dance that Cassie was soooo busy coordinating and buzzing over like a busy, busy bee.

It actually sounded fun. It was a seventies themed dance at an off-campus bar, Rusty's, that turned a somewhat blind eye to the drinking age. But of course, this couldn't be just a regular party, a drink-up like anyone else would put together. No, with Cassie at the helm there had to be some noble cause that would benefit. There had to be ambassadors. What did that even mean? I guess it was an excuse to pair themselves up with the boys they wanted to sink their claws into.

"You want to come with me tonight?" Declan asked, turning around to face me.

Cassie smiled, sugar-sweet. "Yes, please come! Just give us until ten or so. The committee has to take care of business first. There is *so* much to do," she said, rolling her eyes as if she didn't love every single minute of it.

I ignored her, kept my impassive stare fixed on Declan. "I'll pass. I'm going with Fiona, Colin and Terrence to watch Lauren's Dance Ensemble thing tonight."

"No!" General Cassie decreed. "Colin is on the committee. He's an ambassador. Declan, he *has* to come!"

"I think Colin would rather watch his girlfriend dance around in a leotard than strategize about decorations," Avery chimed in.

"You're right, Avery," Declan said. "And why exactly do *I* have to come tonight? If I say pink hearts and you girls say red hearts, I'm thinking you'll go with red, right?"

Paige was channeling Lucifer himself when she smiled and said, "Tonight we're measuring you guys for your costumes."

"My costume? I was planning on jeans and a tie-dye shirt."

"That is *not* happening. We'll take care of everything, don't worry. You just have to be there tonight," Cassie said in an end-of-discussion kind of way.

He looked back to gauge my reaction. I had to rein in my bitchy smirk as best I could. *Yeah, Cassie and Paige will take care of everything. They'll measure you, dress you, blow you...whatever.*

The subject matter in this class was bo-ring, so after the dumb chatter died down in front of me, I busied myself answering text messages. I asked Victoria if she wanted to come with us to watch Lauren and then go out for apps and drinks after. She said yes and said she'd ask Brandon. Wonder what Victoria's reaction would be when he told her where he was going instead. Then I responded to my cousin Dylan, who was making plans to come up on Saturday to watch the hockey game with his friends.

Dylan was trying to fill every minute, to keep occupied and keep his mind off his misery. He was a hockey fan and all, but I knew him. Ever since his break-up with Kasia, he was taking the work hard-play hard thing to a new level. Every time I called he was either traveling for work or partying. I knew he was miserable but he'd never confess to it. It was like Dylan Cole had a switch he could turn on and off. When I asked about Kasia, he'd just say she was in the past. That was that.

I didn't even find out about the break-up until Aunt Margot told me, and then two days later there was a picture of him on some gossip site, his arm wrapped around CeeCee Tate with the caption:

Cole's New Love Interest? How could he be happy with someone like her? She was a far cry from Kasia in beauty, brains and balls.

"Who are you in deep conversation with?" Declan asked, tapping on my desk. Class had ended and everyone was packing up to leave.

"My cousin, Dylan. He's coming up this weekend to watch the game with his friends, so I guess I have no choice, I *have* to go."

"Ouch," Declan said as he laid one hand over his heart. "That hurts." He added, "I'll have to be on my A game."

"Oh my gosh," Avery gushed, "your cousin is, like, so freaking gorgeous. Is it true that Dylan Cole and his girlfriend are broken up?"

"How do you even know that?"

I asked but I already knew. Since my mini-nervous breakdown before Christmas, the entire campus now knew that I was related to Vince and Dylan Cole, a fact I'd hoped to keep under wraps.

Sometimes I had to remind myself that their lives played out on the big screen. Dylan Cole wasn't a movie star or anything, but as a young, good-looking soon-to-be CEO of a major corporation, he was a celebrity in his own way. Dylan was in the newspaper, he was on gossip sites, and random people took his picture when he was out in public. It was disturbing.

"I read about it somewhere. I *am* a business major," Avery said in her own defense.

"Have you spoken to Kasia?" Declan asked. He knew how I felt about her, how I must be missing her.

When the girls moved out of the row, I said, "Once, right after it happened a few weeks ago. And she just sent me a package, a few things from her spring line. It just feels all wrong, though, you know?"

"Like a divorce? Like you have to side with someone?"

"Yeah." I nodded. "I mean, I'm pretty certain Dylan was the one who screwed things up, even though Kasia swore it was mutual. But he's my blood. At the end of the day, I have to support him in any way I can."

"It's hard to feel like you've lost a friend, though." Declan squeezed my shoulder. "I've gotta run to practice now. So I'll definitely see you on Saturday?"

"Yeah, but I'm going out with Dylan and his friends afterwards."

"Oh," he said, looking disappointed, but then brightened up when he asked, "You're coming to that Valentine's Day thing, right?"

"Definitely. If only to see what *costume* you're wearing."

He hung his head. "It's a charity thing. Coach likes us to do that kind of stuff. You know, right, that I...That I pay no attention to them?"

"You're free, last I heard. That means you can do what you want with who you want."

He looked up at the ceiling and let out a frustrated breath, shaking his head. "It's whomever, with whomever you want."

"Thank you, grammar police."

"And that's not true, because if I *could* do whatever I want with whomever I wanted, then I would be with you." When I lowered my head he said, "And I don't just mean physically, Anna. But I do want that more than you can imagine." He waited until I looked up at him. "I miss you as my friend. So much has been happening lately. Confusing things, things I can't figure out on my own, you know? And I find myself wanting to know what you would think about it, what you would do. You're one of the few people who don't have an agenda when it comes to me. You may not trust me, but I trust you completely."

Declan saying the word trust brought all those hurt feelings to the surface again, but I tried to put them aside. "I am your friend, Declan."

"But you're not all the way there yet."

I shook my head slowly, looking down at the floor. "I don't know why I can't shake it. That morning...What you did? It still hurts like it was yesterday. I can't forget."

"That morning and the months leading up to it...It's all my fault. But you have to believe me, I *was* breaking up with Tess. When she just showed up like that...God, it was all a mess. I didn't want to hurt her in that way. I had to get her home, make sure she was all right. Do you understand?"

I'd been holding back for so long, but listening to him speak her name with care and concern broke me. "Tess, Tess, Tess. *Her* feelings always." I pushed at his chest with all the force I could muster. "Protect *her* feelings while you could give fuck-all about mine!"

"No, Anna." He took me into his massive arms, crushed me to his chest and wouldn't let go. I was shaking with sobs. He was stroking my hair, kissing the top of my head and whispering to me, "I'm not asking you to forget, but I'm *begging* you to please forgive me. Please."

After what seemed like forever, I wriggled out of his arms and took a step back. "I'm trying to move past it, but it's hard. I need time. Taking some time isn't a bad thing."

"No," he smiled weakly, "it's not." He kissed the top of my head again and stepped back. "But if you meant what you said...If you are my friend, for real, then it's not weird if we eat lunch or dinner together sometimes, right?"

"I guess not."

"Are you doing anything Friday night? I don't have an ulterior motive, I swear," he said as he held his palms up to face me. "I really do need your advice about something and I also like to eat Italian food the night before my games. I've developed a superstition."

Exhausted from my outburst, I managed a weak smile. "And, if I recall, you're very fond of spaghetti and meatballs."

"Ah, but I was a mere child then. I've moved onto pasta carbonara."

"That's what's annoying about boys. Carbonara is like pure fat on a plate. *You* can eat that and stay all muscle. If I ate food like that I'd have a booty the size of Idaho."

His dimple was deep when he smiled like that, like he was truly happy. "You think I'm all muscle, huh?"

"That's *all* you got from that entire statement?"

"Nope. I was also thinking your booty is bootylicious as is, but you'd look nice with a big giant booty too."

"You're twisted."

He looked at his watch. "Speaking of food, I have two minutes to shovel something in before practice. So we're on for Friday. I'll text you. You're going to love this place, Anna," he said as he walked away backwards. "It's a little hole in the wall in the North End. The baked clams are orgasmic."

"How could I turn that down?"

"Yeah," he winked, "I'll take what I can get in that department these days, too."

* * *

DECLAN

I tried on a few different shirts before settling on the dark blue button-down that looked pretty similar to the other shirts I'd just put on and thrown off.

It was like I'd been given a second chance, a gift, and I was nervous that I'd make a misstep, that somehow I'd screw it up again.

When Anna opened the door I must have had a giant smile plastered across my face, because damn, she was so beautiful.

She was all about fashion, but tonight it looked like she'd taken care *not* to dress up. She had on jeans and a plain sweater, but she still looked unbelievably good to me. And she had her long hair pulled up into a high ponytail, the way I liked it best. It showcased her face and gave me access to her neck—one of my favorite spots on her body to kiss. Don't get me wrong, her ass and her breasts? I worshipped them. But there were a few times during dinner when I was completely distracted, thinking about kissing and nipping that spot she liked, right below her ear.

In the spirit of friendship I extended the invitation to Fiona. And while I truly enjoyed the girl's company, I was praying she'd decline.

"No thanks, Declan. I happen to have a date tonight, too."

"Nice. Who's the lucky guy?"

"A friend of yours."

"Could you be a little more specific?"

"No. I don't want to jinx it. If it's a good date, then I'll spill."

Anna smiled at her, then at me. "She won't even tell *me*. Can you believe that? I told her she has to text me every hour just so that I know she's alive."

When we walked into Giuseppe's, I could tell right away that Anna liked it. The place was tiny, with red-checkered tablecloths, cheesy plastic flowers on every table, and candles melted into those old chianti bottles that had twine twisted around the bottom half.

"Oh my God, it smells incredible in here."

"I like a girl who likes garlic."

"You might not think that later on when you're kissing me goodnight."

She looked embarrassed then, like she regretted mentioning anything about kissing.

"If you let me kiss you goodnight, a little garlic isn't going to scare me off."

"Declan! I was starting to wonder if you were coming." Giuseppe's wife nodded her head in the direction of the back. "It's a game tomorrow, so he's been expecting you." She looked to Anna and smiled. "And who has taken Brandon's place?"

"Mrs. DeMarco, this is my friend, Anna."

"Hello," Anna said.

She grabbed Anna roughly by the waist and turned her around, a complete three hundred and sixty degree rotation. Anna stood there, eyes wide, as Giuseppe's wife appraised her from head to toe.

"Graziosa, bella, perfetto," Mrs. DeMarco declared before smiling warmly and leading us to our table. She turned to me, right back to business. "The usual tonight?"

"Yep. Some baked clams first, though. I told Anna she'll never taste any better."

"Anna, what about you?" Mrs. DeMarco asked.

"Um, should I look at the menu?"

"No menus," I said.

"What do you like?" she asked.

"Tell Giuseppe to surprise me."

Mrs. DeMarco looked to me. "I knew I liked this one."

"This one?" Anna teased after Mrs. DeMarco went into the kitchen. "How many girls have you brought here?"

As soon as the words left her mouth, her smile dropped and she looked pained. I knew she was thinking about Tess.

"No one. I've never been here with another girl."

"Oh," she said, one side of her mouth curving up into a reluctant smile as she looked out the window.

I took her hands across the table. "I'm glad you said yes tonight, even if we're here just as friends. I meant what I said, I've really missed talking to you."

She squeezed my hands back. "Can I guess what's been on your mind?"

"Go for it."

"Are you thinking about whether or not you should leave? To play professionally, I mean?" She added, "Fiona mentioned it."

"Yeah, and I can't talk to most people about it. Everyone thinks you're whining about having this great opportunity, and it's not like that. It's—"

"Impossible. To choose, I mean. How can you *know* you're making the right choice?"

"Exactly," I said, breathing a sigh of relief.

"Are you happy when you're at school?"

I stroked my thumbs over the backs of her hands. "Very happy."

"Will hockey be there for you as long as you don't have some career-ending injury?"

"Most likely."

"And when you envision your life, can you see yourself without hockey? Can you imagine yourself in a suit and tie, coming home to a family at the end of the day, coaching your kid's little league team? Can you see that as fulfilling, or do you see it as boring or suffocating?"

"As long as I'm with the person I love, I can totally envision that life as fulfilling." My inner dialogue was going something like this: *You, Anna. If I'm with you then it will all be good.*

She looked down at the table to hide her blushing cheeks, but I could see that she was smiling. "Then you're set either way. Being a pro athlete will end when you're a relatively young man anyway. As long as you know that everyday life, life after the pros or without it, is something you can deal with and something you can look forward to, then it'll all be ok."

"I want to stay at school."

It's like the decision just came to me, clear as day. I felt light, sure and happy.

"Then that's what you'll do." Her words shored me up, both steadfast and tender. "And you'll take each year as it comes."

Dropping her off that night, I settled for one kiss, one slow brush across her soft lips. I didn't want to risk anything by pushing her too far.

I thought of Mrs. DeMarco's words as I walked back to my dorm: beautiful, graceful, perfect. Yes, that was my Anna.

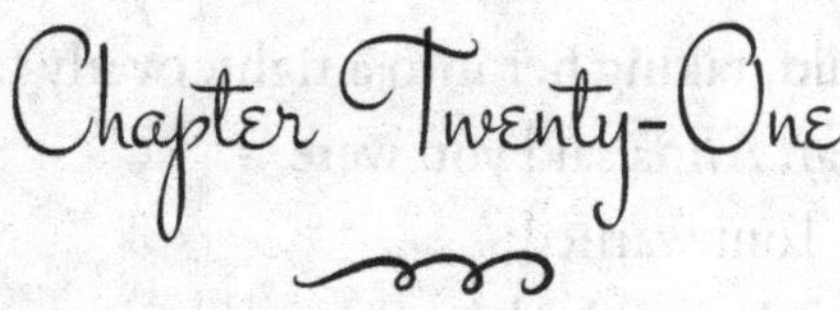

Chapter Twenty-One

ANNA

I wasn't going to be able to hold out much longer. I wanted to wait, I really did, but every time I caught sight of him, every time his touch grazed my skin, every time he said something sweet and loving to me, my resolve weakened.

That night when he dropped me off after dinner, he left me outside my door, kissing me just once before leaving. I cried myself to sleep that night, lonely and aching to be with him again.

Why was I holding back? Because as much as I hate to admit it, I still couldn't move past that morning. I still felt that burning shame, still felt the sting of betrayal as if it was yesterday. I couldn't forget. Guess I wasn't ready to forgive yet either.

He was softening me, though, day by day.

"Anna Banana, my Anna Banana."

Oh Lord, Dylan was beyond buzzing when he showed up at my

dorm at six o'clock. Tom and Ben were behind him, Tom with raised eyebrows and Ben shaking his head in what looked like an apology.

The girls on my floor didn't notice his drunken state, though. They were blinded by his good looks, his charm and the sleek chauffeured car idling just downstairs.

"Fiona," he said, taking her into a tight, overly familiar hug, "you are even hotter than Anna said you were."

"Down boy," Tom warned.

"I'm so sorry," I mouthed to Fiona. She waggled her eyebrows and smiled in response.

I closed my door, essentially blocking the prying eyes of every girl in my dorm. I grabbed two water bottles out of the fridge as Tom and Ben introduced themselves to Fiona and strategically placed their bodies between her and Dylan.

"What time did you start drinking?" I hissed as I shoved a bottle at him.

"I've had two, maybe three. Relax."

"Drink the water, Dylan, and no more booze until we go out *after* the game, all right?" Tom was stating fact, not asking.

"Yes, Dad," Dylan teased. "So Fiona, do you like older men?"

She thought he was hilarious. "Only *really* old ones. Like sixty-five or seventy, you know?"

"Don't encourage him, Fiona," I begged.

"Aw baby, come on. I have to wait, what, forty-one years to get my hands on that sweet ass of yours?"

Ben said, "Shut up. You're embarrassing Anna, not to mention insulting Fiona. Cut the crap or else I'm throwing you back in the car and we're heading home."

"All right, I'll behave," he said, winking at Fiona before he downed one water bottle and then downed the other. He slapped himself in the face and then decreed, "It's all good."

Amazingly, he did sound somewhat better. Cautiously, I opened the door and the five of us made our way downstairs to the car. Tom ordered Dylan a giant soda when we got to our seats, and by the time the puck was dropped for the face-off, Dylan had dialed back the obnoxious considerably. Just to be sure, I sat myself between him and Fiona.

I put my hand on Fiona's knee and whispered, "I'm so sorry. I think the past month has been really tough on him."

"Please, I can think of worse things than being admired, ogled and borderline felt-up by Dylan Cole." When I glared at her, she held up her hands laughing. "I'm joking!"

I've known Tom and Ben for years. They've been friends with Dylan since kindergarten I think, and they were the same age as Will, so they've been in and out of my life for a long time. They were great company, as usual, and as the game wore on, Dylan was civil again as well.

"Hey, that defenseman keeps looking over here." He reached over me to squeeze Fiona's knee. "He's not trying to move in on my woman, is he?"

Maybe I'd spoken too soon.

"Uh, yeah, why does Walker keep staring at you?" My eyes went wide. "Is *that* who you were out with last night?" Her smile told me everything I needed to know. "Oh my God! I love the idea of you two together. That's freaking perfect!"

"Well hush," she warned. "It's just that, the *idea* of us for now. I mean, I like him...He's gorgeous, he's sweet. It just feels too good to be true. I don't want to believe in it yet, hope yet, you know?"

I completely understood, and sent up a silent prayer for my friend because Walker was a good guy and she deserved the best.

No goals for Declan tonight but he had a great game with two assists.

Fiona asked, "Can we wait a few minutes until they get out? I just want to congratulate Walker and you can introduce the guys to Declan."

"Declan?" Dylan asked, surprised. "What's up, Anna?"

"We're taking things slow. We're just friends for now."

"Puh-lease. The boy is head over heels in love with her," Fiona chirped.

"You're a traitor!" I snapped at her.

"We'll meet you girls by the gate in twenty," Tom said. "I think we can safely let Dylan consume a beer now, right?" he asked, looking at Ben.

There were some other people gathered, waiting by where the players exited the locker room. Victoria spotted us and made her way over. She looked testy.

"What's up, Vic?"

"What's up? I'll tell you what's up. Do you know that witch Charlotte measured Brandon for a fucking costume for that bullshit Valentine's Day dance? I overheard Charlotte, Paige and Cassie laughing, comparing the guys' cock sizes because they measured their inseams! Can you fucking believe that? I'm going to kill him. I'm all for people being cordial and polite, but I think he's been a little too accommodating when it comes to those...those..."

She started to cry.

"It's ok," Fiona and I said at the same time, gathering her into a group hug.

"He likes her. I know it. He likes the attention. I don't kiss his ass like she does."

"Vic, come out with us tonight. Forget about all of it for a while."

As we were walking her towards the gate back to the car waiting outside, I saw Paige. Her back was pressed against the corridor wall with her chest pushed out suggestively. My cousin Dylan had her caged in, his hands on either side of her head. He was leaning in, about to kiss her.

"What the fuck are you doing?"

"Oh, hi," Paige said, sweetly.

"Get in the car, Dylan." He looked like he'd just slammed back a few shots, glassy eyed and lazy. "Now!" I shrieked.

She raked her nails over his chest as he backed away, and when he looked as if he was going to move in on her again, I pushed between the two of them and got up in Paige's face. "You are a bitch!"

Victoria, who didn't even know who Dylan was, read the situation accurately and forcibly led him out the door to where the other boys were waiting.

Fiona came for me, grabbing my upper arm. "Come on, Anna. She is *so* not worth it."

The six of us rode to the restaurant in silence. When Dylan slumped over and started snoring, Tom looked to me. "Welcome to my life, Anna. He's been a mess this past month."

"We're sorry," Ben said. "We should have kept a better eye on him tonight."

"It's not your fault, guys. I feel so bad for him."

Tom kind of rolled his eyes, as if to say Dylan had made his own bed. And while I'm sure that was the truth, I felt fiercely protective over him anyway.

We left Dylan sleeping in the car, the driver keeping watch over him, and the five of us had dinner together. Tom and Ben are really funny guys. They even had Victoria laughing inside of ten minutes, so the night wasn't an absolute wash.

Victoria came back to our room after. She didn't really have a close bond with her roommate.

"What should I do?"

"Is it that obvious to you?" I asked.

"Yes, no...I'm not sure. I don't have much experience with serious relationships. I'm crazy about him and I thought he felt the same way. He did, I know it. But now...Lately I just don't know. It's like he can't stand not being the star anymore. He's not getting a minute of playing time and he's so bitter about it. And those girls..."

Fiona said, "Be careful. Charlotte and that whole crew have a way of making you think something is going on while the guys are clue-less. Brandon might be totally oblivious to what's happening and to what you're feeling."

"They're like spiders looking to snare those boys in their webs. I'm in Finance with Cassie. She's all over Declan. He seems oblivious, like you said, Fiona, but she's preying on him. It's sickening!" When Victoria took in my expression, she back peddled. "Cassie does that to *all* the boys, Anna. She rubs Terrence's shoulders, blatantly flirts with Colin...That's how she is with all of them."

"Well, Saturday is that party." Fiona slapped her butt as she looked in the mirror. "I don't know about you, but I'm going to be looking *good* when *I* walk in."

"I hate that I'm agreeing with you, Fiona. Agreeing to objectify myself," I said, laughing.

Victoria looked defeated. "I'm not going."

Fiona shook her head. "Fuck that, Victoria."

"Do you know they're coordinating their outfits? Each of the eight *ambassadors,*" she scoffed, "is being dressed to match their girl."

"Who's matched with who?" I corrected myself. "With whom?" Damn Declan and his grammar lessons.

"I don't know aside from Charlotte and Colin. Lauren told me. She didn't really seem to care because I think she feels a hell of a lot more confident in Colin's feelings than I do in Brandon's. When I asked Brandon he acted like he didn't know what I was talking about. I hate to sound so weak, like I'm accusing him of something. I feel so pathetic."

"I got some very good advice from an old friend. I'll tell you what he told me. You're waiting for him. Don't. Wait."

She looked down at her phone. "He hasn't texted me since the game ended. We're done."

"Maybe you are, Victoria, but you're not rolling over for those girls. I don't care what you feel like. You stick with us this week. You're going to laugh, look good and have fun, you hear me? Suck it up and fake it. And when you walk into that dance and he sees you, if he still wants the plastic version of a woman—what Cassie and Paige are—then you're better off finding that out now."

I didn't see much of Declan that week aside from class. He had a heavy practice schedule and I was busy with my classes. I wasn't really looking to spend time with him either.

Tuesday when I walked into class right before the professor closed the door, I saw Paige sitting next to Declan, whispering in his ear. He was leaning back, away from her, but it still irked me. I saw there was an empty seat on Declan's other side but I chose to sit on the opposite side of the room, away from them all. He kept craning his neck to look my way throughout class, but I pretended not to notice. What did Paige tell him? Some bullshit about my cousin, no doubt. Maybe playing it off like he was the aggressor.

God, I could kill Dylan sometimes. It wasn't like him to be so reckless, to leave himself vulnerable for unflattering pictures or compromising situations. He called me the next day apologizing profusely, and I accepted, of course. I was hoping Dylan and Kasia would work it out, but now I was fairly certain that wouldn't be happening. I was so sad for him. She was the one, and he'd let her slip through his fingers.

Declan was waiting for me after class. "Hey, what's up? I saved you a seat."

"Didn't want to interrupt the tongue fucking your ear was getting."

"Anna!"

"Let me guess," I said, sporting a lip pout. "Was she telling you all about big, bad Dylan Cole taking advantage of innocent little Paige?"

"No, she was telling me some stupid shit about that dumb dance that they think is top secret. What are you talking about with Dylan?"

"Nothing." I looked down at the floor. "She just took advantage of a very crappy situation after the game on Saturday. You know her act."

"I do. She tried to maul me twice within the first month of school."

"Nice."

I was about to snark it up and ask Declan who his partner was for the dance, but then thought better of it. That would be weak on my part and I wouldn't be heeding the great advice I'd just given Victoria. Declan had done nothing wrong, I reminded myself.

Next class, I took the seat Declan saved for me. He and I traded drawings and notes during class like we sometimes did, but it was different—it wasn't easy between us. How could it be with one of those girls turning around every five minutes to remind Declan about some pointless detail pertaining to the dance? At one point he said to Paige, "Enough! I have a game on Saturday. You think I give a crap about this dance?"

Cassie affected a hurt expression but she nodded, defending Declan with so much false sincerity that even I almost fell for it. "He's right, Paige. Declan has so much on his shoulders already. The dance isn't as important as the game."

She was good, I'll give her that. And after that performance, of course the stupid boy felt the need to reassure her, to make amends. "Cassie, I know you girls have been working really hard on this. I didn't mean to make it seem like it's not important. I just have the game to think about, that's all."

She licked her lips and then practically sing-songed, "*Don't* apologize, Declan. You're *so* sweet. And don't worry, Saturday night you don't need to do anything besides show up and look hot. With me on your arm that won't be so hard, right?"

He was paired up with Cassie.

The professor was calling out to everyone about a paper that was due at the end of next week. People were getting up, talking and filing out of class. Declan sat stock still, same as me. He didn't pack up. He didn't even look up until everyone around us had cleared out.

Unfortunately I *was* looking up, so I saw Charlotte's barely contained glee as she said something to Cassie that was likely at my expense.

"Do you get off on it, Declan?" I asked evenly. He didn't respond. "Do you need it? The adoration, the fans? Does it make you feel like a man?"

"Anna," he said as he let out a tired breath.

"Don't," I snapped as I shoved my arms into my coat.

"Wait a fucking second and hear me out. That sounded like it was something and you *know* it wasn't."

"It *sounded* like you have a date."

"Fuck," he said, raking his fingers through his hair.

"Do *not* act like you need to explain yourself, to placate me. I'm not some pathetic, clingy girl who *needs* you, ok? I'm not Tess, so get over yourself."

Yeah, I hope that one stung.

I grabbed my things and left the classroom before he could catch up to me. And I didn't look back so I don't even know if he tried.

My heart wasn't in it as Fiona, Lauren, Victoria, Colleen and I scoured the mall for outfits on Friday.

I knew I'd messed up.

* * *

DECLAN

I wanted to put my fist through something.

When I walked into the locker room and tossed my gear against the wall, Walker took in my expression and demanded, "What the hell, Banks?"

"Nothing...Just Anna driving me fucking crazy. Same shit, different day."

Walker's roommate, Bertrand, chimed in, "I know you don't want to hear this, but did you ever think about satisfying some of the very serious tail that's making itself available to you right now? Maybe you should take some time to just enjoy it...Some good old, no strings attached sex."

"Whenever women are referred to using the pronoun *it*, I can guarantee you the advice isn't worth shit," Walker cautioned.

Callaghan added, "Girls like the ones following you around are the kind that like it that way. They're using you just like you're using them."

I rolled my eyes. I hated that asshole but I wasn't about to start a fight in the locker room the week of our semi-final game. I got up and left. Walker followed.

"Hey," he said, grabbing my shoulder and turning me back to face him. "Anna's a *good* person, the kind of girl who has your best interests at heart. It kind of pisses me off that you're using that *same shit, different day* line about her. You *want* one of those girls who would fuck any one of us? You want some puck bunnies kissing up to you, wearing your jersey...Is that it, Banks? Then dump Anna's ass. I could name a dozen guys right now who'd line up to treat her like gold."

"I'm not into those girls."

"Really? Last weekend after the game, I recall seeing that girl Cassie with her tits practically pressed into your face, pouring a shot into your mouth. Maybe you were too drunk to remember, but I saw you. Would you have let her do that if Anna was there?" He looked disgusted. "Yeah, I didn't think so. Truth is, if Anna was *my* friend, I'd advise her to stay away from your dumb ass."

It was washing over me again, the misery, the regret, the feeling of just never being able to get it right. "I love her, Walker. I really do."

"Then fucking act like it." He waited a moment and then shook his head. "I get it, Declan. You think I haven't been in the same position? Freshman year I met a really nice girl, Sarah. We went out for over a year. I was crazy about her. Sophomore year, though, I started getting caught up in everything...All the people kissing my ass, the drinking, the partying, the girls. Sarah dropped me and I fully deserved it. And those girls who were so hot? Tempting me when I was with Sarah? They started to look pretty ugly real fast. When I begged Sarah to get back together, she wanted no part of me. *She* had her shit together and she didn't need me. Junior year I was a mess. I had a different girl in my bed every weekend and I was fucking miserable. Those girls want you for the image, they don't want *you*. And screwing around like that? It leaves you empty. *You* are about to lose *your* Sarah. Understand?"

I sat alone for a while and then took a few minutes to send some texts before stepping out onto the ice. First text was to Cassie:

Count me out for Saturday. I'll be there, give whatever support you need, but I'm with Anna. Not walking in with anyone else on my arm.

The next one was to my father:

Can you and Diana come for the game next weekend? There's someone I want you to meet.

The last one was to Anna:

You are everything. Do you understand me? I love you.

Chapter Twenty-Two

ANNA

When I casually mentioned the seventies-themed party to Aunt Margot during one of our weekly video chats, she insisted on coming up Saturday afternoon with her friend Bunny to help us girls get ready. Apparently, she had some decade-appropriate clothing and accessories that would be "just fabulous."

Turns out Margot and Bunny could have made a career out of being make-up artists. They were seriously awesome and the girls loved it.

By the time they were finished with me, my hair was a sexy mass of glossy ringlets and my make-up was better than I ever could have done it, with a liberal dusting of gold shimmer over my shoulders leading down into my cleavage.

I wanted them to leave before we got dressed, but no such luck. In my opinion, the clothes we'd purchased for tonight were more provocative—translation: slutty—than we'd ever wear in real life. So I squeezed into my tight black leather pants and donned the gold lame halter top that exposed my belly and the majority of my back. Margot

271

suggested the double-sided tape to prevent what would have been a certain wardrobe malfunction.

"Anna, you cannot wear a bra with that top. It will ruin the effect." My thoughts exactly, I mused, as Margot inspected me from every angle. "But unless you dance without moving at all, you're going to be flashing some serious nipple. And we can't have that, am I right?"

"Yes ma'am," I said, as all of my friends collapsed into laughter.

"Margot and Bunny, can you come here every weekend?" Lauren gushed as she eyed herself in the mirror. "I look freaking awesome!"

As I slipped into my black high-heeled booties, I thought to myself that we all did look pretty great. Fiona had on a tube dress that barely covered her cheeks, showing off the best set of legs on the east coast, Lauren was a very sexy hippie, and Colleen, who decided to channel Daisy Duke, looked positively combustible. But my heart felt heavy as I looked in the mirror one last time. The tight clothes, the make-up, the hair. Competing for Declan's attention and hoping to drive him wild? This act was getting old.

I thought back to the text he sent me yesterday. He said he loved me, that I was everything. It was all well and good, but talk is cheap. The fact that he felt some kind of warped duty to appease a girl like Cassie, that he was concerned with letting *her* down and not me? It was nothing more than history repeating itself.

Then I was back to that Sunday morning when Danielle was so broken up about Frank. I never said it out loud, and I told myself I wasn't being judgmental, but I did judge her. *I would never let a guy use me that way.* I remember feeling just the slightest bit superior, but now I felt like an idiot.

I'm done.

Never again.

Declan wasn't all in, and I vowed that I'd never allow myself to be with a guy who didn't love me as much as I loved him.

After my aunt and her bestie *finally* left—I think Bunny was hoping for an invitation to tag along—we had a few drinks in the room and then made our way to Rusty's.

We decided to make a semi-late entrance so that we didn't have to watch the stupid homecoming court-like procession of our men with those scheming girls. I hate to admit it, but I knew the sight of him walking in with Cassie would have torn me in two.

No such luck.

As we stood at the top of the stairs about to walk down into the large open room, I scanned the crowd and saw no sign of them. We were definitely turning heads as a group as we walked in, though. There were many tongues-a-wagging, but it was no consolation. I only cared what he thought. In fact, the feeling of my breasts bouncing with every step I took and the knowledge that my pert nipples were probably saying hello to everyone in the room left me feeling overexposed.

The music changed mid-song and the lights dimmed. The only lights were the ones reflecting off the giant disco ball that was now spinning as *Bad Girls* by Donna Summer blasted from the speakers.

"How fucking appropriate," I yelled to Fiona.

There were eight couples in all. Avery entered first with some guy from the football team. I had to admit it, she was ok. She smiled when she saw me and gestured to my outfit, dragging her finger from top to bottom. "Love it," she mouthed. Next up was some sopho-more that I didn't know paired up with Chris Gallagher. *Yuck*. Three more couples and then the trio of evil descended, one after another. Paige was first, escorted by Colin. I couldn't say anything about her cheesy outfit, given that I was flashing ample side boob myself, but she had herself pressed up against Colin like she was his Siamese twin. Paige must have wanted to scream because the entire time she was on his arm, Colin had a big-ass grin on his face, waving wildly in Lauren's direction. He mouthed the words, "You look hot," to her. I wanted to cry it was so freaking cute. Next up was Charlotte on Brandon's arm, and that was, well, painful to watch.

The guys were dressed in polyester suits with wide-collared shirts unbuttoned down to mid-torso, gold chains, porn mustaches—you name it. Brandon sauntered down the stairs with her, hamming it up and playing his two minutes of fame for all it was worth. I glanced over to the bar and saw Victoria knocking back a shot with Fiona. It had to hurt because Charlotte looked good. I mean, the girl was pretty. And just like Brandon, she was loving the attention. Ugh, and they must have worked on some stupid choreographed routine. When they hit the bottom step, they did a few hustle-inspired moves before he flung her out in a spin and then whipped her back in, dipping her as he ran his finger down the center length of her torso, tits to navel. I was so angry for Victoria. What had come over him? Charlotte playfully swatted his hand as he raised her up. All innocent, she was. Yeah right, as if half the guys in this room hadn't already copped a feel.

I was bracing myself, felt tears pricking at the corners of my eyes. If I did start bawling, the copious amounts of mascara Margot piled on would make me look exceedingly pathetic. For this and a myriad of other reasons, I fought to control my emotions.

I didn't want to look. I wanted to run but I was stuck in place, just waiting to be annihilated. The two of them were at the top of the stairs, backs to the crowd. There was Cassie, hair stick-straight and glossy, her body on full display in a backless jumpsuit. She turned first, the low-cut top swaying with the movement in a way that nearly gave everyone a full view of the goodies. There were whoops and cheers from Cassie's loyal subjects, and she looked pleased as punch taking it all in from up on high.

How could he do this? How could he hurt me again and again and again?

No more.

I was out.

"What's your sign, baby?" a voice purred in my ear. Sweet Jesus, I thought my legs were going to give out from underneath me. "I've been watching you for the past ten minutes, staring at your ass in these leather pants." His body was so close behind me that I could feel him pressing into my exposed lower back. He slid his hands up my abdomen, stopping just short of his target. "And these...bouncing, teasing me every time you move...driving me fucking crazy." His breath was warm against my neck when he whispered, "Will you let me? Tonight? Will you let me love you again?"

I turned to face him, taking in the giant permed wig, the blue tinted sunglasses, the tie-dyed shirt and jeans. He slid the wig off his head and removed the sunglasses. "Me, Anna. Please say that you still want me."

I turned around again, just to make sure my mind wasn't playing tricks on me. Cassie's eyes were on us, her smile tight and forced. And the guy on her arm wasn't Declan, it was Frank Collagrazzo.

Declan looked defenseless waiting on me for a response. I wrapped my arms around his neck and whispered in his ear, "I've always wanted you. Always."

I Want You Back by the Jackson Five came on, and Declan put his wig back on lopsided with one hand as he led me out onto the dance floor. I would have been content to bail on the party, but spending the next hour dancing with my big, goofy giant was the most fun I'd had in a long time. The fact that Cassie, Paige and Charlotte watched our every move like three bitter sourpusses made it even better.

Declan had me tucked in close to him in the back of the taxi. I thought he was leaning his head down to kiss me, but instead he whispered, "I love you. I swear that I'll never take you or us for granted again. What I said the other day, that you're everything? I mean that with all my heart. I love you...Always have."

Then he did kiss me—a slow, romantic kiss. When we pulled up outside our dorms, he paid the cabbie and then looked to me, his expression cautious but hopeful. "Will you spend the night with me?" And I said yes.

His hand shook as he tried to get his key into the lock. "Damn," he laughed, "I'm nervous." He let out a steadying breath and then unlocked the door, ushering me inside. "Are you sure, Anna? I don't want to screw anything up by pushing things too far, too fast."

I pushed him back a step, so that he stumbled and fell onto the bed. He sat up and went to say something, but I said, "Stop talking," putting my hand on his shoulder to steady myself as I got myself out of those ridiculously high-heeled booties.

I lifted his shirt over his head and paused for a moment to admire him. His body was strong and powerful, and he was mine. And with his eyes fixed on me, I felt powerful too. I took a step back and made a show of shimmying out of my tight leather pants. I knew what I was doing. I knew how I looked in nothing but black lace and that gold halter top that moved and shimmered with every breath I took. I could see his lower body reacting and smiled when he twitched uncomfortably, waiting for me to set the pace.

"Are you keeping your jeans on, Declan?"

He swallowed when he stood up to undo the buttons on his fly, and didn't take his eyes off me once as he pushed the jeans down his legs and then stepped out of them. He was a work of art, a perfectly sculpted male specimen, and in that moment I wanted nothing more than to feel his skin on mine. I pulled on the string at my back and the one at my neck at the same time, and watched as the scrap of gold fabric fell to the floor. I looked up to see Declan staring at my breasts as if he was in a trance when he murmured, "I want inside of you so badly."

I wasn't nervous. His words, they made me hot with need. I slid the snug fabric over his ass and down, pausing to take him in my mouth as I moved back up his body. "Aw, fuck," he hissed, lacing his fingers into my hair, guiding me gently. In and out, in and out, in and out—the salty taste of him and his strangled groans of pleasure made it as good for me as I knew it was for him. It wasn't more than a few seconds before he had me by the elbow, dragging me up the length of his body and then moving me back with him onto the bed. He caged me in, hovering over me as he used one hand to help me out of the little I was still wearing. When he lowered his body down onto mine, I spread my legs to make room for him. I wanted him there, wanted him resting between my hips, his cock firm against my belly. I wanted his tongue in my mouth, wanted the open-mouth kisses he laid on my breasts.

I wanted.

Declan laughed after that first time. "I promise I'll make it up to you. I've been waiting for you for so long, thinking about you this way at least ten times a day...I was afraid I'd bust inside of a minute and I did."

But that second time—that was slow and heavy and breathless and oh so good.

"Forever, Anna. I'll love you for the rest of my life."

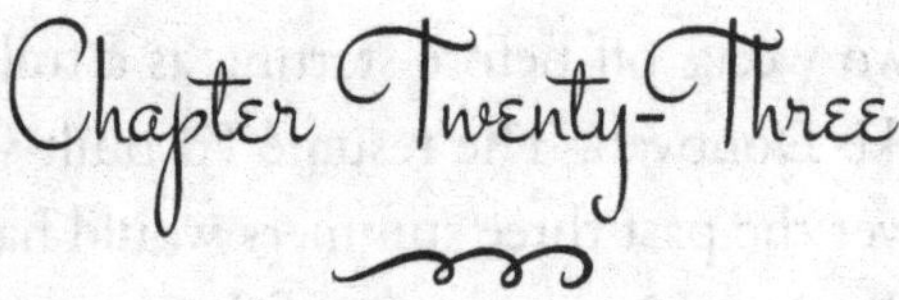

THREE YEARS LATER...

ANNA

Four years of classes, parties, grinding out papers and projects, staying up all night studying for exams, and staying up all night with Declan.

Every memory, every wonderful person who made their way into my life—I couldn't believe this was it.

We would all be leaving our little bubble come tomorrow. Fiona was going home for a few weeks but then she was moving to New York...with me! Fiona landed an entry-level job at a publishing house, hopefully on her way to becoming the next great American writer. And I certainly didn't kid myself thinking that I was the big draw to New York City. I knew she was coming for Walker.

Those two managed to make it through the past three years, through countless separations when Walker shuffled between teams during his two seasons in the NHL. He finally called it a day and went to work as a financial analyst, and was now happily settled into Wall Street life.

The rest of our friends were starting careers, starting graduate programs, or as in Lauren's case, starting their own business. She was always the most fearless of us all.

Me? I had two weeks off before starting as a full-time employee for Kate and Luke Donovan. The resumé I'd built working side by side with Kate over the past three summers would have made it easy to snag an entry-level position with one of the more established firms in New York, but I didn't want that anymore. I wanted responsibility, I wanted to be creating plans that were used, and I wanted to be handling projects now instead of working as a gopher for the "real" architects. I knew Kate had enough confidence in me and my abilities to give me those things.

My graduation present from Vince and Margot was a beautiful two-bedroom apartment on the Upper West Side. It was entirely too extravagant, but arguing about it was pointless. I knew Vince and Margot considered me as much a daughter as Dylan was their son. They wanted to do this for me, so I let them. The apartment was in Dylan and CeeCee's building and less than ten blocks from Declan.

I was so ready. Ready to start my life in New York with my best friend by my side, a great job lined up, and the love of my life waiting for me.

My Declan.

In some ways he was my warm, comfy sweater. Especially on those nights when I needed to talk, vent, cry or grieve. But Declan was so much more. He was scratchy burlap when we challenged one another, a down comforter ready to wrap me up safely when I fell, and silky satin when he made love to me.

Declan made me feel it all.

I stood in front of the mirror for a moment, my fingers running over the words Declan had inscribed on my locket.

I knew what I wanted.

I wanted forever with him.

* * *

DECLAN

This was how it was always meant to be. Anna was my happiness. Did we argue? Yes we did, and her hot temper was something to behold. But we were equals. I loved her and she loved me—I knew that. We relied on each other, shared a bond that was strong and meant the world to me. But I also knew that Anna could manage just fine on her own. She didn't need me.

Sounds cold, but to me it was a life-affirming truth. It was such a relief to be with someone whose happiness wasn't entirely, one hundred percent reliant upon me. Anna had friends, a family she loved, and the makings of a fulfilling career. She was a whole person, with or without me. And the fact that she didn't *need* me? It drove me to make sure that she would always *want* me.

I was thinking about our life together as I made my way up I-95 on my way to Boston. I was driving my new Jeep, the only other big purchase I'd made aside from my apartment. And since I was living in the Big Apple, the apartment was a *big* purchase.

Sometimes I stood in place, imagining the space my two feet took up to be a square foot. I marveled at how much that tiny piece of real estate actually cost in Manhattan. I didn't really sweat it, though. Once the season ended, I decided I needed a place of my own. Splitting my time between hotels when I was on the road and a cramped rental in New York that I shared with another rookie had been all sorts of miserable. I mean, the guy was nice and all, but he turned out to be an absolute slob with a thing for puck bunnies. Not exactly the ideal roommate. And the contract I signed with the Rangers made the cost of my apartment seem like it was nothing out of the ordinary.

The cost of Anna's interior design and decorating? Now *that* was hard to swallow, but I gave her free rein and in the end I was glad I did. The result was a space that was masculine, yet warm and comforting. It made me happy to come home at night, especially when she was here visiting.

She came down a lot this past winter, catching as many of my rookie season games as she possibly could. I'm not going to lie, playing in the pros was no joke. It wasn't as easy to duck checks in this league, and I had my ass handed to me on more than one occasion. Even though I scored enough goals to make the organization pleased with their decision to sign me, the transition wasn't piece-of-cake easy. Looking up into the stands and seeing Anna there gave me the boost I needed during some of those more trying games.

Anna was comfortable in this big city. New York was where she wanted to be, so she was dancing like a wild woman, hooting and hollering backstage when the Rangers called my name last summer at the NHL draft. Having spent the past three summers working for Kate and Luke Donovan, she knew the city like the back of her hand. I wasn't completely sold on it yet, being a New England boy through and through, but it was starting to grown on me.

Anna loves those quirky off-Broadway plays, strolling through museums for hours, seeing concerts and checking out new, exotic restaurants. There's always something pretty exciting to do here, but I don't really need all that. My best nights, I told her, are the nights after my games when we come back to my place, order in, and sit in front of the fireplace together talking.

I loved her more than anything.

In two days they would all be graduating. It was bittersweet for me. I wasn't that far off from graduating myself, but I wouldn't be crossing that stage dressed in my cap and gown—not yet.

After Anna and I finally settled into being a couple—or got our timing right, as she would say—she helped me set up a plan for myself along with the Dean of Academics. Every off-season during the summers, I still had to train but I squeezed in as many classes as I could. I did it just as a precaution, in case I made the decision to leave school and go pro early. At the rate I was now going, after this summer I'd only need about nine more credits to earn my degree.

I wrestled with the decision after sophomore year when the recruiters got more persistent, but I decided again to stay in school. My junior year I broke the all-time scoring record for the school and we won the NCAA championship. Then I was ready. After talking it over with Anna and with Coach, I was satisfied and confident in my decision to leave.

The time apart from Anna was rough. We were kind of used to it from the summers, when I was in Boston and she was in New York, but when I left school permanently, it felt empty. Moving on without her by my side was hard. The constant traveling that first season sucked, and having to make do with phone calls and online chats as I camped out in one hotel room after another was a poor substitute for sleeping with her body curled up and tucked into mine. She supported me every step of the way, though, and Anna making the effort to come and see me, sometimes dragging a half-dozen of our friends along with her, just made me love her even more.

I stopped by the guys' place first. Our crew from freshman year was still together, and I knew each and every one of them would be a friend for life.

Gross.

My sneakers gripped the sticky floor with every step I took and there were beer cans covering every surface. Lampshades were missing, darts were lodged in the wall surrounding the dartboard, and a pair of rumpled boxer shorts were wedged between the couch cushions.

I miss this place.

As I swiped one arm across the counter, steering the cans into the garbage can I was holding underneath, Colin came down the stairs in his underwear, yawning and scratching his balls.

"Guess you had a party here last night?" I asked.

"Senior Week is kicking my ass," he said as he looked around surveying the damage. "I can't believe I have to be ready to go out again in like four hours. Leave that crap, Declan. Have you been by the girls' place yet?"

"No. I figured they'd be dolling themselves up and all that."

"You're probably right." He yawned again and then his eyes went wide. "Shit, I almost forgot. Lauren's going to kill you when she sees you." Now he was smiling. "You know that necklace you asked her to swipe? Apparently, Anna's been all weepy and freaking out since she realized it's gone missing. She's made the girls turn their place inside out like five times looking for it."

"Damn. I feel bad now."

I did feel bad. I thought back to that day a few years ago when she finally opened my Christmas gift. It wasn't long after that Valentine's Day dance, and I remember feeling really grateful and flattered when she asked me to come home with her. She wanted me to meet her aunt and uncle properly, and to be with her when she visited Will's grave. It meant more to me than she could ever know.

Later that afternoon, after inhaling the best cheeseburger and onion rings known to man, we were hanging out in her room listening to music and looking through old pictures when she got up and pulled the small box out from her desk drawer.

"I want to open it now, Declan."

She took her time undoing the ribbon and loosening the tape on the wrapping paper. When she opened the box, she smiled when she held the locket in her hand, running her fingers over the surface before popping the latch. There was a picture of us from that first summer at camp inside. We looked so much younger with our goofy grins, our arms slung around one another's shoulders, our heads tilted towards one another.

She took in a deep, ragged breath and covered her mouth. "What? Where did you even get this picture?" Then she looked to me smiling. "I love it, and I love you."

My intention was to surprise her with the new and improved version after she crossed the stage on Graduation Day, but I never saw her without that locket, and knowing she might be upset called for a change of plans.

"Is everybody decent?" I called out as I let myself into their place with my hand over my eyes. Everyone except Anna was sprawled across the couches. After getting the hellos out of the way, I asked, "Aren't you girls supposed to be out getting manicures or getting your hair done or something? I thought the day of the Commencement Ball was like an all-day primp fest."

"Not," Fiona said. "You are looking at a bunch of girls who need an hour, tops, to look fabulous. Besides, your girlfriend hasn't even woken up yet."

"Really?" I got right to it, taking the stairs two at a time.

"Wake up, sleepyhead," I chirped as I whipped off her covers and laid myself right on top of her.

"Jeez. Do you actually get wood that fast or were you hard before you got here?"

"Just hearing that you were still in bed gets me standing at attention."

"Whatever," she said lazily as she kissed me. "I like it."

After she threw me off of her to go brush her teeth, we spent the next hour together in bed, getting reacquainted after not having seen each other for an entire ten days.

Just as we were about to get up, Anna pulled me back down to her but couldn't meet my eyes. "Declan, I have something crappy to tell you." The look on her face was so dire.

"Go ahead, it's ok," I said.

"I've been looking for my—"

"Locket?"

She nodded, her lips trembling and her eyes glassy with tears. I pulled her in close to me. "I'm sorry, Anna. I wanted it to be a surprise. I took it."

I released her slowly, just in case she was feeling the need to beat me up, but she was sniffling and smiling when I looked down at her face. I grabbed my shorts from the floor and dug it out of my pocket. "I wanted to give it to you tomorrow with your other present, but here goes...Happy Graduation. I'm so proud of you and I love you."

When she sat up, her breasts and the way her long hair hung in waves, resting right along those sweet, rosy nipples that I love so much, had me thinking about other things besides the little velvet bag she was now anxiously waiting for me to hand over.

"Hey, put a shirt on or else I'm putting those babies right back into my mouth."

She dug a tank and her underwear from between the sheets and shimmied back into them. "Hand it over, Banks," she said, giggling.

She caressed the surface, just like she did the first time I gave it to her, and then she popped the latch. Now there were two pictures. The more recent shot was taken last summer on the beach—Anna in her bikini, me standing right behind hugging her close. When I first saw the picture it reminded me of those happy, goofy grins we were wearing in the original shot. It was nearly seven years later, but we looked as happy to be together now as we were then.

I knew I was happier now than I'd ever been in my life. Being with Anna just made my life...great.

"Turn it over."

With the words engraved on the back, I wanted to tell her what she meant to me and what I wanted for our future.

I knew what I wanted. I wanted Anna, I wanted a home with her in it, and I wanted children—lots of them.

Anna and I would raise our family with love.

I watched her as she turned it over and read the words. She

looked up at me and nodded as tears pricked at the corners of her eyes.

FIRST LOVE

TRUE LOVE

FOREVER LOVE

"Forever, Anna."
"Yes, Declan...Forever."

* * *

A Note From Lily

Thank you for reading *Let Me Heal Your Heart*. Anna just about broke *my* heart when she emerged in *Let Me Go*. She's damaged and hurting, but fierce in the way she takes on the world. Like her cousin Dylan, Anna's story seemed to take on a life of its own while I just happened to be there to record it.

And Jeremy Rivers? I knew he had his own story and was just waiting for me to tell it. Jeremy and Carolyn's story, *Let Me Fall*, is up next:

Shame, secrets, and the lies we tell ourselves...

In the weeks leading up to graduation, Carolyn Harris was the single-most hated member of her senior class. The girl who drove the school's golden boy to his demise. The girl who did something sordid and shameful. Exposed in a cruel and very public way, everyone said she got what she deserved.

She used to be the perfect girl, the apple of her parents' eye. But a secret, once revealed, sets a devastating chain of events into motion, destroying everything and everyone in its wake.

They say you can't judge a book by its cover, and Jeremy Rivers is all kinds of wrong for Carolyn on paper. He's angry, unpredictable... He's trouble. But the boy who loved her before her world fell apart loves her still, and with his help, Carolyn is going to learn that everyone—even a girl like her—deserves a happy ending.

Critical praise for *Let Me Fall:*

Kirkus Reviews: "With her character-driven plot and fast-moving storyline, Foster easily keeps readers engaged. Although the ending isn't surprising, the journey toward that resolution is fraught with unexpected twists. Foster's prose is easygoing and readable, but she still tackles weighty issues in this romantic story, ranging from bullying and sex shaming to mental illness and living with learning disabilities. An involving tale of love and redemption that will satisfy discerning fans of the new-adult genre."

Publishers Weekly: "Smart and attractive Carolyn Harris and academically-challenged football star Jeremy Rivers find their lives intertwined in a wealthy Connecticut town in this gripping tale that effectively straddles the line between young adult and romance. Both the sweetness of young love and the dark underside of high school cliques are effectively depicted by a well-developed cast of characters shadowed by tragedy but reaching for independence and happiness. Readers will find themselves deeply engaged by Carolyn and Jeremy and the twists and turns of this genuinely engrossing story."

Visit the website to learn more:
www.LilyFoster.com

Also by Lily Foster

THE LET ME SERIES

Let Me Be the One

Let Me Love You

Let Me Go

Let Me Heal Your Heart

Let Me Fall

When I Let You Go

THE BLACKBIRD SERIES

When the Night is Over

Your Hand in Mine

Ghost on the Shore

All Your Life